PORTRAIT OF SEBASTIAN KHAN

A NOVEL

BY AATIF RASHID

7.13 BOOKS
BROOKLYN, NY

Printed and distributed by 7.13 Books. First paperback edition, first printing: March 2019

Cover design: Olivia Croom
Author photo: Aatif Rashid

ISBN-10: 1-7328686-0-3
ISBN-13: 978-1-7328686-0-1

Library of Congress Control Number: 2018962338

On pages 253-4, a passage in the Qur'an is taken from the following book: Arberry, A.J., translator. *The Koran Interpreted.* New York: Touchstone, 1955.

For information about permission to reproduce selections from this book, contact the publisher at https://713books.com/

"To fast, to study, and to see no woman—
Flat treason 'gainst the kingly state of youth…"

—William Shakespeare, *Love's Labour's Lost*

PROLOGUE

Sebastian Khan stares at his reflection in the window: black, wavy hair, light-olive skin, high cheekbones and aquiline nose. It's the kind of face young women find attractive, dashing and mysterious in its racial ambiguity (the genetic result of two half-Pakistani, half-white parents), aged eighteen years and two hundred and thirty-one days, and accompanying a figure that likewise strikes a desirable chord in the female heart, tall but not too tall (five feet, eight inches), hipster-svelte but not emaciated (one hundred and forty-five pounds), attired in a white-buttoned blue blazer, slim-fitting crimson chinos, and dark-brown leather shoes, all worn with a pose of aristocratic nonchalance. It's the eyes, though, that give the image its aesthetic harmony, large, dark-brown eyes, of a brown so dark and deep that it swallows up the pupils, confident, graceful, hypnotic eyes, framed in dark-rimmed glasses that only magnify their power, and containing in their swirling depths all the infinite wisdom of a young man.

The window belongs to the Philadelphia Museum of Art, and beyond Sebastian's reflection lies that city, its red brick buildings strewn with autumn leaves, the skies above gray and cloudy. But Sebastian sees only his reflection. He runs a hand through his hair and notes via the window as a girl, mid-twenties at the oldest and dressed with art-student chic, glances up and lets her gaze linger on him as she walks down the marble-floored museum hallway. He listens to the echo of her shoes and smiles when her steps briefly slow as she passes behind him.

Sebastian turns from the window and walks down the hallway to the adjoining room. He's in Philadelphia for only a few more hours—the Model United Nations Conference he was here for is over, and his team's plane will soon depart back to San Francisco, and tomorrow he'll be back in his freshman dorm in Berkeley—and so he wants one more time to gaze upon the painting, which has always been his favorite.

Before the next room he finds it, hanging unceremoniously by the doorway, overlooked by all the passersby eager to plunge headfirst into the twentieth-century rooms beyond (though not by Sebastian, who, like the painting, prefers to remain here, firmly rooted in the nineteenth century): *The Thorny Path* by Thomas Couture (1873). The painting centers on a woman who is almost naked, wearing draped around her body only a single white sheet that nevertheless manages to leave exposed both her breasts. She sits enthroned atop a carriage, which with a jaunty tilt of her head she wills forward, through a shadowy forest path. Below her, each clutching a rope that leads back to her magnificent seat, are not horses but men: a nobleman, a soldier, a scholar, and a troubadour. Despite the surrounding darkness, the woman shines, as if with divine light.

As a whole, the image is meant to be an allegorical critique of the decadence and immorality of nineteenth-century French society, or so the description beside it says. But Sebastian cares little for Couture's rather obvious didactic intent. In fact, his gaze barely lingers on the woman (naked though she is) and instead focuses on the men before her. The nobleman is fat and tired, his stomach hanging grotesquely out before him. The soldier is defeated, his sword pointed at the dirt and his face turned away in shame. The scholar is distant, a pen in his hand and his gaze faraway. Only the troubadour has his head held high, his expression proud and glowing as he pulls the carriage forward. To Sebastian, this troubadour becomes the unintended center of the piece.

Sebastian is not stupid (a straight A student, in fact), and so he does immediately recognize the painting's stern morality and the not-so-subtle reference to the transience of youth in the form of the old crone, hunched in the carriage behind the semi-naked woman. But he choses to ignore it all, the crone and the larger message. Art for him is about the perceiver and not the artist, and Sebastian reads the painting not as one of shame or sadness, but as a celebration of the troubadour's spirit. Alone of all these men, the troubadour pulls the carriage with purpose and optimism, happy to bear a burden as exquisite as this woman.

Sebastian had a similar interpretation of another Couture favorite of his, *Romans during the Decadence* (1847). Couture intended that piece as a moral condemnation of drunken debauchery, yet to Sebastian, the piled naked ladies and men in laurels and togas lying amidst columns and marble statues were altogether a beautiful celebration of bodies and worldly pleasure. But Sebastian often ignores the obvious thematic elements of art. He is the kind of young man who reads *Frankenstein* as a defense of ambition and views *La Dolce Vita* as a glorification of the hedonistic life. His favorite literary figures are Amory Blaine, Julien Sorel, Don Quixote, and Don Draper. Most tragically of all, he believes *The Picture of Dorian Gray* to be a celebration of the Epicurean spirit of Henry Wotton instead of a critique of decadence and aestheticism. And so, what can one expect when a young man like that gazes up at a painting such as this?

7

Staring at it thus, Sebastian only reaffirms his decision to study Art History. To him, nothing is more beautiful than that which is real and yet still immortal, like these figures in this painting. He imagines the actual model for the troubadour, a young man once, but aging quickly even just a few years after posing, lines appearing on the forehead and around the mouth, the rosy cheeks and lips fading to yellow, the beautiful locks of hair thinning and falling out, the fine, erect, Apollonian figure flattening and developing a gut, the knees starting to ache from any prolonged period of standing before eventually giving out entirely. Now, of course, the model is long dead, his bones turning to ash somewhere in a Parisian catacomb. But the figure in the painting will always be young. And so, in that troubadour's upturned face, Sebastian imagines his own eyes reflected back. As far as he's concerned, a piece of art is just a mirror, and Sebastian can't help but long to be young forever too, to have his reflection in the window proceed unchanged, Dorian-like, through the ages.

In truth, though, Sebastian's love of art is more complex than simple youthful yearning—because when he was twelve, his mother died, and nineteenth-century paintings like this one provided him a refuge from the pain of her loss. Sebastian may insist that his tastes are due entirely to his devotion to the ideal of beauty and not at all to anything as bourgeois as childhood trauma. But that is simply another of his classic misinterpretations. And so, even Sebastian sometimes pauses when staring at this painting, detecting hints of mortality in the immortal canvas and wondering— is this young troubadour not deceived? Is this bard of love and beauty not just caught up in the lie of his own song?

CHAPTER ONE

THE VOYAGE OF LIFE: YOUTH (1842)

The old man has white hair, long, unwashed, and matted against his neck, and he wears a blue T-shirt and a green jacket, both too big for him. He is clean-shaven, though, with no hint of stubble, and so if he is homeless, which Sebastian suspects he is, he must have a razor tucked away wherever he sleeps (and, of course, a mirror too). Sebastian imagines him rising each morning from the doorway he calls home, resting his mirror against a nearby windowsill, carefully shaving, and then smiling at his reflection, the wrinkled cheeks now smooth, or at least as smooth as wrinkled cheeks can be.

The man sits on a bucket, in the middle of Sproul Plaza, holding up a whiteboard that reads in large, neatly written dry-erase handwriting 380 DAYS TILL THE END. He is, as Sebastian has learned through some googling, a follower of a famous radio evangelist who incorrectly predicted the end of the world in 1994 and then, citing a mathematical error to explain his inaccuracy, re-predicted the same apocalypse for May 21, 2011—five days after Sebastian will graduate. Yet despite this modern Cassandra's well-timed prophecy, students pass by him indifferently, white Apple headphones in their ears, backpacks and messenger bags slung over their shoulders, books and papers clutched under their arms, a river of bodies moving steadily down the red-stone promenade towards the distant, rusted green arch of Sather Gate.

A few other possibly homeless men stand nearby, one holding up a sign calling for Obama's impeachment, another reading aloud from a Bible in a sonorous voice that rises above the flowing crowd and joins the choirs of birds that chirp from the leafy trees. The Berkeley sky is overcast as always, but Sebastian knows it's May by the warmth in the air and by the way the sun peeks through the murky gray and by the way the students walk, with a slightly brisker pace, eager to get through their final classes and start their summers, eager for the sun to fully emerge from behind the clouds and for the grass to bloom and for the rainy spring to end, eager for the season of barbecues and vacations and summer internships that may help them get a leg up in the suffering economy to begin.

But Sebastian doesn't share their enthusiasm. It's the end of his junior year now, and he feels all the melancholy of a young man nearing the precipice of his youth. He turned twenty-one recently, and if being legally allowed to drink wasn't sign enough of his approaching the end, the thought of what will happen a little over a year from now is, because then he'll have to cross the stage at graduation and the world of college will shimmer into hazy memory, left only for the nostalgic remembrances of crotchety old men (among whose number Sebastian will, by that point, be included, since in 380 days he will have reached the ghastly age of twenty-two). And today of all days, when Sebastian is hosting at his apartment a party during which Berkeley's Model United Nations club will drink merrily and celebrate the end of another year and the graduation of another class of fine public speakers departing into the wide recession-era world, the sense of his own impending doom is all the more intense, because though the homeless man intends his sign as a genuine apocalyptic prediction, Sebastian Khan, purposeful misinterpreter of all things, views it as a narrower prophecy, of the doom of the Class of 2011, who in a year will leave their glorious youth behind. Only earlier today, his American Romanticism professor discussed with them Thomas Cole's *The Voyage of Life* (1842), four panels, each a stage in human life, *Childhood, Youth, Manhood,* and *Old Age. Youth,* of course, was Sebastian's favorite, a vivid, shining image depicting a young man dressed in fine red attire, standing in a boat with lush forests on all sides and reaching out towards the sky, where the image of a grand palace materializes in the clouds. But in the next painting, *Manhood,* the palace is gone, and the young man, now older, has his hands clasped in terrified prayer, while around him the water is dark and overhead the sky swirls with storm clouds. What if that is now Sebastian's future? What if college is the palace, and soon it will be gone along with his youth? He imagines his own face in the homeless man's wrinkled visage, faint signs of fleeting youth mirrored tragically, wistfully back.

"You're not listening, Sebastian," Viola says.

They are sitting on the steps of Sproul Hall, facing the plaza. Across from them looms the Martin Luther King building, casting its comforting shadow over the promenade. A few students sit at tables, still advertising their clubs and student groups, though by this point in the year, they are as effective as the homeless men shouting nearby. Viola meanwhile has been reading aloud from a book she's been assigned in her Medieval History class, a series of dirty French stories called the fabliaux, usually tales of lewd priests or of peasant women cheating on their husbands with young traveling clerks. On warm afternoons like this, lounging between classes, Sebastian often enjoys nothing more than listening to Viola playing the troubadour, her mellifluous voice bringing out all the subtleties of the Medieval texts (even in translation). But the homeless man has drawn his attention, and even the most gracefully spoken dirty stories of the French peasantry can't wrest it back.

"I'm listening," Sebastian says.

Viola clearly doesn't believe him.

"What's the story about, then?" she asks.

"A priest who fucks a peasant's wife."

This is largely a guess on Sebastian's part, a general approximation of fabliaux subject-matter based on Viola's previous readings.

"That was the last one," Viola says. "We've now moved onto 'The Fisherman of Pont-sur-Seine.'"

"Ah. Sorry. What's this one about?"

"A fisherman and his wife. The fisherman thinks the wife loves him only because he has a big dick. She insists that no, it's his great personality—"

"Are those her words?"

"Essentially. Anyway, one day the well-endowed fisherman is out fishing and finds a dead body washed up on shore. It happens to be of a priest who was caught fucking someone's wife in a neighboring town and who, in fleeing, fell into the river and drowned. By some miracle, his penis remained erect, and so the fisherman decides to test his wife's declaration. He cuts off the priest's still-erect penis and brings it back to his wife and tells her that he was accosted by some evil knights who said they were going to cut off one part of his body but that, because they were feeling generous, they would let him choose. He chose his penis, since his wife had said it wasn't the only reason she loved him. Predictably, the wife becomes upset at the thought that her husband's giant cock is gone and decides she doesn't love him anymore and starts looking into ways of divorcing him. He then reveals to her his own un-severed penis and tells her to admit the truth about why she loves him. She admits then that she only loves him for his dick and they have good sex and live happily ever after."

Viola smiles and looks expectantly at Sebastian.

"Charming," he says.

"I know, right? A more realistic depiction of marriage than a Jane Austen novel."

"Jane Austen novels are realistic enough," Sebastian says.

"Are they? Elizabeth Bennet marrying Darcy for his personality?"

"It's not for his personality. It's for his big house and money, which is just nineteenth-century-novel code for a big dick."

"Well, I prefer the directness of the Middle Ages."

Viola turns back to her book of fabliaux. The wind tussles her shoulder-length blond hair, and Sebastian notices that the color of the sky behind her matches her mirthful eyes, which scan with pleasure the lines of the fisherman's story. She wears a navy-blue blazer, not unlike Sebastian's own, with the sleeves rolled up to reveal the white lining, along with a black- and white-striped shirt, a black skirt, and black boots. Sebastian imagines her dressed as she is, sitting in a small, thatched-roof peasant house in thirteenth-century France, happily married to a well-endowed fisherman, while he himself sits brooding and Darcy-like in his nineteenth-century Georgian estate, next to a pale English wife who looks smilingly up at their mansion's tall marble columns.

The bells of the Campanile begin to clang, signaling 4 p.m. Viola sighs, folds up her book of fabliaux, and stands.

"Have to get to class."

"Lecture on the fabliaux?"

"On eleventh-century monasticism."

"So not quite the same then."

"You'd be surprised. Anyway, see you at the party tonight!"

She smiles, waves, and disappears down the steps of Sproul, into the river of students. Sebastian watches her for a moment, her sprightly walk, the jaunty tilt of her head, and then turns back to the homeless man. In the air around them, meanwhile, the bells of the Campanile continue their steady, ominous toll.

❋

That night, Sebastian's apartment fills up with alcohol and wild, enthusiastic members of Model UN. The compact space pulses with the energy of almost fifty undergraduates, their laugher resounding off the white walls of the two-bedroom. The apartment itself is located on the third floor of a building on the corner of Addison and Milvia, in Downtown Berkeley, one block from Shattuck and its bar-restaurants and restaurant-bars. Because it's only 2010 and the latest tech boom is only in its early stages—Facebook is still relatively new and cool, Twitter people are still trying to figure out, and Instagram is still just a future billionaire's work-in-progress—housing prices in the Bay Area have not yet reached the exorbitant levels of the future, and so despite the apartment being a prime plot of real estate, the rent is still relatively cheap (at least by Sebastian's haute-bourgeois standards): $2,200 a month, utilities included, parking extra (though, of course, Sebastian has no car and has never actually learned to drive, preferring to live as European an existence as he can). Sebastian's father is ultimately the one who pays his half of the bill, via an online system that Sebastian has only logged into once, a year ago, to fill out a maintenance request after the electric towel warmer in the bathroom briefly malfunctioned.

In the kitchen mixing drinks is Sebastian's roommate Harry. His full name is actually Hari Kumar, but due to the classic neuroses of an upper-middle-class minority, he prefers Harry and tells people he's mixed race like Sebastian, even though his parents, Jawal and Priya, are both from India.

Sebastian and Harry moved in together about two years ago, at the start of their sophomore year. Their apartment is decorated like most college student dwellings, with all the familiar IKEA pieces including the $150 navy blue sofa (the Solsta), the $25 coffee table (the Lack), and three of the $25 bookshelves (the Billys). Yet there is a clear clash of identities in the space, the modern minimalist chic of the building's architects and the contemporary Scandinavian furniture offset by Sebastian's own love of the past, the black-and-white photos of European cities he purchased on his trip two summers ago hanging on the walls and the lamp in the corner he bought from an antique store, a mid-century modern with a square, off-white lampshade that looks as if it's been taken from the set of *Mad Men*. The pale gloom it casts across the party is like light from another world, and when combined with the electronic music playing from a MacBook on the kitchen counter (a playlist put together by Harry, a fan of obscure and alternative Scandinavian bands), it imbues the party with the apartment's inherent tension, the clash between past and present, the reminder of the reality of time.

Normally, Sebastian never notices this tension, as the fusion of nostalgia for the distant past and love of the bourgeois present is the most accurate summary of his own sensibilities. But tonight, he can't help but see it. He leans against the wall next to the antique lamp, face shrouded in pale light, sipping a mixed drink (an Old Fashioned, of course, in un-ironic tribute to the great Mr. Draper), but is too preoccupied to appreciate the pleasant taste on his tongue, the sharp whiskey and the sweet afterthought of sugar. He thinks of the homeless man and his sign, and it doesn't help that he's only further reminded of the impending end when, in gazing at the merriment around him, he can easily pick out the senior members of the club, those who pretend to laugh, smile, and drink in the carefree way they've been doing for four years but who clearly can no longer enjoy themselves like the non-seniors can, because they know now that uncertainty awaits after they walk down the stage in their caps and gowns and accept their (fake) diplomas (while their real ones are processed and sent by mail). Rebecca Chen, for example, outgoing Model UN President, is one of the few to have a job lined up, though it's not what her freshman self would have envisioned after four years at Berkeley: she'll be moving to Greenville, Mississippi to join Teach for America and teach English to low-income middle schoolers. It's a noble cause, and Rebecca has been sharing the news with pride and trumpeting her own selflessness and commitment to serve the less fortunate. But Sebastian can see in the way she drinks more hesitantly tonight and in the way her smile always fades when she thinks no one is looking how she really feels beneath that bubbly, effervescent exterior. This is Rebecca Chen, after all, fashionista, consumer of fine whiskeys, fluent speaker of five languages (Sebastian, envious, only speaks one, English), a cosmopolitan dreamer who envisioned herself eventually working some sophisticated job somewhere like Geneva or Singapore and who joined Model UN as a freshman because she liked the idea of wearing pantsuits and flying off to fancy hotels across the world on the University's dime. It's the same reason Sebastian joined in his freshman year, the idea that for a weekend one can pretend to be someone else, a diplomat of some far away country power-brokering in hotel lobbies with the leaders of the free and the not-free worlds. It's fake, of course, but Sebastian and Rebecca and all the others like it precisely *because* it's fake. They can fly to Boston or Chicago or The Hague, put on suits and ties and pocket squares, saunter down escalators to mezzanine-level conference rooms, sit at long tables lined with placards for their countries and pitchers of ice-cold water periodically refilled by the hotel staff, then spend the night drinking at fancy bars with leather seats, and yet all the while know that in a few days they'll be back on a plane, dressed casual-hipstery once again, soaring home to the cozy embrace of the Berkeley bubble. It's all of the glamor of international diplomacy without any of the responsibility. Sebastian can't imagine what Rebecca must feel now, knowing that the situation will be reversed, that now she'll have the immense responsibility of turning around the lives of underprivileged adolescents but without any of the trappings that may make such a thankless job tolerable (though Sebastian has never been there, he imagines that Greenville, Mississippi is nothing like The Hague). And so he stands, contemplative, melancholy, next to the pale glow of the old lamp, his Old Fashioned half-empty, his eyes roving across the room like the lights of the world's last lighthouse, watching the old ships pass him by and anchor at port, where they wait to be decommissioned.

It's from this pose that he first sees her—Fatima Ahmed, as he'll later learn her name to be—seated on the IKEA Solsta and staring at him. She's as separate from the party as he is, quiet amidst the laughter, a tableau of stillness against the general swirl of bodies, sitting rigid and in place while the students around her sway drunkenly side to side or throw their heads back to down shots. In the way she looks at him, eyes wide, a faint flush in her cheeks visible even in this light, he knows she's intrigued by him, not an uncommon occurrence at a party but surprising tonight of all nights, when Sebastian is not his usually vivacious and charming self and instead stands sullenly against the wall. Perhaps, though, it's the very melancholy that makes him attractive to her. If Sebastian never saw the homeless man and if his mind were far, far away from thoughts of the end of days and if he were laughing in genuine merriment like the others around him, she might have paid him no notice. She doesn't know Sebastian, and so maybe when she sees him standing there looking pensive, moody, and detached, she imagines he's always like this, the wallflower, the introvert, the wise young man too mature to partake

17

in the revelry surrounding him. If only she knew the truth of the thoughts beneath that wavy-haired head, that those dark-brown eyes hold within them more of a longing for youth than all the departing seniors combined.

Sebastian makes his way towards her, gliding through the laughing throng, his eyes never leaving hers. She isn't his normal type, far too somber and frowning—but today isn't a normal day. He sees the homeless man's sign floating above a stone promenade and imagines how one day the apartment around him will be empty.

He reaches the sofa and sits, leaving a few inches of space between them.

"Hi," he says.

"Hi," she says.

Sebastian sees she has no drink in her hand.

"Not drinking tonight?" he asks.

"I don't drink."

Sebastian is briefly awed. Temperance is not a very popular ideal on a college campus and meeting a practitioner is often more unlikely than meeting a 9/11 truther or someone who voted McCain. She does in some ways resemble those women who founded temperance societies in late-nineteenth-century America, with strong, arched, and bushy eyebrows, a broad forehead, hair tied back in a loose ponytail, small glasses that sharpen her already sharp gaze, a blouse buttoned all the way up to the top, and a long, flowing skirt that falls past her knees, a garment which in the age of miniskirts seems as archaic as the ideals of courtly love and traditional marriage.

"Are you allergic?" he asks.

"What?"

She looks confused.

"Are you allergic?" Sebastian repeats. "To alcohol?"

"Why do you think I'm allergic to alcohol?"

"Because you don't drink."

Her eyes narrow. "I'm Muslim."

"Ah."

Sebastian's eyes widen, with surprise and interest. It's obvious now that he knows. Her skin color is like his mother's was, and she looks like a grown-up version of the Pakistani girls he remembers from the Islamic classes at the mosque he used to go to as a child. Sebastian, of course, has long since abandoned Islam. His mother was the religious parent, holding onto the Pakistani half of her heritage in a way Sebastian's father never did and insisting Sebastian go to Islamic school on Sundays. But when she died, when Sebastian was twelve, he started going less and less, and eventually not at all. Religion seemed an insufficient answer to life's tragedies. Instead, Sebastian turned to art, an interest his mother had often encouraged in him. At the library one day, soon after her death, he found a book on the Pre-Raphaelites and, flipping it open with a longing for his mother clutching at his chest, he discovered a print of Rossetti's *Proserpina*. He was drawn at first to the way she reminded him of his mother, the slender fingers, the black hair, the faraway look in her eyes, but after a moment, he began to focus on the colors abstracted from any meaning, the fiery orange of the peach, the deep red of the lips, the velvet and oceanic blue of the dress. They were like nothing he'd ever seen in suburban California, windows to another reality, a refuge from the melancholy of his new, mother-less world. After that, Sebastian lost himself in the art of the nineteenth century, in Romantic and Pre-Raphaelite and Victorian images of slender women standing in vivid landscapes, with wild hair and sadness in their eyes. In the abundance of color and sensuality, Sebastian found something almost spiritual, an alternative to the dreary present, a glorious past where emotional pain didn't exist. Those paintings filled a void that Islam, with its rejection of visual depiction, never could. And so Sebastian passed his adolescence in a state of blissful impiety, skipping mosque class to go to museum exhibitions and reading Walter Pater instead of the Quran (Sebastian's father, who never particularly liked Islam, or any religion for that matter, wasn't at all bothered by his son's spiritual decline and fall). Yet still, despite his apostasy, whenever Sebastian passes by the Muslim Student Association table on Sproul Plaza and sees the group of them praying at the top of the steps of the Martin Luther King Building and placing their foreheads on the felt prayer mats rolled out across the ground, he feels a surprising swell of emotion listening to their collective "Allahu-Akbar" echo down the promenade. In those moments he thinks of his mother, who taught him some Arabic words as a child and whispered them to him as he went to sleep, comforting, lilting phrases that she said would blanket him and always keep him safe. Now, with this Fatima who declares herself Muslim and doesn't drink and has his mother's skin tone, and even looks a little like Rossetti's Proserpina, with her sharp nose and fierce expression, Sebastian is overwhelmed with a strange feeling, something he's never felt for any of the many women he's casually courted (women who have almost entirely been white), something beyond simple lust, a longing for his mother and a culture he'd long ago rejected.

"I'm Muslim too," Sebastian says.

Fatima's eyes flicker down to his drink.

"I slip up sometimes," he adds. "But honestly, I don't drink that much."

Before Fatima can confirm the truth of what is, in truth, a complete lie (one of many Sebastian will inflict on poor Fatima), Viola appears in front of the Solsta, holding a whiskey bottle by the neck and clutching a handful of shot glasses in her other hand.

"Sebastian!" she says. "Drink up! You told me we'd finish this bottle last night and there's still half left!"

Before Sebastian can explain himself to Fatima, Viola thrusts him an overflowing shot of whiskey. A few droplets slosh onto Sebastian's coat, joining an earlier whiskey stain higher up on the lapel. Sebastian attempts a sheepish smile in Fatima's direction, but Viola interrupts him for a toast.

"To Sebastian Khan! Binge-drinker extraordinaire!"

"I don't drink that much—"

"He once blacked out from wine!" Viola says to Fatima. "From wine! It was boxed wine, but still…"

Fatima stands and brushes out the creases in her skirt.

"I should find my friend," she says, as diplomatically as any Model UN delegate.

She disappears into the crowd by the kitchen, her ponytail waving back at Sebastian before vanishing into the churning sea of bodies. The sharp smell of whiskey drifts up from the shot glasses Viola still holds.

"Who was that?" Viola asks. "Also I didn't know they made skirts that long anymore."

Sebastian doesn't laugh. Viola sighs and shakes her head.

"Oh, Sebastian," she says. "You can do way better than her."

"She's not bad."

"She looks like a librarian."

"I like libraries."

Viola shrugs and raises her shot glass. "I guess if anyone can convince her to drop that skirt, it's you. To Sebastian Khan, incubus extraordinaire!"

Sebastian sighs but raises his shot glass (not exactly opposed to the flattering nickname). Viola clinks hers against his, and whiskey splashes out across their hands and down onto the carpet. The dark, swirling liquid reminds Sebastian of the color of Fatima's skin. Sebastian leans his head back and downs the shot. The drink is bitter. Viola drinks with a jerk of her head and starts coughing and then laughing. She holds up the still-half-full whiskey bottle.

"More?"

Sebastian shakes his head and stands. "I've had too much."

"You've had two drinks. Are you an old man already?"

"Maybe," Sebastian says, thinking of the homeless man and his sign.

He moves past Viola and towards the kitchen, looking for Fatima amidst the crowd. Snatches of conversation drift by his ears, references to coursework and whether Obama has been a good president thus far and various upcoming unpaid summer internships. The whiskey shot races through him, and his heart pounds with a renewed purpose, so hard he can hear it pressing out against his eardrums. It's rare for him to feel this kind of frantic desire for a girl he's just met. He's experienced enough with seduction to know the importance of being disinterested, but tonight, Sebastian can't help himself. As his heart pounds and the sweat builds under his wavy strands of hair, he thinks of freshman year of high school, when he was fourteen and he and the girl in his geometry class who'd made eyes at him for several months (Chelsea, a senior) finally had sex in the back of her dad's Honda Accord, in the empty parking lot at the top of Old Ranch Hill, in one of the city's parks, late at night when the only lights were the gas stations down in the valley and the few cars that zoomed along the distant highway, going west towards San Francisco. His heart beat furiously then and his brow was dripping with sweat, even though the whole thing lasted less than a minute (to Chelsea's disappointment). Now, in the crowded apartment, Sebastian feels fourteen all over again.

Across the room and near the balcony, he sees a flash of a ponytail and the whipping of a long skirt. Heart racing, he moves towards it, crafting in his mind possible lines he might say—but he's interrupted by a strong hand on his shoulder, and he looks over to find fellow junior Imogen Lin steering him into a conversation with freshman Nathan "Nate" Hale.

"Sebastian!" Imogen says, with practiced eagerness.

"Imogen," Sebastian replies, with a false smile of his own.

Imogen doesn't particularly like Sebastian, so he knows she's only using him now to save herself from a prolonged conversation with Nate. Chubby, with a cherubic face, innocent blue eyes, and already thinning hair, Nate is nothing at all like the nimble clandestine operative he happens to share a name with, and he stands now in his characteristic pose, with his chest thrust forward and his hands on his lower back, something that only further pushes out his stomach. He has no drink in hand, but his eyes glisten with the recognizable drunken stupor, and he sways awkwardly, like a lopsided buoy. Imogen, meanwhile, pale skin, black hair, half-Asian, half-Persian features (and thanks to her Anglophile parents the whitest of names), characteristic dark eyeliner, and polished, professional attire, stands with her arms crossed, her gaze level and sober, in one hand a whiskey cocktail which she swirls more than drinks, in the other hand her phone, which she always holds at parties to remind everyone that she's a busy person who might get an important call or text at any moment. Today, it's her new iPhone 3GS, gleaming and futuristic in the room's murky light (technologically savvy Imogen is one of the few college students to even own a smartphone; old-fashioned Sebastian, for example, still has his Motorola Razr flip phone from high school).

Sebastian faces Imogen and Nate but keeps an eye out for signs of Fatima off near the balcony.

"We were just talking about the election," Nate says to Sebastian. "Congratulations."

"Yes, congratulations," Imogen says, voice dripping with disdain.

"You were a worthy opponent," Sebastian returns, with an equal measure of disdain.

Like all things that ultimately don't matter, MUN elections are taken very seriously by college students. A week before, UC Berkeley's Model UN club gathered in a small classroom for a three-hour meeting during which members

23

gave impassioned speeches about why they should be President or Head Delegate or Treasurer or Secretary, citing their commitment to the club and their previous credentials and their visions for the future of UCBMUN, all with Obama-esque eloquence. Sebastian stood (not "ran"—he treated elections with a languid, European flair, a policy which suited his nonchalance) for Head Delegate, the head of the travel team, citing his three years with the club and his oft-stamped passport. He barely eeked out a win over the competitive perfectionist Imogen (who unlike Sebastian very much "ran" for the position, printing out fliers and making an "IMOGEN LIN FOR HEAD DELEGATE" Facebook group where she posted her resume and asked fellow MUN-ers to offer suggestions for the club's future). Harry, meanwhile, won his election for President uncontested and Viola won hers as Vice President in a landslide, beating out the sweating, stammering, and severely overmatched Nate, who everyone was surprised chose to run at all.

Sebastian notices that now that her rival is here, Imogen has tensed, her pupils dilated, her mouth slightly open. She's the only person he knows who responds to competition with such a militant passion, an almost sexual urgency. He finds her charming enough, though he's long since abandoned thoughts of sleeping with her. Once, in their freshman year, the two were flirting at a bar during the UPenn conference, but the conversation quickly devolved when Sebastian gave her a backhanded compliment, telling her that her debate skills had improved considerably since the beginning of the year. She responded with vitriol, telling Sebastian not be a condescending prick ("Who, me?" Sebastian asked) and declaring from then on that she would out-debate Sebastian at every conference. Imogen then made a Google Doc and started tallying each of the club member's conference awards and to this day has made sure she's always on top. Sebastian finds this competition amusing and treats it with a vague and frivolous interest—but to Imogen, who's been in Model UN since middle school and is one of the rare few in the club who wants to be a diplomat in the future, it's an ideological struggle as significant as the Cold War, two incompatible views of the world pitted in a life or death struggle.

"So what are your plans as head delegate?" Imogen now asks Sebastian.

"Should I have plans?"

Imogen glares at him, brow furrowing, eyes narrowing, and nose wrinkling like she's sniffed something unpleasant. "Of course you should! The club's finances are a mess! Our own conference lost money last year, and we can't afford to send the same number of people off to away conferences as we did this year, unless we win enough awards to convince the ASUC to give us more University funding, which will mean more training sessions—"

"It'll work out," Sebastian says, looking past her and out towards the balcony.

"You can't just say that without doing anything! You have responsibility now. You won an election—"

"I know, Imogen I was there too—"

Nate, whose head has been bouncing back and forth between them, laughs (far louder than the joke deserves). "Yeah, Imogen, he was there!" he repeats.

Imogen lets out an exasperated sigh and downs her whiskey in one swig. "Honestly, Sebastian, I don't even know why you do MUN when you obviously don't care—"

"I've told you before, I do it for the theatre of it all, the chance to pretend to be someone else for a weekend."

"Well not everything in life is a fucking play."

Sebastian ignores her and looks back over to the balcony, through Harry's room. Harry is sitting there, on his swivel chair, pontificating to a group of younger members about political philosophy ("The UN is absolutely based on Plato's theory of forms, since both agree that there is

an ideal government, somewhere out beyond the cave…”).
Past Harry, Sebastian can see Fatima, standing out on the
balcony, alone, looking out across the city.

Sebastian pushes past Imogen and Nate, his eyes locked
on Fatima. Imogen notices and shakes her head.

“Another soon to be attempt for the great Sebastian
Khan?” she asks.

“And another soon to be success,” Sebastian says.

Imogen, still frowning, turns away and goes to refill her
drink. Sebastian feels pleased to be rid of her, but then finds
that Nate is following him into Harry’s room.

“You going to try to pick her up?” Nate asks.

Nate speaks very loudly, almost at shouting pitch,
and Sebastian is glad the apartment is noisy enough that,
despite this, only the two of them can hear. As always,
though, he can’t bring himself to be too angry at Nate, who,
red-cheeked and starry-eyed, stares back at Sebastian like a
stray dog grateful for the faintest glimmer of attention. Nate
idolizes Sebastian, always choosing to be in his committees
at conferences and trying to copy his style of debate, not to
mention his manner of flirtation (though when Nate tries
to smugly catch the gaze of his fellow delegates, he comes
across more Humbert-Humbert-creepy than Don-Drap-
er-suave). Yet even Sebastian recognizes that in the end,
there’s very little that’s substantively different between the
two. Nate may be two years younger (and considerably
fatter), but the stupidly optimistic, underlying spirit is the
same, and when Sebastian stares into his pale blue, childlike
eyes, he imagines himself looking back.

“I’m just going to talk to her,” Sebastian says, in answer
to Nate’s question.

“I don’t know how you do it…”

His eyes droop sadly to the ground. Sebastian senses a
way to get rid of him.

“It’s easy. Look.”

Sebastian scans the room, and his eyes land on a girl,

standing towards the side of the room, a drink in hand, staring uncertainly out at the party. Her hands shake a little, and her shoulders slouch, and Sebastian sees that she's shy, possibly a little unhappy, probably a little desperate too. She's not unattractive, and if Sebastian's mind wasn't elsewhere, he may have even considered a half-hearted attempt to flirt. Instead, he nods his head towards her and looks at Nate.

"What do I say?" Nate asks.

"Just be yourself. Be honest."

Sebastian claps Nate on the back, pushing him towards the timid girl and then wheels quickly into Harry's room.

"Sebastian!" Harry says. "We're debating Epicurus vs the Stoics—"

"Not now," Sebastian says (they've had this debate before, and Sebastian is a devout Epicurean).

He can see Fatima through the glass door, still standing by herself. The wind whips at her hair, and Sebastian imagines a painting, hanging in a museum, of her staring pensively down at the street, while behind her partygoers gather and laugh. Harry follows Sebastian's gaze and understands. He turns back to the others seated before him and continues his lecture series, his scholarly, pedantic voice describing how "the problem with Lucretius is that there's no moral aspect to his philosophy."

Sebastian steps outside onto the balcony and closes the door behind him. He's greeted by a cold wind and the smell of burnt-out cigarettes. In the distance he hears a few cars zooming down Shattuck. Except for Fatima standing by the railing, the balcony is empty.

She looks over at him, her face still set in her resting frown. "Not drinking anymore?" she asks.

"No."

Sebastian leans against the balcony next to her. Her eyes narrow but she doesn't move away. The black metal railing is cold, colder than the nighttime air (though not nearly as cold as Fatima's icy stare). It's just before midnight, and down below, on Addison, a crowd emerges from the Berkeley Rep, milling about with an audience's post-performance energy, all dressed in sports coats and corduroy pants and with the well-maintained skin and hair of older people who've lived lifetimes in relative affluence. The theater itself, like everything else on the street, has similar marks of wealth: large, rectangular glass windows, reinforced with beams of steel, and a brick facade, obviously false (nothing is made purely of brick in earthquake-prone California), but to Sebastian beautiful for that very reason, because what better way to build a theater than with a deceptive exterior? Beyond the theater, Addison continues to Shattuck, where the multicolored lights of the buildings shine into the night, PiQ (Pane Italiano Qualita) with its outdoor seating designed to mimic a European cafe (and thus one of Sebastian's favorite haunts), Half-Price Books across the street, the strange restaurant that serves both Mexican and Pakistani food further down Shattuck, and the newly opened bar/restaurant/gastropub on the corner, too expensive for college students to frequent (but where Sebastian often goes regardless), with a crowd of wealthy urbanites gathered outside to smoke. Beyond Shattuck stretch the rising hills of Berkeley's campus. The moon sits high, and the sky is open and free of clouds. The stars remain invisible, drowned out by the city's lights, but they aren't necessary. Tonight Sebastian can see the city as clearly as he needs to, the beautiful urban sprawl of restaurants and cafes and apartment buildings, the construction cranes paused for the night, in the midst of throwing up another powerful, looming, glass and steel building, a sign of all that the place may one day be, yet for Sebastian another sign of regret, of a world that in a little over a year he'll suddenly lose.

The city lights flicker across Fatima's face and light up her skin. The wind pulls a strand of her hair down across her dark eyes, and Sebastian resists the desire to brush it away with his fingers and let his hand rest against her cheek.

"You're missing the party," Fatima says. "Don't you have a whiskey bottle to finish?"

"I don't feel like drinking any more tonight."

He's not lying now. He glances back through the door of the apartment. Harry, the scholar, remains seated on his chair, gesticulating wildly to his faux-lecture hall. Beyond him, Nate, stomach presented out to the world, stands next to the timid girl, awkwardly close, and even from this distance, Sebastian sees the wariness in her body language (Nate attempts to place his hand on her arm, and she quickly pulls away). Near them, seated on the sofa is Imogen, on her phone, still sober and alert despite having another whiskey cocktail in her hand, checking emails from one of the several other clubs she's an officer of. And then there's Viola, ever the troubadour, standing on the chair and belting out the lyrics to a song while alternating shots of whiskey and vodka (Viola doesn't like gin—"I'm not a fucking old person."), a mixture which she will the next morning seriously regret. Sebastian imagines each of them pulling the carriage, leading the woman down the thorny path.

"Have you seen the new homeless man on Sproul?" Sebastian asks, turning to Fatima.

"I don't keep track of them."

"Well, there's a new one. Old guy, white hair, clean-shaven. He thinks the world will end in a year."

"A lot of people have crazy ideas."

"But think about it. In a year, we graduate."

Fatima looks unperturbed. "It's just a coincidence."

"But it's still significant, right? It still means something."

"Does it?"

"Yeah! The end of college, the end of the world…"

Fatima laughs. "The end of college isn't the end of the world."

"No, not literally, but…it's the end of some kind of world. I mean, for four years we've lived in this bubble of privilege, taking whatever classes we feel like, spending our days at cafes reading, eating at restaurants almost every night, going to parties every weekend, getting paid by the university to fly off to Model UN Conferences and stay in swanky hotels—"

"I think you and I have had very different college experiences."

"Okay, sure. Maybe you didn't do Model UN."

"Also, I'm a junior transfer, so for me it's only been a year, not three."

"Oh." Sebastian is surprised, having never met someone with a college experience so different from his own. "Well then you must feel the loss even more, since you'll only be here two years."

"No, I think two years will be enough. I didn't apply here to enjoy myself and put my life on hold. I came here with a plan, knowing exactly what courses I needed to take—"

"What do you study?"

"Computer science."

"You want to work in tech?"

Sebastian says this inadvertent disdain, as if Fatima has said she wants to become a dentist or a nun.

"Yes, I do," Fatima says, frowning. "I'm already applying to jobs in Silicon Valley."

Sebastian is surprised again. It's never occurred to him that someone still in college can apply to jobs in the real world.

"What do you study?" Fatima asks.

"Art History," he says. "But I've taken enough English and History courses that I'll probably do majors in those too."

It's now Fatima who is surprised. Sebastian imagines it's because she's impressed at his array of coursework, though as her next question suggests, perhaps more pragmatic thoughts flutter through her head.

"What will you do with all those?" she asks.

"No idea," Sebastian says with the most carefree of shrugs.

They pause a moment and stare at each other, as if contemplating how two people of the same religion and (partially at least) the same ethnicity, both American and raised in the same cultural milieu and both born around the same time, can end up so different in just twenty-one years.

"So did you ever want to study anything else?" Sebastian asks. "Anything besides computer science?"

"Not at all. Ever since high school I've known I wanted to work in tech."

"So then you've never felt the fear either?"

"What fear?"

"The fear of the real world. The fear that you feel at the end of junior year, when three-quarters of this life has gone, and you realize that in three hundred and eighty days you'll be thrown out via the graduation stage in a cap and gown, off into the world. The fear that everything here, all the carefree happiness you've felt, will disappear like some palace mirage you imagined in the distant sky, leaving you and your boat to drift out into the deadly, open water, where the sky is dark and the only things around you are rocky crags and dead trees…you've never felt that fear?"

Fatima laughs. "No," she says. "But I think I understand."

Fatima is smiling, and Sebastian feels pleased with himself at having overcome her earlier coldness. Maybe she's never met someone so apparently improvisationally eloquent (in truth, Sebastian has said variations of these lines before, to Viola and Harry). She's also probably never seen Thomas Cole's paintings (or even heard of Thomas Cole) and so perhaps imagines that Sebastian has invented the metaphor of the boat and the water and the palace in the sky all on his own. He considers mentioning the painting and correcting any misunderstandings on her part but then decides not to. In her widened eyes, he sees that she's intrigued and that the initial spark that led her to stare at him as he wove his way through the crowded room and sat beside her on the IKEA Solsta is still there, magnified now by the depth he's revealed to her, the melancholy over the end of college that she seems to think is a sign of maturity.

He reaches out to shake her hand in a gesture of exaggerated politeness.

"I don't think I've learned your name," he says.

She looks amused at his theatrical formality.

"Fatima Ahmed," she says.

Her voice wavers ever so slightly, but enough that Sebastian notices, and when they shake hands, the shudder in her body at the contact of their skin is slight but perceptible. He smiles, as much with his eyes as with his lips.

"Sebastian Khan," he says. "A pleasure to meet you."

CHAPTER TWO

THE MAGIC CIRCLE (1886)

She is blond, the girl who walks across Memorial Glade, blond and tall and wearing a gray summer dress. Each step she takes displays the full extent of her long legs, and when a breeze blows down across the grassy field, the hem of the dress lifts slightly to reveal the briefest hint of black underwear. She walks purposefully, her wavy hair and the leather satchel slung over her shoulder swinging rhythmically with her movements, and Sebastian watches as she moves up the stone steps and into Doe Library, through the main entrance over which looms the watchful bust of Athena. Her black boots echo loudly against the stone, a steady clip, and as Sebastian's eyes rise from her body up to the neatly ordered neoclassical facade of the library, ten huge rectangular windows interspersed with faux-Corinthian columns and one larger window just above the entrance, he imagines he can hear the echo of her boots resounding through time, to Ancient Greece, when women in flowing peploses strode confidently up to the Acropolis, their sandals clipping across the stone with the same timeless sound.

"Does it even matter that I'm here?" Fatima asks.

They're sitting together, under a tree at one end of the glade. Fatima angrily closes her book (Frank, Robert H. and Bernanke, Ben S. *Principles of Microeconomics*. New York: McGraw-Hill, 2008.), whose thud drowns out the echoing footfalls in Sebastian's head.

"What?" Sebastian asks, innocently.

"You know what."

"I was admiring the view. It's a beautiful day."

Fatima frowns.

"You have a thing for white girls, you know. Every girl you've dated besides me has been white."

When Fatima says dated, Sebastian knows she really means slept with. In the literal sense of the word, Sebastian has actually dated only two other women besides Fatima, Emily in high school and Madeline in college, both as white as their names suggest. In the broader sense, though, Fatima is also correct, as all the other women Sebastian has "dated" have either been white or white-looking. Yet Sebastian sees no problem with this erotic homogeneity. From an artistic point of view, he simply likes the look of white skin: it's like a piece of sculpted marble or a blank sheet of canvas, and it contrasts beautifully with the wild splash of color from a lustrous head of hair. He certainly doesn't believe his preference is a sign of anything deeper, such as the psychological trauma of losing a mother who identified more with the Pakistani half of her heritage, or the unconscious lessons gleaned from a father who, after his wife's death, also dated only white or white-looking women, or any of the political and social forces of a post-9/11 America that might perhaps lead someone to value white skin over others. No, as far as Sebastian is concerned, it's simply an aesthetic choice.

"Well, that must mean you're special," Sebastian says now to Fatima, in reference to her observation.

He reaches out to play with her hair, but Fatima turns away. Sebastian's charms may have won her over four months ago, on his balcony at the end of junior year, but now the summer is over, and it's two weeks into senior year, and Fatima appears less enamored with Sebastian's soft eyes and breezy words.

"I'm sorry," he says.

He does his best to look contrite, though inside he feels irritated. Fatima has been upset before at his (supposedly) wandering eye. Admittedly, eyeing the girl just now across Memorial Glade was a blatant and unambiguous wander, but the previous time was quite different. They were at La Note in Downtown Berkeley on their second official date (their first was an informal gelato at Naia the week before, three nights after the party). Finals were over by then and the restaurant, like most of Berkeley, was almost empty, the only diners besides them a late-twenties couple talking about their mortgage and an old man in the corner, quietly drinking coffee and staring up at the vintage posters of Paris and the Alphonse Mucha prints that lined the off-white walls of the dimly lit interior. Fatima seemed to be enjoying herself, although she wasn't eating much of her food (poulet au champignons in a white wine sauce—later she admitted, to Sebastian's horror, that she didn't really like French food). But when the waitress returned to refill their carafe of Bordeaux and Sebastian started speaking to her in French, Fatima became jealous, as she herself didn't speak French and was therefore under the impression that Sebastian's poor attempt to practice his lessons from French 2 ("Merci" was the only word he really got right) was a sort of sophisticated and flirtatious bantering, especially when the waitress put her delicate, long-fingered hand on Sebastian's shoulder and let it sit there for, what was to Fatima, a moment too long.

"What was that?" Fatima asked, afterwards.

"What?" Sebastian said, with genuine innocence this time.

"You let her flirt with you."

"I let her? Fatima, I can't control how people act around me."

In truth, the waitress had seemed to Sebastian more amused than flirtatious, though he decided not to correct Fatima's impression. Fatima didn't mention the incident again, but it remained a sour stain on an otherwise lovely dinner (which was sour only where it was meant to be, specifically the vinegar-based dressing that came with their salads). Now, on Memorial Glade, Sebastian thinks of that dinner as he stares contritely back at Fatima. After a moment, she sighs.

"Just don't do it again," she says.

The wind around them picks up. It's September but still warm out, and the leaves are only just beginning to drop from the trees, which remain relatively unchanged from a few months back and give no sense that time has passed and is still passing. In his heart, though, Sebastian feels every minute tick by, and if he ever forgets, there's always the homeless man, still seated prominently on Sproul Plaza with his whiteboard sign (now at 244 DAYS TILL THE END). Sebastian thinks of Keats's season of mists and mellow fruitfulness and wishes he lived elsewhere, a place where autumn meant more than just an extended summer, where he could see time passing in the world around him and reassure himself that it wasn't just he who felt the change. Whenever he goes to the East Coast at this time of year, he experiences all the mesmerizing wonder that so many colors can bring, as well as the sadness of the young and beautiful leaves suddenly dying.

He turns to Fatima. "So. The party tonight?"

Fatima shakes her head. "I have too much on my mind to just stand around and watch people drink."

Her eyes drift far away, and Sebastian can tell she's thinking of her email inbox, where the rejections have been piling up.

"By the way, did you take a look at any of the links I

sent you?" she asks. "A lot of those places accept applications in the fall."

"Not yet," Sebastian says. "But I will."

The truth is, he feels it's far too early to even think about applying for jobs.

"Please look at them, okay?" Fatima says. "If we're really going to move to San Francisco after graduation, then you'll need to take this all much more seriously. We'll never afford rent if I'm the only one who gets a job."

Moving to San Francisco is not something to which Sebastian has explicitly agreed (by this point, they've only been dating for a little over 100 days, and while FDR may have accomplished much in that length of time, Sebastian has no doubt that even he would have been wary if a woman talked of moving in after only a few months of "going steady," or whatever they called it back in 1932), though his silence has acted as a tacit form of assent, and he has to admit that a significant part of him, the part that was attracted to Fatima in the first place and that is currently deeply troubled by the sight of the homeless man and his sign, is glad that Fatima has planned out this future, of the two of them living together in the city, Fatima working for a tech company as an engineer, Sebastian working at some investment bank or management consulting firm that hires people from all majors (even Art History), as long as they're smart and confident (which Sebastian certainly believes himself to be).

"And we'll live in a nice apartment in SOMA," Fatima said to him, one night towards the middle of summer, when they sat on his rooftop and drank wine (at least, Sebastian did) and stared out at San Francisco's distant towers, "one of those new glass and steel buildings with the big windows that let in all the natural light. And each evening, before we go to bed, we'll sit out on the terrace and watch the sun set over the bay. And on weekends, we'll have little parties on our rooftop, with a few friends from work, and we'll all talk about how we're moving up in the world, and college will be just a pleasant memory, almost forgotten…"

It is comforting, Fatima's bourgeois palace in the air, especially in the face of the world's impending end. But to Sebastian, it never feels concrete or substantial and is instead just another dreamlike fiction, as unreal as a Model UN conference—and when Fatima tries to make it real, to remind him that the apartment and the view and that upwardly mobile set of friends will require hard work, diligence, job applications, financial planning, etc., Sebastian chafes, because after all, there is another part of him, a part that's not at all like the one that fell for Fatima and that in the face of the world's end doesn't seek out an actual future but wants instead to retreat back into the world of college, to be a freshman again, and to this part of him, Fatima's dream and all its adult connotations is not a dam halting the progress of Thomas Cole's river, but instead a confirmation that the homeless man's prophecy has come to pass, that the world has ended and Sebastian's boat is now plunging headlong into tumultuous waters and towards the black skies of manhood and old age.

The bells of the Campanile toll. Fatima stands and puts the economics textbook into her backpack.

"I have to get to class."

"Will I see you at the party tonight?" Sebastian asks.

"I already told you, I'll be busy. But have fun. And call me afterwards."

Sebastian stands and kisses her. He wonders if to Fatima, the kiss is comforting and warm, because for him it's perfunctory, cold, and passionless. He is aware of the coldness of the inside of her lip and the hesitation on the tip of her tongue. He thinks of their first kiss at the start of summer, outside her apartment on the south side of campus after their informal date at Naia. She was uncertain then too, but Sebastian put his hand gently on her arm and felt the brief shudder in her body, and so he leaned close and placed his other hand behind her neck, and under the streetlight, as a few students sauntered by, she leaned forward and they kissed. Her lips were warm in the night air, but more than that, Sebastian felt the thrill of something stolen. The kiss felt transgressive because she'd told Sebastian over gelato that she never kissed someone on the first date, and yet here she was, just a few hours later, unable to resist. The sense of victory and fulfillment reminded Sebastian of a Model UN Conference, when he convinced a majority to vote for his resolution, or when he won an award at the end of the weekend.

The warmth of that night and the thrill of that kiss lingered over the summer, which he and Fatima spent together, wandering the empty paths of Berkeley's campus hand in hand, Sebastian regaling her with tales of his three years here, Fatima listening to him, enraptured by his eyes. They even made the occasional foray to San Francisco, to get Blue Bottle coffee and Three Twins ice cream at the Ferry Building and then walk along the Embarcadero down towards AT&T Park while Fatima sketched out for him her dream of their life together, how from their apartment they would look out onto the Bay Bridge and the ocean every morning. In those days, Sebastian hadn't felt afraid of that future. It was the summer before school restarted, and so time never felt real anyway. The world was paused and even the homeless man was on vacation, having taken his count-down with him.

Sebastian remembers how once, just before the summer ended, when students were returning to school and there was a sense of anticipation in the air, but also when it was still late August and the air was still warm, he felt genu-inely in love with Fatima. They were at Jupiter, eating pizza and drinking beer (at least, Sebastian was), seated outside on the patio in the cool evening light. They'd been dating for three months at that point, not a terribly long time, and so perhaps the love he felt was just the beer, warm inside his stomach, though Sebastian wanted to believe it was her, Fatima, who kept him spellbound for three hours, animated and vivacious, leaning forward on the dark-green wooden table where their pizzas sat steaming, her eyes dilated and sparkling, her breath scented with garlic and mozzarella, her hands occasionally brushing her hair behind her ears.

"Anyway, to me computer science isn't just the latest fad, the latest way to make money. It's something I actually enjoy. I think computers are the next frontier of human exploration. We've discovered the Earth itself, and we've even flown up into space. But the computer world, it's this other reality that exists on a different plane entirely, in between the atoms themselves, in the very equations we use to create it, a whole infinite universe that we barely understand. Honestly, sometimes I feel like I could live in that world forever."

It was the first time Sebastian ever heard Fatima speak in such a way, authentic, emotive, propelled by a genuine desire that went beyond the trappings of the real world. In that brief moment, it seemed as if it didn't matter whether she ever had her apartment in SOMA or a long-term relationship or all the bourgeois comforts she'd been taught to want, and for the nano-est of seconds, Sebastian glimpsed who she really was, the actual processor that made her hum to life. But now the warmth and thrill have gone and the summer feels an eternity ago, and as Sebastian watches Fatima walk away across Memorial Glade, he feels a sharp pang of longing for those carefree days, ultimately all too brief and few, as if they never happened at all, as if the couple sitting at the wooden table and staring into each other's eyes were two different people in a different world entirely.

Soon Fatima disappears into the crowd of moving students. Sebastian looks up at the clock on the Campanile. Professor Walter's office hours begin in half an hour, and Sebastian has promised to drop by. Walter is one of the few professors Sebastian gets along with, mainly because he doesn't treat him like a student at all and especially not someone in need of guidance and instruction (Sebastian, as one can guess, has a problem with authority). Moreover, Walter's class on Aestheticism was one of Sebastian's favorites from freshman year, and the two kept in touch, Sebastian not wanting to lose a rare kind of mentor figure, and the professor not wanting to lose track of his most brilliant (at least, in that particular class) pupil, whose essay on Keats's "Eve of St. Agnes" (not officially an Aesthetic text, but one Walter considers foundational or, in his words, "Proto-Aesthetic") is still, as he often says, "one of the most *inspired* pieces of undergraduate writing I've ever come across," not only making a compelling, moving argument but managing to infuse into what was only an academic paper some of the beauty and sublimity of the poem itself. With an enviable verve and panache, Sebastian argued in five dense and flowing pages that the poem was not just a cliched romance of two lovers running away together or a subtle rumination on the passing of all things but instead a celebration of the power of writing to immortalize sensory experience and preserve youthful love. Ultimately, as he wrote in his final sentences, "the beadsman's foreshadowed death in the final stanza is not meant as a harbinger of impending woe for Porphyro and Madeline. They have fled, 'ages long ago,' and thus are outside of time itself. They exist only in the poem, where they are preserved like the figures on Keats's Grecian Urn, 'for ever panting and for ever young.'"

Sebastian turns back to the library facade and stops. There, in the second window, at the end of one of the long tables that stretch across the north reading room on the second floor, is the girl in the gray dress. She sits, laptop open in front of her, headphones in her ears, body angled slightly towards the window. Her legs are crossed and the dress has fallen back to reveal tanned skin that extends all the way up to her mid-thigh. One of her black boots dangles slightly above the other, dark against the light wood of the chair and swaying ever so gently, as if waving tantalizingly down to Sebastian. Adjacent to her, past the next window, is the bust of Athena, looking broodingly down from over the entrance of the library. Sebastian feels Aphrodite would be more appropriate, not just given the immediate circumstances, but in light of everything that college has come to signify. He recalls how once he and a girl had sex in the main stacks down in the library basement—Alice her name was, someone he met at a party in freshman year, a daredevil of a girl who after learning that Sebastian had never had sex in a public place told him in a private moment that she would "help [him] with that rite of passage," if he was willing (which he was). On the chosen day, she met him under the statue of Athena, her blond hair up in a bun, an eager glint in her eyes. They didn't speak a word as they walked down the stairs and along the long hallways and over to an obscure section of nautical maps. She turned the wheel at the end of one of the beige shelves, and she and Sebastian slipped into the small space and moved to the end of the row of oversized volumes stacked atop each other to fit the narrow space. The lights overhead flickered and hummed with a persistent drone, and the metal of the shelf was cool against Sebastian's asscheek as he hoisted Alice up and towards him. She muffled her face in his shoulder to staunch her heavy breathing, and he remembered the strawberry scent of her hair that he now associated with those rows of moveable shelves. They finished quickly (or, at least, he did), doing their best to keep the metal from creaking too rhythmically, and afterwards they walked back through the stacks and up the stairs, their cheeks flushed, their hair tussled, trying hard to avoid the glances of students who looked up from their books or the brief and possibly judgmental flicker of the security guard's eyes as they passed through the gray detectors and back under the bust of Athena and out into the open air, where Sebastian tossed the used condom into a trashcan outside the Free Speech Movement Cafe.

Sebastian stares at the girl in the gray dress now as she sits cross-legged on the other side of the window, and he imagines he smells strawberry amidst the musty scent of old maps.

❀

"Oh don't move to San Francisco after graduation! The city will always be there, but you will be twenty-one only once!"

Sebastian sits in Professor Walter's office, looking across the desk at the venerable older man who leans back in his vintage leather office chair. Professor Walter is only fifty-six, but to Sebastian he may as well be a man from the days of Roosevelt (Teddy not Franklin), one who grew up before electricity was common, possibly even contemporaneous with Otto von Bismarck. Walter's hair is graying near the temples (though his mustache retains its rich, dark-brown color), and he wears the loose slacks and baggy dress shirt of someone of an older generation not accustomed to how fitted clothing has become in recent years (nevertheless, Sebastian does admire Walter's color palette, a gray blazer and brown corduroy pants, something that evokes faded grandeur and a time when academics still wore tweed and were paid livable salaries). Walter's office is decorated much like him: relics of the '60s and '70s line the walls, movie posters from the era (*The Graduate, Annie Hall, Jules et Jim,* and *La Dolce Vita*), photos he's taken of his travels across Europe (one of a church in Prague that Sebastian has himself visited and one of James Joyce's apartment in Trieste, near where Walter lived for a year in his twenties), and a degree from Harvard, framed and prominently displayed (Sebastian applied but never got in, though Walter assures him the place is not what it used to be). Papers, meanwhile, litter the desk in haphazard and uneven stacks, and a small bust of Epicurus sits at the end, looking over everything with a pleased expression.

"What did you do after college?" Sebastian asks.

"Well it was The Seventies, so the economy was much like it is now," Walter says. "*Stagflation* was the word of the day. Today it's all about *subprime mortgages* and the *deregulated financial industry*—" (the way Walter speaks, halting, lilting, one can hear the italics in his voice) "—but back then, our conception of why our generation was suffering was of a different sort. We all spoke of OPEC and Vietnam and looked fondly back to the dream of the Great Society."

"Did you have a job lined up?"

"Of course not," Walter said, disdainfully. "I didn't actually want to *work* after college! And that's what I don't understand about your generation. I have hundreds of requests from my former students asking for recommendation letters to all sorts of jobs and *programs:* graduate school programs, MFA programs, programs to travel abroad. When I was your age, if we wanted to travel we simply went, gathering up our things, spending all our savings on the ticket, determined to figure out how to eat and where to sleep when we arrived. We didn't need a *program* to apply to in order to travel."

"Our generation has been raised on programs," Sebastian says. "By elementary school, I was enrolled in soccer camp, the Boy Scouts, swimming lessons, the youth orchestra…"

"It sounds exhausting. I can't see why it appealed to you."

"It didn't appeal to me. But my mother and father believed it was all good for me, exposing me to different things, even if I didn't show the slightest interest. Your generation might have hated programs back in the day, but you made sure to heap them on your kids."

"I never had children, Sebastian, and you know that," Walter says, smiling.

"You have hundreds of children, new ones each year!"

"Yes, yes. So then my advice to you and all my other

surrogate children is to forsake these programs. Go *do* something, Sebastian! Don't stake your future on some application your girlfriend makes you fill out. She is just your girlfriend, right, and not your fiancée?"

"Just my girlfriend…"

"Good. Keep her that way, Sebastian. You don't want to be married at your age. Most of my friends who were married are now divorced, and I'm telling you, the few of us that didn't, we were the happy few, smart enough to see that it was foolish to bind yourself to one girl when a whole two decades and more of freedom awaited us! I know I may not look it now, but in my youth, I was quite handsome, and I took *full* advantage of that freedom. After college, for example, I went to Europe, because all of us went to Europe at one point or another (it was cheaper then), and in one of the hostels in Barcelona, I met a fellow traveler, American too, and I believe I fell in love, and she may have felt the same way too, but she was from Minnesota or Wisconsin, somewhere like that, and was going to work in Chicago, and I knew after that night we'd never see each other again, and so I let myself *enjoy* the temporality of it and not get caught up in those misplaced desires for long term commitment and stability. And the very next night, on the train to Madrid, I met another American traveler, from California this time, and we had a lovely three days in Madrid before she too left. But of course I didn't mind, because I knew there was more to come, more encounters with more women, on trains, in hostels, in foreign cities… that is *life*, Sebastian! Encounters in rooms between untethered individuals all freely roaming this grand Earth. Don't take it for granted. Don't throw it all so easily away for the sake of some girl…"

Sebastian leans against the wall of Viola's apartment, a

clear plastic cup of vodka and cranberry in his hand. He's in a hard liquor mood tonight, Professor Walter's advisory reminiscences having galvanized in him a desire to follow his youthful impulses (and what is more youthful than drinking large quantities of Trader Joe's brand Vodka of the Gods—$10 for 1.75 liters—on a Thursday night). The microwave clock reads 11 p.m., but Sebastian is already four drinks in, even though the party is still in its early stages (traditionally these sorts of gatherings end around 1:30 a.m., with the stragglers trekking out to La Burrita or, if past 2 a.m., to the Asian Ghetto, the small stone courtyard of mostly non-Asian restaurants that stay open past their stated opening hours to cater to the crowds of drunk college students desperately trying to stave off impending hang-overs with greasy food that would give middle-aged men heart attacks but which the students can make up for with a few vigorous hours at the gym.) The mood of the party is casual, upbeat, like the music that plays in the background, overlaid atop the buzz of conversation, nothing too loud or too wild just yet, but mellow, hipster-rock, enough to get the head bobbing and foot tapping but to still allow for conversation and drinking and the occasional aloof pose as one glances across the room and takes in the crowd. Viola herself is playing the good host, drifting among her guests with her own cup of Vodka of the Gods, encouraging the various partygoers to stay energized and take more shots, and effortlessly landing a few well-placed witticisms that charm the particular circle before she dematerializes and moves on to the next with enviable ephemerality.

The ostensible reason for the party is to celebrate the publication of one of Viola's short stories in the aptly titled *Arcana*, a literary magazine for the serious, erudite type that in its heyday in the mid '80s had a sizable readership but now is kept afloat by the goodwill of older individuals (who are all too busy to actually read the stories) and a few college professors who teach at MFA programs and encourage their students to subscribe and submit to magazines like this one but also secretly know that literary magazines don't actually publish quality. Case in point is Viola's story, which she describes as "just a lark, like Wodehouse but with millennials," and which was only accepted because Viola happened to meet one of the magazine's interns at a party of a mutual friend in San Francisco over the summer, an intern who, after some casual flirtation, agreed to put in a good word for Viola with the editor.

Harry, Imogen, and Nate are at the party too. The latter two are in a circle of other Model UN-ers, Nate and the others listening while Imogen lectures them on some international relations issue of grave significance. Harry meanwhile is talking about music to a girl he's trying (unsuccessfully) to flirt with. Sebastian wants to give him advice ("Let her talk for a minute, and don't lean in so close—with your height it looks creepy.") but his mind is elsewhere, on his conversation with Professor Walter, and on Fatima, probably still up typing away at another application. She texted him earlier in the night (*What time do you think you'll be home?*) and so far, he's left the message unanswered. He looks at it now and frowns at the word "home" and its implication of a joint domesticity that he certainly hasn't encouraged. Somehow they've settled into a rhythm where he will stay over on weekends and she on weeknights, and if for some reason Sebastian wishes to sleep in his own bed any night from Friday to Sunday, Fatima will look upset and ask him what's wrong (and he doesn't have the heart to tell her that he likes sleeping by himself, that he enjoys the freedom of kicking out at night, untucking the sheets, spreading himself across the twin bed without the discomfort of another body in his way).

Sebastian slips his phone back into his blazer pocket and looks across the party and around at Viola's apartment. It's smaller than his own, and the building older, but the peeling paint and the cracked wood paneling on the cupboards in the kitchen and the old-school mechanical fan on the ceiling give it an old-world charm, especially with Viola and her roommate Sarah's sense of décor, mainly thrift-store pieces (the one exception being the blue IKEA Solsta, the same one Sebastian and Harry have in their apartment) along with posters of old movies, Sara's choices more conventional (the original *Star Wars* and *Raiders of the Lost Ark*) and Viola's somewhat more controversial (Ken Russell's *The Devils* and Antonioni's *Zabriskie Point*)—though unlike Sebastian and Harry's contradictory, clashing apartment, Sarah and Viola's is fully in the past, a crumbling Italian villa, like the one from *The English Patient*, a refuge against the outside world and the steadily marching forces of time.

Above Viola's desk hang several rows of postcards from the various museums she's visited, a decorating technique she's borrowed from Sebastian, who has a similar wall in his room. A particular postcard from the Tate Britain, which Sebastian and Viola visited together on their trip through Europe the summer after their freshman year, catches Sebastian's eye: Waterhouse's *The Magic Circle* (1886), of a dark-haired woman in a long blue dress standing before a boiling pot in a rocky, arid landscape and drawing a circle around her, while white smoke rises up towards a dark, hazy sky. The actual painting is six feet tall and meant to be imposing, but in the well-lit, white-walled galleries of the Tate, it seemed innocuous, whereas here, in the darkened apartment, amidst the pulsing music and the animated babble of the party, a six-inch version is so much more ominous. And yet, at the same time, Sebastian finds the painting strangely comforting, in the same way he does the rest of the apartment. The pale blue of the woman's dress, the white, wispy smoke, and the hazy colors of the background are classic Waterhouse and evoke that timeless, murky past, when everything was magical, when the world was more alive.

Sebastian thinks of the first time he was in this apartment, September a year ago. Viola and Sarah had just moved in and were throwing a party to celebrate, much like the current one, with many of the same people and much of the same atmosphere. The books on the shelf are now changed to reflect Viola and Sarah's new classes, but otherwise the general mood, the vodka they're drinking and the musty, woody smell and the warmth of all the bodies and the cool currents of air drifting in from the open windows and the way the curtains rustle as laughter brushes up against them, has remained the same.

At that first party, leaning against the wall near those curtains and peeking carefully behind them to gaze onto the sleepy Northside streets of Berkeley was a girl, Madeline, incongruously attired in a black miniskirt and black gloves, blond hair streaked with blue to match her eyes. She clutched her drink in a peculiar way, with two hands, her gloves obscuring the liquid, as if any exposure to light would make it lose its magical quality. It was alluring the way she held her cup and stared out the window, wide-eyed, not innocent, but curious, and ultimately, *youthful* (emphasized the way Walter would say it). When Sebastian walked over to her and leaned next to her and peeked out with her behind the curtain and dropped a largely banal line ("So what are you drinking?"), he didn't expect the earnest, sharp response ("Ambrosia! The best thing you'll ever taste! Try some..."), and when she looked at him with those open blue eyes and offered him a sip of the drink with her gloved hand, it wasn't she that was charmed, as Sebastian intended when he first approached.

Besides Madeline, the only other girl Sebastian has fallen in love with was his high school girlfriend Emily, though she was never present with him, not the way Madeline was. Emily's eyes were always looking out towards the distant future, towards college, and in that way she was not unlike Fatima. But with Madeline there was no future. Like the apartment, she existed firmly in one unchanging moment. Their first date was also at La Note, but back then, in September a year ago, it was Sebastian's first time there, and the place was another restaurant entirely, not forlorn and abandoned as it had been with Fatima but filled with students and laughter and the tinkling of glass, and with waitresses dressed in elegant black drifting gracefully between the tables and setting down plates of ratatouille and bouillabaisse and bottles of Bordeaux and Burgundy, and of course with Madeline herself, lively, vivacious, brimming with energy, shoving pieces of baguette into her mouth as she told Sebastian about her favorite current class (Romanticism) and how she'd recently studied abroad (Edinburgh), leaving him dazzled that he'd met someone as blissfully in the moment as he was. How foolish of him to have tried to recreate that experience with Fatima.

Viola approaches Sebastian, her hand clutching the neck of the Vodka of the Gods bottle. She pours him a refill without waiting for him to ask.

"Fatima not coming?" she asks.

"What do you think?"

Viola shrugs and pours herself another helping.

"Have you two had sex yet?"

Subtlety is not one of Viola's strong points, nor something she particularly values. The question triggers for Sebastian another memory, this time after his and Fatima's date at La Note, how, without discussing it, they returned to his apartment and stood out on the balcony, much as they had the night they met. Sebastian poured himself a glass of wine (Fatima, of course, didn't have any), and after a few sips, he leaned over and kissed her. She was tentative and uncertain, as if she were only going through with this because she'd already relented once. But the kiss was still pleasant, and after a moment, Fatima reached up and grasped Sebastian's neck and pulled him towards her, and for an instant Sebastian thought this might be the consummation of the strange desire he'd felt for her these past weeks. But when he grabbed her by the waist and tried to slip his hand up her shirt, she pulled back and knocked over his wine glass, which shattered against the balcony and sent shards of glass and droplets of wine spilling over the edge and showering the sidewalk below (luckily the only pedestrians were farther down the street, loitering outside the Berkeley Rep for a cigarette between acts).

"Sorry," Fatima said. "I'm not ready to go that far yet."

Now, in the face of Viola's question, Sebastian doesn't answer, though his silence is confirmation enough. Viola shakes her head and raises her cup of vodka.

"Then I toast to your impending year of celibacy!"

"It's not going to be a year—"

"Please. I know girls like Fatima. She's a virgin, right?"

"She won't confirm or deny—"

"She's a virgin then. And she'll not want to lose that virginity casually, especially if she's held out this long. She's probably been raised in a traditional household, and as much as she tries to liberalize her views, she'll never shake that foundational understanding of sex, that virginity is an actual *thing* that she has, the source of her feminine fucking mystique, and that once she gives it up, she gives up the thing that will help her get a husband, a goal which she's also probably been taught is the be-all-fucking-end-all of a woman's existence. If I could, I'd sit her down and tell her to fuck you, Sebastian, since I'm sure she'd enjoy it, but I doubt it would do any good, since she's probably also been taught that women like me, the liberal, liberated ones, are the fucking DEVIL!"

Viola waves her arms in a ghostlike manner.

"You're assuming a lot," Sebastian says.

"Am I wrong?"

Sebastian takes a drink. Viola smirks and leans in close.

"You know, Sebastian, in the past, people weren't as pious as we think. In my Enlightenment History class, we read an excerpt from Casanova's autobiography, this chapter in which he seduces this nun."

"Not exactly unexpected for him."

"No. But the crazy thing was that this nun already had a lover, some gentleman from the town, and Casanova had to work his away around their scheduled meetups. Not only that, the Abbess of the convent knew about this gentleman caller and didn't mind, as long as the nun kept it on the down-low. It was all understood, a 'don't ask, don't tell' sort of thing for straight women."

"What's your point?"

"My point is, your girlfriend is more repressed than an eighteenth-century nun. But you, my dear Casanova, don't have to be." Viola gestures theatrically around the room. "There are plenty of women here who might lift their habits for you…"

The music changes, to something more upbeat and electronic. Viola dances back towards the center of the room where a circle is forming. Her eyes linger on Sebastian before she turns, closes her eyes, and loses herself to the music. The circle gradually expands around her, and her blond hair swirls as she dances, and Sebastian is reminded of a scholarly article he read in one of her course readers about the *Malleus Maleficarum,* a treatise from the fifteenth century written by two German clergyman as a guide to combatting witches. The treatise described in detail the rituals of these supposed witches, which involved magic circles and strange incantations. Sebastian imagines Viola appearing to nuns during their prayer sessions, whispering into their ears about attractive young noblemen in the nearby town.

It's then that Sebastian looks up, past the magic dance circle and towards the window, where he sees a figure standing, sipping a drink and peeking out behind the curtain. She is blond and wears a gray dress and tall black boots, and he realizes immediately that it's the girl from Memorial Glade.

Berkeley is a school with over 35,000 students, and the Glade is one of the campus's most popular spots, and so one particular girl who strode across it and into the library and into Sebastian's mind appearing suddenly at this very party seems to him like some kind of miracle, or else the opposite of one, perhaps the result of Viola, who with her witchcraft conjured up this girl just to tempt him. As Sebastian downs the rest of his vodka from his plastic cup and walks towards the girl in gray (because of course he will approach her now—how can he not?), he notes how the pose she holds looks familiar, the way she grips her drink with both hands and peeks behind the curtain, and he feels suddenly overwhelmed with a rush that has nothing to do with the vodka. He reaches the window and sets the empty cup on the nearby dresser. The cup falls off but makes no sound as it clatters to the ground, and Sebastian doesn't notice or stoop to pick it up. He remains transfixed by the girl, who still seems unreal, otherworldly. Behind him, Viola continues her wild dancing.

"So what are you drinking?" Sebastian asks.

The girl turns, and he hopes for the same, magical reply from a year ago. Instead she stares at him, as if transfixed herself.

"You have nice eyes," she says.

She reaches out and brushes a strand of hair away from his forehead. Sebastian feels a thrill at her touch, but also wishes she said what Madeline said.

"Yours aren't so bad," Sebastian says, with his practiced smile.

The girl returns a smile of her own. Sebastian is about to ask her name but then stops. What if it isn't Madeline? What then? Will the spell around him be shattered, and will this tiny apartment come hurtling back from the past? Will Sebastian remember with thudding clarity the homeless man and his sign? Will a single uttered name, the wrong name, be like a thunderbolt from above, like one of the religious invocations from the *Malleus Maleficarum*, a blow that will dispel the enchantment and leave Sebastian in a foggy, moral stupor? Is it not better to let the dance continue and imagine that she's not actually real? The girl is already leaning towards him, intrigued, expectant…

It's here, with this other-Madeline inches away from him, her eyes flashing with that familiar gleam, that Sebastian thinks suddenly of Fatima. He imagines where she must be right now, sitting alone in her tiny studio, bent over her IKEA table as she reads *Principles of Microeconomics*, her eyes flickering now and then to her phone, her mind unable to concentrate as she waits for Sebastian's text. Sebastian imagines the drunk revelers outside her window on Telegraph shouting obscenities to the sky and the occasional solitary car swishing by along the street, its lights tracing patterns across her open curtains. He imagines her listening to its passing sound and thinking of the Doppler effect and constructing the equation in her mind. Sebastian should be with her, listening to these sounds of the Berkeley night. But he is elsewhere and in another time entirely, in Viola's apartment by the curtain, inches away from the girl in gray, but simultaneously a whole year back, with Madeline at the end of their first date. They raced home from La Note that night, hand in hand, and as the elevator brought them up to Sebastian's floor, they kissed furiously against the mirrored walls, their stomachs fluttering as they were carried upward. Sebastian pulled her down the hallway towards his door at the far end, her palm warm against his, and as he fumbled for his keys, she grabbed him by the neck and kissed him again, and only after a moment did they stumble inside. Harry was off at some party and the place was empty, and they didn't even wait to get to Sebastian's room, shedding their clothes in the hallway and pressing each other up against the walls of the entryway. He thinks of that night now as he leans towards this girl, this other Madeline, and though he knows it won't be the same, that it can't be the same, that life only moves in one direction (an oft-quoted sentiment from his idol, Don Draper), Sebastian imagines that maybe here in this apartment the rules don't apply, that time might flow backwards, that in the midst of the music and the dancing and the Vodka of the Gods and Viola's hair swirling in a golden aura around her face and the postcard of the dark-haired woman looming on the wall and Walter's emphatic, italicized advice repeating in his ear and the girl in gray's ravishing stare reminding him of the past, here he can reclaim that lost moment, turn the clock back a year, add 365 days to the homeless man's countdown. And so, before he knows it, his hand is on other-Madeline's cheek and they're leaning towards each other and kissing. Her lips are warm, even as a cold wind from the open window enters the apartment and rustles the curtain.

It all happens so fast that it doesn't even feel like a choice, as if some sinister magic compelled poor Sebastian towards the inevitable. But later, when everything has gone wrong and he looks back to this moment as his first step down the dark and tragic path, he will recall how, in the nano-est of seconds before their lips touched, he first felt the chill from behind the curtain, the outside world seeping slowly into that time capsule and reminding him in one thunderbolt of everything, of Fatima, of that shared future she believed in, of how six months ago, he and Madeline broke up in a storm of tears (hers not his) and shouting because of what he did with another girl at another party, and he'll know that in that moment there was no magic in the apartment, no witch's spell—only him, Sebastian Khan, making a choice, as always.

CHAPTER THREE

THE POET AND THE SIREN (1893)

She sits at the front of the conference room on a black leather office chair, centered along a long table and elevated onto a makeshift stage, a gavel laid before her. Her dark-red hair shines with a glamorous polish under the hotel's fluorescent lights (it's not a natural color and clearly dyed, yet to Sebastian alluring for that very reason), and she wears her black blazer and white blouse with a stately, ambassadorial elegance (she is not the only one, as the entire conference room is filled with similarly dressed and chattering Model UN delegates doing their best to look like diplomats and not privileged college students).

Below the table, however, she looks different. Her legs are crossed seductively, her black skirt is a little too short, and the suggestive pose of one black-heeled leg crossed over the other seems to invite Sebastian to uncover the secrets hidden underneath her professional exterior. It reminds him of the elaborate staging of the whole room, the fact that outside the windows of the hotel are the streets of Santa Barbara, and tonight these well-dressed and professional-seeming "delegates" will transform into rowdy undergraduates, eager to consume the fabled delights of Isla Vista, home to California's premiere "party school."

Her name is Lorelei, as the placard on the table indicates, and she's the Committee Chair and a student at UCSB. Sebastian wonders whether she's like the majority here, choosing the college for its "social reputation," or whether she's the rarer commodity who actually researched the professors and chose to make this college her academic home because of some particular scholar with whom she wished to work (even at Berkeley, supposedly a "smarter" school than UCSB, it is rare to meet an undergraduate with that level of intellectual rigor—Sebastian himself only chose Berkeley because he likes the city, its cloudy atmosphere and casual mix of bohemian and bourgeois worlds, and also because he didn't get into any of the Ivy Leagues). She may be anything, this Lorelei, any type of student. Underneath the facade of Model UN, it is impossible to tell.

Next to him, Imogen, dressed in a similar black blazer but with long, ankle-length slacks and hair bound tightly into a bun, frowns.

"You're staring," she says.

"I'm just admiring the room," Sebastian says.

"It's creepy."

"It's charming."

As if in confirmation of Sebastian's assessment of himself, Lorelei catches his eye and smiles.

"See?" Sebastian says to Imogen. "She agrees."

"The only difference between charming and creepy is how a person looks."

"Then it's a good thing I look the way I do."

Imogen's eyes narrow. "What would Fatima say if she were here?"

There's a savage menace in her tone, and Sebastian knows Imogen doesn't really care about Fatima and is only saying this to make him feel bad.

"It's just harmless flirting," he says, doing his best to sound flippant.

Delegates continue to stream into the room and fill up the arranged rows of seats. The clock on the wall reads 5:58 p.m. The committee's first session is set to start soon. At the front of the room, a sign stands off to the side of the stage and reads in hastily scrawled pen "SOCHUM —Social, Cultural, and Humanitarian Committee." The more prestigious conferences such as Berkeley's or those on the East Coast usually have their signage typed, but this is UCSB's first conference and so Sebastian doesn't fault them. Most of the "delegates," after all, aren't exactly here for a rigorous, authentic simulation of the United Nations, except perhaps Imogen, who's researched every aspect of her country (Latvia) from its government structure (parliamentary republic) to its GDP per capita (12,082.06 USD in 2009) to its average rainfall (20 inches in Riga). Sebastian knows considerably less about his country (Libya), except that its leader, Muammar Qaddafi knows how to make a theatrical speech.

On Sebastian's other side sits cherubic-faced Nate, his pants two sizes too small, his jacket one size too big. On his lap is a placard for Serbia, though in his desire to mimic Sebastian, Nate has done absolutely no research. He stares around the room with the wonder of someone who's never been in a committee before, lips slightly parted, eyes wide with terror and awe, even though as a sophomore he's already had a year of Model UN experience. Despite Nate's awkwardness and almost practiced lack of grace, Sebastian can't help but envy this wide-eyed outlook, this ability to see everything as if it were the first time all over again.

Imogen flips though the committee's background guide, prepared for them in advance by Committee Chair Lorelei. The two topics are "Prostitution" and "The Refugee Crisis in Palestine," and the committee will decide with a vote on the first day which of the two they'll discuss throughout the conference. Imogen expects the committee to select the latter ("It's a incredibly serious and relevant issue," she said earlier), but Sebastian hopes, for the sake of a more lively and entertaining discussion, that prostitution wins the vote.

"It's not meant to be a joke," Imogen says, when Sebastian brings this up. "Prostitution is directly linked to human trafficking, and in many places, making it illegal has only hindered government regulation that would prevent these women from getting exploited—"

"So you're in favor of legalizing it?"

"I'm not. Even legalization creates ethical and moral problems and makes men think women are commodities they can buy and sell, like groceries. But prostitution is legal in Latvia, so I have to argue that position."

"Is it really legal? We should visit."

"I'd kill myself before traveling the world with you."

"Aren't we technically traveling now?"

"This is different."

"Is it really?"

"This is work."

"Is it really..."

Imogen shakes her head, exasperated, and changes the subject. "Are you going to take this seriously enough to win an award? This is a pretty low-level conference, and if we really put our minds to it, we can come out with Best Delegation—"

"You act like it's under our control."

"It is under our control."

"Awards are subjective. It's up to her."

He nods at Lorelei, up at the front of the room. Once again, she smiles at Sebastian, and once again, Imogen frowns.

"All I'm saying is, try and take it seriously," Imogen says. "This actually matters."

Sebastian lets Imogen have the last word, because he knows the truth and doesn't feel the need to convince her that what she's said is ridiculous. Despite his position as Head Delegate, Sebastian knows that winning Best Delegation at a Model United Nations conference is the very last thing that "actually matters" and that Imogen's desire to win and imbue a conference with life or death stakes is just another response to the fear of college ending, a different response from Sebastian's, but stemming ultimately from the same source, another attempt by youth to act out against the ticking of time. After all, Imogen too has seen the countdown (now at 217 DAYS TILL THE END).

Lorelei takes the gavel and raps it on the table three times.

"Delegates, please take your seats and come to order."

Her magical voice quiets the room instantly. The delegates find their seats, and all eyes turn to her, though none more eager than Sebastian's. He is transfixed by her voice, which is more powerful even than her smile, a sonorous, melodious voice, filling the room and reverberating off the walls.

"My name is Lorelei, and I'd like to officially welcome you to SOCHUM, here at the First Annual UC Santa Barbara Model United Nations Conference."

Lorelei bangs the gavel once more on the table, and like her voice, the sound carries across the room, rich, echoing, and a little ominous.

The committee chooses prostitution as its topic, and Lorelei's announcement of the result of the voting is greeted with cheering and hooting, enough that Lorelei has to bang her gavel and remind everyone to treat the topic with the gravity and respect that it deserves (though even she smiles as she says this, something Sebastian appreciates, as it reveals that she's not uptight like Imogen, who remains, as always, frowning). From there, the committee progresses smoothly, with the bulk of Saturday's sessions consisting of individual speeches in a formalized setting, followed by the more informal unmoderated caucuses, in which the delegates separate into blocs to write (slightly) different resolutions that will then be debated for the remainder of the session. Usually these blocs have very little to do with the topic itself. In this case, the committee inexplicably divides itself between pro-Western and anti-Western countries, with a small, third bloc that takes the topic seriously and is proposing legalization as an effective means of combatting the issue. Imogen is obviously spearheading this latter group, while Sebastian, as Libya, has joined the anti-Western bloc, bringing together a group of Islamic countries who want to try and link prostitution to a moral decline brought on by US and European neocolonialism (Sebastian only ever embodies his Muslim identity in a Model UN conference, and even then only an exaggerated version of it), though aside from making a few bold yet ultimately substance-less speeches and lingering on the peripheries while the more serious members of his bloc type up their resolution, he does little to contribute to the group and instead spends the sessions carefully developing a relationship with Lorelei the chair, one which begins with a few questions about procedure ("Should we list the sponsors in alphabetical order, or by order of importance?" and "Do we need any perambulatory clauses or is it okay if we just have operative ones?") and continues with some well placed compliments ("I'm impressed your doing this all without any assistant chairs." and "Your voice is perfect for this. Naturally authoritative.") and finally develops into consistent conversations throughout the day. Nate, who has no idea whether Serbia is in favor of legalizing prostitution or not or whether it's even pro- or anti-Western ("Isn't it somewhere in Western Asia, near Russia?" he asks. "That's Siberia," Imogen says), accompanies Sebastian on these chats with Lorelei, awkwardly leaning in between them, his mouth slightly open and his eyes studying everything Sebastian does and every reaction he gets.

They stand by one of the tables on the conference room floor. Lorelei leans with her back against it, surveying the room. Sebastian leans nearby, on one arm, and Lorelei can't help but forgo the room and stare instead into his dark eyes. Sebastian, meanwhile, finds himself drawn to either the perfume she wears or the smell of her shampoo, a flowery and breezy scent that reminds him of the ocean and feels somehow familiar.

"Did you select this topic?" Sebastian asks.

"Oh no," Lorelei says, laughing (a musical, melodic laugh, gently decrescendoing notes that drift into Sebastian's head and linger there like a song). "Our Secretary General did. He just assigned me to chair. Me and my naturally authoritative voice." She smiles coyly at Sebastian and leans in closer. Nate notices and leans in closer too.

"What's your opinion on it?" Sebastian asks.

"On prostitution? Well, I think if we want to prevent human trafficking, we have to legalize and regulate it."

Sebastian agrees but decides to be contrarian for the sake of a livelier discussion. He recalls what Imogen said. "But what about the moral and ethical problems? Won't making it legal lead to men thinking of women as objects rather than as people?"

"But don't men already view women as objects?" Lorelei looks at Sebastian knowingly. "You find us beautiful and you desire us, and that's never going to change, no matter how many laws a government passes."

Her fragrance is even stronger now, an ocean breeze along a sandy shore, and Sebastian knows he's smelled it once before.

"But isn't that desire mutual?" Sebastian fixes his eyes on hers. "Don't women also desire men?"

Lorelei laughs. "Sometimes. But it depends on the man."

It's only later, when the unmoderated caucus is over and Sebastian and Nate have returned to their seats, Nate having gushed with sufficient praise at Sebastian's flirty bantering with Lorelei ("Holy shit, that was fucking *magical!*"), and Lorelei is back up on stage, her legs crossed once again under the table, that Sebastian remembers where he's come across her perfume. He was with Fatima in the Walgreens on Telegraph, accompanying her to pick up some toiletries (Sebastian lingered briefly by the prominently displayed condoms, but Fatima shook her head). They stopped by the shampoo and Fatima pulled one down from the library of choices before them.

"What do you think?" she asked, opening the top for him to smell.

Sebastian doesn't remember the brand now, but he recalls the smell with perfect clarity, a bold, flowery, beachy scent that brought to mind seagulls chirping and a warm sun beating down while a mermaid's song drifted out on the ocean breeze and across the rolling waves, a place a world away from the fluorescent lights and dull pop music of the Walgreens.

"It's not for you," Sebastian said, closing it and handing it back. "It's too intense."

Fatima didn't seem hurt and simply shrugged. "Yeah, I think you're right."

Sebastian feels startled that he's thinking of Fatima now, when his mind is far, far away from Berkeley and his life with her. He never told Fatima about other-Madeline, the girl in the gray dress. She disappeared that night at Viola's party after the music faded, and Sebastian walked back home alone, through the dark streets, past a few sleeping homeless men and late-night-burrito places packed with drunk students. In his mind, she wasn't even real, just a spirit conjured up by Viola and her magic circle. But conjured or not, she was significant, because with her, Sebastian crossed a threshold, and what a year ago would have been nothing, casual banter with an attractive chair, a few exchanged smiles, what he described to Imogen earlier as harmless flirting, now reminds him of Fatima in the most visceral of ways, and Sebastian knows that he can't pretend Lorelei into non-existence as he did with other-Madeline, that she, sitting up on stage, is already more real and that a hundred other undergraduates can testify to her corporeality, to the way she crosses her bare legs beneath the table or the way her resonant voice echoes through the room.

Sebastian knows all this, rationalizes it all in his mind, convinces himself that the harmless flirtation is over—but then looks up and sees her crossed legs, her shimmering hair, and suddenly smells flowers and sand and an ocean breeze and hears the sweet crooning of a siren song.

The party that night begins innocuously enough, with the student delegates gathered at the quiet hotel bar for a few drinks. The roughly sixty of them are spread out across the lobby, seated on the leather sofas or else standing in groups, all chatting amiably and holding glasses of whiskey sours and other "fancy" drinks that they order with relish from the bartender, a middle-aged man who knows better than to check their IDs (the hotel bar will triple its normal haul on this night). The hotel receptionists, meanwhile, watch nervously as the group of students get progressively noisier and work their way to drinks two and three and four, while a few of the hotel's regular patrons (older men on business trips who go to the bar to pick up married women to take back to their hotel rooms) frown at this sudden infusion of youth and vitality into the sterile surroundings. The mellow, uninspired lounge music that usually plays in hotel lobbies, soundtrack to the seedy goings-on of the hotel bar, can barely be heard above the laughter and animated conversation of these sixty college students. So far, however, nothing rowdy has happened, no glasses smashed, no delegates fallen drunk to the floor, not a single drop of alcohol spilled onto the leather couches or the tiled floors. But nevertheless the gathering has an on-the-edge quality, an anticipatory buzz that permeates the air, brought on most significantly by the contrast between the faux-posh, upper-middle-class look of the hotel lobby and the casually dressed delegates, who've long since shed their professional attire for the hipster-chic of undergraduates, Toms and Converse and thrift-store-bought leather shoes, skinny jeans and short skirts, corduroy and denim jackets, blazers, V-necks, button-downs, and argyle sweaters, a few bow ties, lots of dark-rimmed glasses, and one or two slightly angled fedoras, all in all a precarious balance of out-of-place youth teetering at the edge of what they've been promised will be a wild night out.

Sebastian is among them, already on his second Sazerac (forgoing the Old Fashioneds for something bolder though still appropriately upscale). Next to him are Imogen (whiskey neat, her first), Nate (a Sazerac, to mirror Sebastian, his second too), Harry (draught of Sierra Nevada), and Viola (vodka tonic, her third), along with various other members from the Berkeley delegation.

"We have the committee wrapped around our fingers," Harry says. "China basically does whatever we say, and we've got the rest of the countries to really hate the United States."

Viola and Harry are partners, representing Russia in the Security Council, a committee of only fifteen countries, with a higher caliber of debate but a much better chance to win an award (as head delegate, Sebastian distributes country and committee assignments to the Berkeley delegation, and Imogen *begged* to be on the Security Council, it being a well-known goal of hers to one day win a gavel at this highest level, but Sebastian told her that Harry and Viola were more likely to win the award since they worked better together and that Imogen would be much better in a larger committee, to match her skill set—"And isn't the goal to win as many awards for Berkeley as possible?" Sebastian asked her, with relish).

"How about you guys?" Harry asks Imogen.

"I'm doing well, considering my country assignment," Imogen says, looking at Sebastian. "I've got a sizable group behind a resolution calling for the legalization of prostitution, but thanks to Sebastian, the committee's become divided between pro- and anti-Western countries—"

"How is that my fault?" Sebastian asks, innocently. "I just did my best Qaddafi impression and made a few well-timed speeches accusing the West of perpetuating the moral ill of prostitution."

"You think dividing the committee is going to get you an award?" Imogen asks.

"No. But she will."

Sebastian looks across the hotel bar to Lorelei, who now leans over the bar and orders a drink (vodka cranberry). Her outfit has changed, the business skirt and blouse gone in exchange for jeans and a gray T-shirt. If it weren't for her red hair, Sebastian would barely have recognized her.

"Up to your old tricks?" Viola asks.

"Yeah he is!" Nate says, leaning over to pat him on the back but accidentally splashing some of his own Sazerac onto the floor.

Imogen frowns and but remains silent, and Sebastian notes the judgment in her eyes. None of them say Fatima's name, but Sebastian can tell that all of them (save for maybe Nate) are thinking of her. Viola, though, doesn't seem to care, and Harry looks at the ground, to avoid, as always, the contentious subject of Sebastian's wandering eye.

"There's nothing wrong with a little flirting," Sebastian says.

He downs his Sazerac and turns towards the bar and Lorelei.

"You better slow down," Imogen says. "Or you won't remember what happens."

"I'll be fine," Sebastian says.

He walks across the lobby. Behind him, Imogen says something snarky and judgmental to the others, but her voice dissolves into the general babble as Sebastian reaches the bar, where Lorelei remains, waiting for her drink. The two Sazeracs are taking hold, and Sebastian feels the familiar buzz behind his eyes, the way the sounds of the world amplify and his focus zooms in on something, in this case Lorelei's red locks of hair. He slips through two taller, laughing bodies and reaches the bar. Lorelei notices him and smiles.

"Libya!" she says. "Hey there!"

"Hey!" he says, as if surprised to see her.

They pause a moment to take each other in in these new surroundings, and Sebastian notices how Lorelei appears captivated by the way he looks in his casual clothes, the blue blazer, the tan chinos, the old-school faux-vintage brown leather watch, and the black and white striped shirt, all worn with that swagger no one else at the bar seems to have. She smiles, and Sebastian feels that second rush, the one not brought on by the Sazeracs.

The bartender returns and slides over Lorelei's vodka cranberry. She pays ($10) and raises the glass to her lips. Sebastian notes the way the murky liquid matches the deep red of her hair. She takes a sip and then offers it to Sebastian.

"Have some," she says.

Their fingers brush as she hands him the glass, which is cool against Sebastian's warm skin. He takes a sip and watches Lorelei as she studies him and waits for his reaction. But before he can speak and tell her she has good taste (or another line to that effect) someone pulls Lorelei away from the bar and says something to her about gathering everyone and heading out. Lorelei nods and looks back to Sebastian.

"I'll catch up with you in a bit!"

"What about your drink?"

"Just have it! You can pay me back later…"

With a wave of her hand and a last flirtatious look, Lorelei is gone, vanished into the crowd. Sebastian chugs the drink, making sure not to splash any down his chin, and then pushes the glass onto the bar. He feels momentarily woozy and realizes the drink must have been a double-shot. The crowd meanwhile starts to move towards the doors, word spreading that the pre-party is ending. A few students return their glasses to the bar, but most don't bother and take their still half-full glasses out with them through the hotel doors. The bartender protests, but no one can hear him over the gradually increasing din, as the students start to murmur with excitement at the prospect of their impending night out, to party with the students of this most elite of party schools.

As they leave, Sebastian passes the others from Berkeley. Viola somehow produces from inside her blazer a fifth of whiskey and several plastic cups.

"Want?" she asks, offering a shot.

"I've had a lot already…"

Viola forcibly pushes a cup into Sebastian's hand. He and Viola down the shots, and she pours each of them another as they move towards the door with the crowd. Imogen shakes her head but holds out her glass. Nate accidentally drops his as they leave, and it shatters against the tile, but the momentum carrying them all out the door is too strong, and he doesn't bother to turn around to try and find the pieces.

After the students leave, silence settles on the hotel lobby once more, and the older patrons and the receptionists and the middle-aged bartender all share a relieved look.

❋

Sebastian's memory of the walk from the hotel down through campus and into the streets of Isla Vista, a community of mostly UCSB students nestled along the strip of beach, is hazy: he remembers taking a few more shots with Viola and then looking up and seeing streets filled with people who seem to pour out from the rows of houses. The noise is incredible, everyone laughing and shouting, and the night air is warm from all the heat generated by the bodies. Shirtless frat boys dance through the street and girls in swimwear lounge on patios, and people stand on rooftops or lean out windows, all with drinks in hand, as if on Saturday nights the whole of Isla Vista becomes one giant party. Nate, trying to match Sebastian drink for drink, has to step away from the crowd to use a bathroom (in one of the frats, whose door is open), but when he emerges, the Model UN procession is long gone, and he finds himself lost amidst a crowd of unfamiliar faces, some of whom, with the kindness of drunk college students, start making fun of him for being fat. Imogen, meanwhile, is talking with Harry about the merits of the veto power in the Security Council ("It provides some semblance of order," she says. "Yes but philosophically," he argues, "it goes against the ideals of democracy and the equality of nations that the UN was supposedly founded on!"), while Viola feeds them all more shots (the fifth of whiskey is gone but somehow she's procured a new fifth of vodka). She dances atop a nearby car, trips and falls into the arms of one of the shirtless frat boys, kisses him on the lips, and then laughing, is pulled away by Harry and Imogen. Sebastian, meanwhile, vision hazy, ears pounding with the sound of steadily advancing feet, follows the image of Lorelei up ahead, her red hair shining brightly in the starlight, her sonorous voice occasionally rising above the crescendo. Once Sebastian finds himself next to her, and she sees him, the two of them wobbling and tipsy, and she smiles ("Libya!") and puts her arm around him and leans her head close, but then is pulled away by another portion of the crowd, and Sebastian barely has time to call after her ("My name is Sebastian!") before he too is pulled to the other side of the sea of bodies, stumbling down the street towards this supposed house party, though of course by now they are satisfied, because *this* is what they were after, this parade through the heart of Isla Vista, this view of the soul of UCSB, this new understanding of what a night out *really* means.

Eventually, they reach their destination, a large former frat house belonging to a group of UCSB students. The frat was banned several years back after a controversial hazing practice (tying new members between mattresses and throwing them off the roof) resulted in a student's death and since then, the more douchey elements of the house have been toned down and replaced with more of a hipster-chic vibe, a mix of IKEA and thrift store furniture, art prints on the walls by Alphonse Mucha and Gustave Moreau, fixed-gear bicycles out front next to a Vespa, and a composting bin in the small backyard. It can almost pass for a place in Berkeley, except that in Berkeley no party would ever be this insane, with people falling down the stairs and puking in toilets only to come out, chug a bottle of Gatorade, and start from the beginning all over again with a fresh shot of vodka.

Sebastian scans the house for Lorelei's hair, but all the red cups distract him. Imogen, meanwhile, turns to Harry and tells him that Nate's missing ("Maybe he's in one of the rooms?" Harry suggests. "Let's check," Imogen says, pouring the rest of Viola's vodka into a cup and downing it in a long swig).

Viola notices Sebastian's restless gaze and grabs him by the shoulder.

"Hey. What's wrong?"

"What?"

"You're acting weird as fuck."

"I'm fine," Sebastian says, not looking at her.

She leans towards him, so their foreheads almost touch. Her breath smells of vodka and her blue eyes are wide open and vivid against the faded colors of the party. The two of them sway briefly together to avoid falling over.

"Calm down," she says, her voice lilting strangely, as if swaying with the rest of her body. "The party's not going anywhere."

"I'm looking for someone," Sebastian says.

Viola gives him a rueful smile. "You're always looking for someone."

"This time it's important. I need to find her."

"Why?"

"Because this might be the last time…"

Sebastian spots it then, the shimmering red hair, over on the stairs, strands of it waving tantalizingly down at him. He pushes past Viola, and she lets him by. Somehow, a beer has appeared in his hand, and he drinks it mechanically, in one swig, watching as Lorelei ascends each step in seeming slow motion.

"Lorelei!" he calls.

But the din of the crowd drowns his voice, and the sound flutters and crashes to the ground like a bird with a broken wing. Sebastian pushes forward, past two guys chugging boxed wine while a group cheers them on, past Imogen and Harry who emerge Nate-less from the adjoining room ("Do you think he got left behind somewhere in the streets?" Harry asks, reasonably. "No, he's here somewhere," Imogen insists.). They glance briefly at Sebastian, who stumbles by them, up the stairs, and towards Lorelei at the top. He grabs at the railing to avoid falling back as a herd of partygoers comes stampeding down (a fellow stair-ascender is not so lucky and tumbles down the steps, his glasses flying off his face as a well-intentioned but unsuccessful hand tries to catch him).

Sebastian reaches the top of the stairs and sees Lorelei's hair whipping around a corner and into a nearby room. He pushes past the beer pong table on the landing and enters through the open door to find her standing, alone in a bedroom, staring at a poster on the nearby wall, a large print of a painting by Moreau.

Lorelei sees him come in and smiles.

"Libya!"

She grabs his hand and pulls him towards her to look at the print on the wall. Sebastian is too mesmerized by the sudden appearance of art to register the physical contact. His vision sharpens, and his brain, as drunk as it is, feels something more than the haze of an inebriated stupor. The room is cold, with none of the oppressive body heat of the rest of the party (save for Lorelei's warm hand), but Sebastian also feels a strange sense of awe, a mystical reverence, as he gazes at the poster.

The painting is a classic Moreau, with the symbolist's recognizable color palette and unsettling proportions. In it, a tall woman looks down at a small young man who lies dying at her feet in a shallow pool of water in what looks like a cave. The woman is naked and crowned with an ivy laurel, and her red hair falls in a long sheet behind her, like a luxurious fur cloak. Her skin shines with luminescent whiteness, and she gazes imperiously down at the young man below her, whose own skin is a sickly, corpse-like gray. His eyes are shut and his mouth hangs open, and he barely has the strength to hold himself up. The cave around him, meanwhile, though vividly colored, is nightmarish and otherworldly, with rocks hanging from the ceiling like streaks of black rain and strange red plants rising like monsters from the still water, while out beyond the distant world grows fainter and fades to nothingness. Sebastian, of course, recognizes the painting in an instant: *The Poet and the Siren* (1893).

In that moment, Sebastian questions the reality of his surroundings. Yes, the owner of the apartment has nineteenth-century French art prints hanging in the entryway, but Sebastian is also drunk, having done more shots and chugged more drinks tonight than he ever has before, and so it's far more likely that the alcohol rushing through his brain has caused him to dream the painting up and that he and Lorelei are staring at an empty wall. It is, after all, an apt painting for him to imagine at this moment, a vivid scene of a beautiful, dangerous women having lured a man to his demise (Sebastian, of course, thinks of himself as the sickly poet, and doesn't imagine that though it was Lorelei's red hair that he chased through Santa Barbara, perhaps he is actually the siren, having ensnared her when he smiled at her under the conference room lights, luring her with those eyes that promise more depth than they contain). Standing there, though, and seeing it so vividly, the siren's well formed body, the cascade of red hair, the profile that looks so much like Lorelei, and feeling her hand in his, a vivid presence radiating warmth into that cold room, he wonders, why not lose himself to this fantasy, if that's what it is? Why not let the painting be as real as Lorelei is beside him?

She smiles and holds up two shot glasses and a fifth of vodka (Sebastian by this point has given up trying to understand the logic of this magically materializing alcohol).

"Shall we?" she asks.

In her whispered suggestion, Sebastian hears echoes of the powerful, resonant voice from committee, a quivering passion hidden in the quietly spoken words, a promise of an experience he may never find again. He tries to think of Fatima, he really does, but she's not here, and his mind is whirling from the alcohol. And so Sebastian takes a glass and listens to the gentle murmur of the vodka as Lorelei pours it inside and watches as she raises her glass to her lips, which are now flushed and match her hair. She bites her lip and waits. Sebastian tilts his head back and gulps down the shot.

He wakes up to the feeling of scratchy, coarse carpet against his face. The back of his head throbs, and he tastes vomit in his mouth. Slowly, he lifts his head and finds he's lying on his stomach on the carpeted floor of their hotel room. His glasses are still on his face, bent awkwardly but still intact. Nate is sprawled out on one of the beds, and Viola and Harry lie (platonically) on the other. The couch where Imogen sleeps is empty, save for a tousled-up blanket. Sebastian hears the bathroom fan buzzing and light creeping out from under the door. Through the blinds at the other end of the room, he sees the parking lot, illuminated by a few streetlamps. Beyond it, the horizon glows white and yellow with the slowly rising sun.

As Sebastian pushes himself to his knees, the bathroom door opens and Imogen emerges, already dressed in her pantsuit, her hair tied in a bun atop her head. Her eyes and her demeanor betray none of the drunken frivolities of the previous night.

"He rises from the dead," she says.

"What happened?" he asks. "How did I get here?"

"You don't remember the taxi ride? When you puked on the back seat and got us all kicked out a mile from the hotel?"

"No."

"Well, you did that, and we had to walk the rest of the way. We used your credit card to pay, by the way, so if you see a big charge, it's the fee for having to replace the leather seats." (The card is in Sebastian's name but connected to his father's account, so Sebastian will most certainly not see the charge, and his father will likely pay it off without even noticing.)

"What happened to my glasses?"

"I think you fell down the stairs at the party."

Imogen smirks at Sebastian's confusion and walks over to her suitcase. Sebastian enters the bathroom and flicks on the light. He stares at his reflection in the mirror. His hair is rumpled and his eyes red, and he's wearing his clothing from last night, but his collar is turned up and there's a vomit stain down the front of his shirt, and one of his buttons is missing. Sebastian fingers the dangling thread.

"What's the last thing you remember?" Imogen calls

from the other room.

He thinks of standing before the painting with Lorelei and taking the shot of vodka. In his mind, he sees flashes of her red hair and lips.

"Drinking vodka," Sebastian says.

Imogen leans into the bathroom, frowning.

"Around what time?"

"I don't know? Midnight?"

"Well, we lost track of you for a good few hours and we didn't really leave till around two. So…"

Imogen leaves the rest unsaid. Sebastian looks back at her, unblinking.

"I don't remember anything," he says.

Imogen stays silent for a moment. Her eyes flicker to the missing button on Sebastian's shirt.

"You should shower," she finally says. "You look like shit."

❖

Committee that morning is a blur. Most of the delegates don't show up, and those who do are either hungover or still drunk, and so no one puts in anything more than a perfunctory effort at debate, except of course for Imogen, who makes rousing speeches encouraging those present to vote for her bloc's prostitution-legalizing resolution (Sebastian finds it surprising that someone so personally opposed to the institution can argue so forcefully and persuasively in favor of legalizing it—a testament really to the instructive of power of Model UN and how well it encourages students to disappear into their roles). And somehow, through her rhetorical brilliance (and the good fortune that most of the committee is absent), Imogen manages in that final two-hour session to gather enough votes to pass her resolution, to the surprise of everyone present.

"Now that's diplomacy," she says, smiling as the room

rings with the tepid applause customary in Model UN committees each time a resolution passes.

Sebastian, though, is not listening and may as well be one of the delegates still asleep in their rooms. Lorelei is among those absent from the committee, and in her place is an assistant chair (a polished-looking Indian guy with gelled black hair). Sebastian wishes she were here, so she can confirm for him what may or may not have happened during those hours when Imogen and the others "lost track of him"—though Viola insisted earlier, on their walk to that morning's committee sessions, that he needn't worry.

"It's a party!" she said. "You were probably having fun! That's all you need to know." She's lighthearted about it because she herself has also blacked out twice. "The first time I definitely had a moment of existential doubt, like, did I flash into non-existence for a few hours, does what I did during that time actually have repercussions, and can I go around pretending it never actually happened? But after a while I realized it doesn't matter, that sometimes that kind of shit happens, and while I should probably avoid doing it again since I've read it kills brain cells, it's not a big deal if things get out of hand, especially in our senior year—so live a little, Sebastian! Think of it as a final hurrah, a last frontier of experience in our college lives!"

"I think it's 'final frontier' and 'last hurrah,'" Harry corrected.

"In a few years," Viola continued, "you'll look back fondly on your crazy undergrad days and that one time you blacked out at that party in Santa Barbara…"

Sebastian wants to be as nonchalant as Viola is. The truth is his memory will never come back, and according to Viola's logic, all reality is purely subjective, and if he doesn't remember anything after that shot of vodka he had in front of the painting, then in reality nothing happened after that moment until he woke up on the floor to the taste of his own vomit. In fact, perhaps this blackout was ultimately for the best, his brain's way of allowing him to enjoy the fruits of his pursuit without the memory and the guilt. It's an admirable series of mental gymnastics, not unlike what his mind did to rationalize kissing faux-Madeline (and at least alcohol is a more valid excuse than "witches"). But for whatever reason, Sebastian can't rationalize away this incident as easily, even though he remembers no actual physical details of any encounter with Lorelei, whereas his mind has often lingered on the softness of faux-Madeline's lips. It's as if, in the absence of those physical details, the guilt itself has become physical, palpable, as real as the warmth of Lorelei's hand and the bitter, wet taste of the vodka sliding down his throat. But then he hears Viola's voice in his head, stating back to him his own dark thoughts: "There's nothing to feel guilty about! Even if you and Lorelei did have sex, you don't have to tell Fatima, since you and her will likely never be having sex, so you don't have to worry about giving her an STD, though maybe you should get yourself checked out quietly, just in case, not that I don't trust Lorelei, but you never know, stuff happens, like my friend Jasmine who had sex only once but still managed to get chlamydia..."

But any comfort Viola's voice brings is only short-lived. Later, at the closing ceremony, when the Berkeley delegation is seated in the hotel ballroom and the committee chairs are at the front announcing awards, Lorelei among them (revitalized from the previous evening, with her slightly-red eyes the only signs of the previous night's celebrations), and when Libya is declared Best Delegate of SOCHUM and Sebastian makes his way up to the stage amidst applause (while Imogen gripes in her seat, having received only Outstanding Delegate) and steps forward to shake Lorelei's hand, he sees a glint in her eyes and a flirtatious smile across her red lips and feels in the way she tilts her head and brushes her other hand through her red hair and whispers "Congratulations..." (her voice soft, purring, musical even in that one word) a strange shudder pass through him, and he knows that though he won't ever remember the prior night, he'll never forget that current moment and all the signs in Lorelei of a shared secret between them.

Sebastian sits back down, the certificate and gavel proclaiming him Best Delegate in his hand. Viola, Harry, and Nate are pleased, and even Imogen, though frowning, is secretly happy, as this means Berkeley is probably guaranteed Best Delegation, since Viola and Harry also won gavels in their committee. But Sebastian doesn't look at any of his friends. Under the sharp fluorescent lights of that room, all he can see is Lorelei's red hair, shimmering as she steps back from the podium and takes a seat.

CHAPTER FOUR

OCTOBRE (1877)

She stands in line, a few blocks ahead of them, leaning against the brick wall under the dilapidated marquee of the old theater, her hands in the pockets of her Gore-Tex jacket, her gaze pointed up at the night sky to watch the snowflakes fall. The faux-fur-lined hood of her jacket is up over her head, but Sebastian can still see her hair, jet black and a sharp contrast to her pale skin, and done up in that 1960s French New Wave way, long and with bangs at the front, so that she looks like Anna Karina.

"She's definitely Sebastian's type," Harry says.

They're in Montreal, standing in line outside the old theatre, which has been turned into a club, "they" in this case being Sebastian, Viola, and Harry. The occasion is the Saturday night party at the McGill Model UN Conference, though this time only these three musketeers have ventured out for the evening, as the forecast predicted temperatures around the 0s (Fahrenheit) with the (faint) possibility of a blizzard, and Imogen, Nate, and the others, unacclimated to wintering in parts of the world which aren't California ("The temperature in Berkeley right now is fifty-five!"

Imogen said wistfully that morning), opted to stay in the warmth of the Le Centre Sheraton. The conference itself is already a lost cause as far as the UC Berkeley MUN team is concerned. Fresh from their victories at UCSB, they flew to Montreal that December brimming with confidence, only to be reminded that the East Coast Ivy League teams are, so to speak, in an entirely different league, chummy old boys' clubs far more rhetorically savvy than the laid back Californians they're used to debating. And so, Sebastian told the Berkeley delegation to forget the awards and focus instead on enjoying the wonders of this fantastic city, which to him was a veritable paradise, a place thoroughly North American yet with a very Old World charm, where French is spoken on the streets and cafes are open till 2 a.m. and the people (women) are thin and beautiful in that European way.

"What girl isn't Sebastian's type?" Viola asks, in reference to Harry's pronouncement.

"Hey now," Harry says. "Sebastian Khan is a very discerning man, with particular and refined tastes. When we're at Trader Joe's, he makes sure to read all the tasting notes for their wines before making a purchase—"

"And yet if its two a.m. at a party, and the only wine left is Two Buck Chuck, Sebastian will still drink."

"Well yeah. He's not a snob."

As they banter about his tastes, Sebastian stares at the girl who leans against the wall and watches the snowflakes tumble down while her friends chat around her. Ahead of her, the line slowly shifts as the bouncers let another group in after checking their IDs and handing out wristbands (the drinking age in Montreal is a generous nineteen, but even those freshman and sophomores who fail to make the cut remain unworried, knowing that inside, the bartenders, hired by McGill specifically for this party, won't really check, and that the wristbands and IDs are just a form of theatrics for the outside world). The girl shifts forward too, away from the wall, and joins the crowd as it shuffles towards the wooden doors. In a few minutes, she also will have passed the bouncers and crossed the threshold from the snowy night into the dark interior of the theater-club. Sebastian imagines trying to find her again amidst a world of flashing lights and dancers and faces blurred by the darkness and the drinks.

"What was her name again?" Viola asks.

"Kyrgyzstan," Harry says.

"Her name, Harry, not her country."

"Oh, sorry. I don't know."

"You said you met her too."

"Rosalind," Sebastian says, his gaze fixed on her. "Her name is Rosalind."

She, Rosalind, is in Harry and Sebastian's committee (the UN Human Rights Council), though they were only introduced on a first name basis earlier today, when Sebastian and Harry ran into her in the seventeenth-century room of the Montreal Musée des Beaux-Arts, standing before a painting by Poussin (*Paysage avec un homme poursuivi par un serpent*, 1637-1639—a classic Arcadian scene, with its sense of balance and harmony and its beautiful landscape, tempered slightly by the yellowish tinge and the sense of dread in the figure of the young man in Greek clothing looking over his shoulder at the serpent following in his wake).

"Oh hey!" Rosalind/Kyrgyzstan said, turning from the painting. "What a surprise!"

The delegates had the afternoon off from committee and most of them chose to stay in the apartment and sleep off the previous night's frivolities in preparation for tonight's. Sebastian, though, wanted to visit the city's museum, and Harry wanted to accompany him. Rosalind herself was there with Kazakhstan, also from their committee, and the four of them slipped into a comfortable group to wander the rooms together, though Kazakhstan eventually grew bored and at one point touched a sculpture by Rodin (*Les sirènes,* 1887-1888, an essentially pornographic depiction of three women intertwined in some kind of embrace) and got their group told off (in French) by a particularly irate museum guard. Rosalind, though, turned out to be as much a devotee of art as Sebastian.

"Have you ever seen the Scuola of San Rocco in Venice?" she asked, as they stood before a Tintoretto (*Portrait d'un membre de la famille Foscari,* 1555-1560—a painting of an austere, bearded gentleman in a flowing red gown, with that characteristic Tintoretto murkiness that suggested a surprising depth of feeling).

"Tintoretto's Sistine Chapel," Sebastian said, remembering the awe he felt gazing up at that ceiling and those walls covered by grand, luscious scenes from the New Testament. "I saw it on my trip through Italy."

"I think it's the only time I've ever felt truly moved in a religious building."

"Though not for religious reasons, I hope."

"Of course not. I doubt I could even tell you what the paintings were actually of. But I'll never forget those swirling colors."

It was difficult to pin down what Sebastian was feeling in that moment, standing before the Foscari gentlemen and next to this girl who suddenly revealed her own surprising depth. He had seen Rosalind before in committee, sitting with her Kyrgyzstan placard a few rows ahead of him, and he had taken brief note of her as he did with every pretty girl in a room. But now it felt like he was meeting her for the first time, seeing her not as Kyrgyzstan but as Rosalind. Sebastian had met plenty of girls who liked art (or at least claimed they did when they learned he studied Art History) but to meet one not at a party under the influence of vodka but in a museum and while sober was so much more authentic, a strange sensation since, as he and Rosalind wandered the rooms of the museum together for the next hour and he began to actually observe her, he soon realized there was also something very *theatrical* about her, the way she walked with careful steps, the way she looked at the paintings with a fixed, poised gaze, the way her left hand rested gently on the blue purse at her side, the way her bangs seemed perfectly arranged across her forehead, as if hair and makeup artists were, when Sebastian was turned away, rushing out to return each wayward strand back into perfect order.

There was one painting in particular, in the eighteenth- and nineteenth-century French room, that perfectly captured Rosalind's nature: James Tissot's *Octobre* (1887). The painting was of a woman dressed in a frilly black dress and a black feathered hat and walking through a forest of orange-leafed trees. She had a green book tucked under her arm, and as she pulled up her dress to wade through the fallen leaves, she looked mysteriously back over her shoulder at the viewer, as if beckoning him to join her. Physically, she bore very little resemblance to Rosalind, as her hair was auburn, not black, and as she was clearly white, whereas Rosalind, despite her pale skin, was more ambiguously mixed race, with her jet-black hair and small eyes (Sebastian briefly considers using Rosalind as proof to Fatima that he doesn't like only white girls (just white-looking ones) but ultimately decides against it). Yet it was the theatrically of the painted woman's attire, combined with that look, the depth in the dark eyes, the way the mouth was set with confidence, that to Sebastian made them appear almost identical, and every time Rosalind glanced at him, he saw that look, beckoning him deeper into the orange forest.

Sebastian didn't comment on the similarity. Instead, as he and Rosalind stood before the painting in silence, he said only that it was beautiful. Rosalind smiled in response, as if understanding immediately what Sebastian meant.

"She is, isn't she?" she said, looking over her shoulder at Sebastian.

Now, he stands on the snow-covered sidewalk and stares ahead at Rosalind and thinks of the painting with longing. Those few hours in the museum's heated halls were a strange, innocent bliss. Even if he did think of Fatima (which he didn't at any length), he wouldn't have felt guilty, because what was he doing besides walking with Kyrgyzstan and looking at paintings? And as for *Octobre*, what better representation is there of the innocence of flirtation? He can stare at the woman as she enters the grove of trees and smile at the "come hither" look in her eyes but be comfortable in the knowledge that the painting ends there, that he will never come hither and that she will always remain as she is, poised on the threshold.

Sebastian sees Rosalind now, at the door to the theatre, showing the bouncer her ID, holding out her arm for the wristband, and then moving forward with her group of friends, through the door and into the darkness. She doesn't look back over her shoulder, but Sebastian imagines she does, beckoning him inside.

"Well, if Sebastian does get laid tonight," Viola says, "Harry, you deserve some of the credit."

"What did I do?"

"From what you told me, you took one for the team at the museum, quietly letting Sebastian and Rosamund—"

"Rosalind," Harry corrects.

"Whatever—quietly letting them go ahead, forcing yourself to hang out with dimwitted, statue-touching Kazakhstan. I'm sure Sebastian appreciates it and will think of you and your sacrifice as he's burying his face in Rosalind's vagina—"

"Stop it," Sebastian says. "Nothing's going to happen."

"And why not?" Viola says, after a moment's pause.

"You know why."

Sebastian leaves her name unspoken. Viola shrugs.

"Your loss then," she says.

There's a silence as the line shuffles forward. Viola is smirking, but Harry looks uncomfortable. Unlike Viola, who has no problem voicing her displeasure with Sebastian's choice of a long-term (Fatima's word) partner (also Fatima's word), Harry always finds even an unspoken reference to her troubling. He's trying to appear nonchalant now, but Sebastian can see in his expression the familiar signs of moral brooding.

Sebastian finally lets himself think of Fatima. It's three hours earlier in Berkeley, and she's probably having dinner, with a few friends perhaps, or more likely by herself, a styrofoam box of takeout Thai food sitting next to her economics textbook. Sebastian texted her earlier, letting her know that he was going to the party and that he would call before he went to bed. Fatima texted back, telling him *Have fun.*

"So what about you then, Harry?" Viola asks. "Are you planning on finding this Kazakhstan on the inside?"

"I don't think so."

"Why not? Didn't you say she was hot? A little stupid, it sounds like, but still—hot is hot."

"I've told you before, Viola. I won't just sleep with any random girl."

"Oh right. Harry 'I'm-still-a-virgin-at-twenty-one' Kumar."

"I know it's hard for someone who lost their virginity at thirteen to understand—"

"Twelve," Viola corrects.

"—but I'm not going to sleep with a girl unless I know she's the one."

Viola laughs and tries to catch Sebastian's eye to share a derisive look of judgment. But Sebastian finds himself strangely moved by Harry, the certainty in his voice, the way he stands stoic in the face of Viola's laughter. Sebastian imagines Harry's "one" somewhere out there, a moral and intellectual saint like him, someone also committed to changing the world and who also always reads the latest National-Book-Award-winning narrative histories and watches PBS and C-SPAN and wakes up every morning at 7 a.m. to jog and listen to NPR and who also likes to read philosophy with their morning coffee (fair trade of course)—and in his heart Sebastian wishes that they do in fact meet to make each other happy.

The three of them reach the door and hand the bouncers their IDs. Sebastian stares ahead, through the darkness and towards the flickers of light and music. He imagines the orange forest and Rosalind, dressed up in theatrical black, waiting somewhere inside.

Immediately around the corner from the door is the old theatre's lobby, now turned into a kind of lounge area. Crimson leather sofas line the walls, tattered and worn to match the old carpeting, a beige that in the dim lighting looks like a light grey. The air too smells like the past, musty, like old wood and settled dust, as if the theatre has only just been reopened after many dormant years. A frieze circles the top of the room along the walls, filled with vaguely masonic-looking symbols and tall, faux-Egyptian figures, two-dimensional men in long conical crowns holding ankhs and staring at incomplete pyramids and disembodied eyes, the kind of decorating motifs beloved by early-twentieth-century theaters longing to convey a sense of mystic power. And yet the once-kitschy frieze is now also a remnant of an earlier time, when the theatre would have been filled with middle-class gentlemen and gentlewomen from the late Gilded Age, attired in suits and hats, chatting amiably while they waited for the players to take the stage. And while these men and women are now gone, the faux-Egyptian figures remain, and if they could speak, they would tell of all the history they've witnessed. By virtue of simply existing for so long, they have in fact become art. As Sebastian looks at them, he thinks sadly once again about the inevitable passage of time.

Sebastian, Viola, and Harry drop their coats off in

coat check (a novel experience for the three California residents—"I hope we don't lose these," Harry says in reference to the numbered tokens they'd been given) and then walk up to the bar that stretches across the front of the lobby. Three overworked bartenders dressed in all black rush up and down, hurriedly splashing vodka and whiskey and gin into plastic cups and topping them all with dashes of cranberry juice and Coke and tonic water, not bothering to check wristbands, hastily grabbing the soggy bills from the counter where they've been unceremoniously placed on puddles of the aforementioned alcohol and quickly scooping up any tips (those golden $1 Canadian coins that to the Berkeley delegation look like Monopoly money and add yet another level of unreality to their Model UN experience) before turning and asking "What can I get you?" in breathless, tired voices. Meanwhile, more delegates stream in from outside, and the lobby and bar grow increasingly crowded.

Sebastian and Harry dutifully wait behind the crowd, while Viola snakes her way through, tossing off a few "excuse me"s and "pardon me"s and flashing a flirtatious smile or two at the guys in front of whom she's cutting. Soon she returns to Sebastian and Harry (who at this point have only managed to move farther from the bar), deftly holding eight drinks between her fingers, spilling only one of them as she weaves her way back through the crowd.

"I think you miscounted us," Sebastian says, taking three of them from Viola's fingers.

"With this line, we might not get another chance," she says.

"I'm sure there are more bars inside the theatre floor," Harry says.

"Better safe than sorry."

Viola downs one of the drinks (a vodka tonic) in one long gulp, and then takes another and starts sipping it delicately. Sebastian and Harry do the same with a drink each, and then slowly sip their seconds (the remaining one Viola gives to Sebastian—"Extra courage, in case you run into Rosemary."—"Rosalind," Harry corrects.). Afterwards, they stand and glance around the lobby. The sofas are full, occupied by student delegates who already look in no condition to walk (Sebastian checks his watch to confirm that it's only 10 p.m.), and the rest of the carpeted floor is crowded with circles of other students, chatting amiably, sipping their drinks at that brisk pace common amongst young people only recently introduced to alcohol (as expected, those drinking the fastest have no wristbands). Other students meanwhile stream through the doors into the theatre, drinks in hand, towards the distant sound of rhythmic, pounding bass. Sebastian recognizes some of the faces in the crowd, but not the one he quietly craves. In his mind it's as if the paintings from the museum have been dumped here haphazardly, their labels stripped away, and now Sebastian has to sift through them and see if his eye can recognize the sharp features and inviting orange glow of the Tissot.

After a moment, Viola gestures to the doors that lead out onto the theatre floor. Sebastian and Harry nod and follow her across the lobby and into the room of light and sound. It takes a moment for Sebastian's eyes to adjust, but when they do, he finds himself surprised at how big a theatre is when all the seats have been removed. A large mass of students covers the old tiled floor, but even then there's plenty of open space along the sides. Above them, the theater's terrace and balcony levels jut out, throwing a small shadow over the entrance. A few bars line the perimeter of the space ("See?" Harry says. "They know better than to have only one place that dispenses alcohol."), and the walls, like those of the lobby, are covered with more faux-Egyptian iconography (and what the theatre's original designers must have believed to be hieroglyphics), though here the heads of the two main ankh-holding figures have giant speakers affixed to them, belting out that generic dance music of the late 2000s, while below one of them stands a DJ bobbing his head with a smug expression. A shallow set of stairs meanwhile descends towards the stage, before and atop which clump the main group of dancers. The light fixtures on the stage have been repurposed with various moving and flashing lights, intended to mirror the atmosphere of a club. Yet from the entrance, Sebastian can't help but see the room as still a theatre. The DJ in the pit is a kind of orchestra, important for the mood but ultimately irrelevant to the main show, while the dancers are both the performers and the audience, playing their parts for each other. The lights that flicker across the floor illuminate dust specks in the air, and it looks to Sebastian as if a mist of enchantment has settled over all their heads.

"Oh no," Harry says. "It's—"

"Hey!" Kazakhstan says, throwing up her arms. "My museum friends!"

She exuberantly hugs both Harry and Sebastian. Her breath smells of vodka. Viola extends out her hand.

"You must be Kazakhstan," she says. "I understand the museum really touched you. "

"It was alright," Kazakhstan says. "Too much art for me." She turns to Sebastian. "Kyrgyzstan's around here by the way," she says. "She was looking for you."

Sebastian's heartbeat quickens, and he feels like he's chugged another vodka tonic. Viola gives him a mischievous look.

"Alas, our Sebastian is behaving himself tonight," Viola says. "He has a girlfriend."

"Is she here?" Kazakhstan asks.

"No," Viola says.

"Then what's the problem?"

Viola laughs and takes Kazakhstan's arm.

"You know, I think I actually like you. Let's go dance!"

Viola and Kazakhstan disappear into the crowd, Viola giving Sebastian one last pointed look. Sebastian glances at

Harry, but the latter is looking at his own shuffling feet, as if avoiding Sebastian's eyes will make him forget the larger moral dilemma lingering in the air.

"Shall we find others from our committee?" Harry asks, after an awkward moment.

"Sure." Sebastian nods, determined not to think about Rosalind dancing somewhere under the misty light.

They move down around the side of the room, passing circles of standing delegates. Sebastian looks back and sees the terrace and the balcony now. Both are empty, and the stairways leading up to them are roped off and guarded by bouncers, perhaps to avoid any lawsuits in case a drunken student falls over the side. But their emptiness creates a strange effect in the atmosphere of the room, especially as unlike the main floor, the red, velvet-cushioned seats haven't been removed and instead line the space in eerie rows. Sebastian imagines a ghostly audience of those theatre-going gentlefolk from the past looking down in judgment on the oblivious college students below.

Harry and Sebastian find a circle of people from their committee, and Harry strikes up a conversation with Botswana about whether their committee topic (Civilian Deaths from Drone Strikes) is something the real UN would ever actually address ("Maybe not," Harry contends, "but I think the point of Model UN is not to be a literal model of the United Nations but rather an idealized one, a Platonic UN so to speak."). One of the other delegates, Paraguay, tries to talk to Sebastian ("So where are you from?" she asks, twirling a finger in her hair), but tonight he is distracted. The atmosphere of the old theatre, the memory of the museum, and that tugging in his chest all lead him to keep turning his head to look off across the bobbing sea of dancers, the girls in jeans and leggings twisting their hips and shaking their hair. For a moment, he imagines that time has rolled backwards and that everyone is dressed in early twentieth-century garb, tweed coats and bowler hats, and that the hall is more well lit, by a chandelier hanging from the ceiling, and that the music surrounding them like mist isn't electronic but acoustic and comes not from speakers but from a small band on the stage, men and women dressed in bow ties and brightly colored, striped suits, strumming acoustic guitars and belting out lively riffs on trumpets. But after a moment, the image fades, and he's back in the modern world.

And that's when he sees it, a sudden flash of orange against the dark colors of the dancing crowd. Somehow, he knows it's her. He hands his remaining drink and a half to Harry and makes his way towards the stage, past a girl who's flailing blond hair catches him in the face, past a guy in a V-neck and a fedora who's pretending to breakdance, past an awkward guy who tries to dance with a girl and is rebuffed with a hand and furrowed eyebrows, and all the while he keeps his eyes trained ahead of him, at the orange flashes flitting in and out at the edge of his vision and the accompanying cascade of black hair.

He steps up onto the stage, which is narrow, cramped, and filled mostly with girls. Sweat beads on his brow and the back of his neck, and above him loom the lights, humming as if their sound is a part of the DJ's set. The main red curtain is open, but the second one, a dull brown one that separates backstage from the main hall, is drawn shut. It's so stiff with dust and age it might as well be a wall. Sebastian follows it, weaving his way through the dancing girls, down towards stage left, where the curtain meets the actual wall— and there, just beyond the lights, he sees her, standing alone, not dancing but looking back at him and smiling.

"You found me," Rosalind says.

She's wearing an orange dress, which she must have had on under that Gore-Tex jacket. Below it she wears black tights and black shoes, which when taken with her black hair give her the sense of being surrounded by a frame. Sebastian is speechless, staring at her and at the murky darkness of backstage beyond her glowing form. The shouting of the dancing crowd behind him seems suddenly far away. The only world he's aware of now is the stage.

Rosalind looks at him, and in her eyes he sees that beckoning look. With the confidence of an actor, he steps forward, takes her by the waist, and kisses her. Her lips are warm and taste like alcohol and fruit. She reaches a hand up and strokes his cheek, and he slips his own hand down and under her dress and rubs her through her tights, feeling a wetness on his fingers seeping through the nylon. She breathes sharply against his neck and digs her nails into his arm.

He takes her by the hand then and steps backstage. Here, the noise of the main room suddenly dampens, and the only light is a sliver between the curtain and the wall. The rest of the space is a dark, empty cavern through which even their faintest footsteps seem to echo. To the right is a set of ropes tied in a complex knot, and to the left an old wooden chest and a wardrobe, both covered in a sheet of dust. Behind the ropes stretches a hallway, leading off to what must have once been the dressing rooms.

As they feel their way towards the hallway, they kick up the long settled dust, which swirls mist-like around them. The air is surprisingly cold, and the only warmth Sebastian feels is Rosalind's pulsing hand and her breath against the back of his neck. He turns the handle of the first door they reach, which creaks open at his touch. Whatever the room once was, it's a supply closet now, stacked with what in the dark looks to be unmarked cardboard boxes and wooden crates. But Sebastian imagines it's a dressing room still, filled with masks and wigs and makeup and elaborate costumes. He leaves the door open so a few rays of light can filter in from the stage. They cast a strange aura around Rosalind's orange dress, just enough for him to see her smooth skin and dark hair.

She leans back against one of the walls and gently pulls him towards her, kissing him again and guiding his hand down to her tights, which he slowly peels back, while her own hands work the buttons of his pants and then tear open the condom that he pulls from his front pocket. Her body is warm in the cool air of the dressing room, and heat radiates off her bare skin as he runs his hand back up her legs and up towards the wet spot between her thighs. He closes his eyes and the feel of her is enough to send him out of the cold darkness of the old theatre and back into the warm halls of the museum, to the nineteenth-century room and to the orange forest. He presses his body against hers and feels her lips against his ear and imagines that in between the sounds of her soft, sharp breathing, he hears the rustling of October leaves.

Afterwards, they wordlessly dress and retrace their steps, down the hallway and back onstage. They pause a moment to let their eyes adjust to the light. Before them stretches the sea of bobbing dancers and in the distance float the empty red seats of the terrace and balcony, like a ship on the horizon. The dusty mist in the air now looks like water, high above their heads so that there's no chance of swimming to the surface.

"Well," Rosalind says, turning to Sebastian. "See you around."

She smiles and puts a hand on Sebastian's shoulder, and then slips back offstage and down into the crowd. Sebastian watches her go, but soon loses the orange dress in the swirl of dancers.

He returns to Harry, who's still talking to Botswana and Paraguay about their committee.

"There you are!" Harry says. "I still have your drink."

Sebastian takes the drink from Harry mechanically. The ice has melted and the tonic water has gone flat. Sebastian sips it and finds it unpleasantly lukewarm.

"I'm going to head out," he says.

Harry looks surprised.

"Everything okay?"

Sebastian nods and hands Harry back the tepid drink. Harry's eyes narrow, and suddenly it's clear that somehow he understands everything. He stares back at Sebastian, aggrieved and disappointed, with that look of moral judgment he usually reserves for Model UN speeches.

Sebastian turns away and walks back along the edge of the crowd, past one of the bars, which is now as crowded as the one in the lobby earlier. The theatre is packed, all the way to the wall, and the pounding bass is louder too. In the distance, the DJ's head continues to bob with satisfaction. Sebastian imagines the music coming not from the speakers but from the Egyptianesque figures themselves. The lights on the stage meanwhile, flash in wild shades of blue and yellow.

At the entrance to the lobby, Sebastian runs into Viola, still arm in arm with Kazakhstan. The two have a fresh batch of drinks (four each) in their hands.

"You're leaving?" Viola asks.

"I am."

"Oh, don't be a little bitch. If this is about Fatima, I promise I'll keep you from fucking Rose of Sharon—"

"Rosalind," Kazakhstan says.

"Whatever," Viola says.

"It's not about that," Sebastian says.

"Then what?"

Viola scrutinizes Sebastian, as if noticing something. The theatre's flashing lights are mirrored in her eyes. Sebastian tries to pull his gaze away, but Viola grabs him by the shoulders (spilling one of her four drinks all over the floor as she does) and then smiles with understanding.

"Oh Sebastian, you naughty boy. You don't waste any time, do you?"

Sebastian pushes past her and towards the lobby. He

can feel the lights of the club, magnified through Viola's eyes and boring holes in the back of his head.

"Why leave now?" Viola calls to him. "What's done is done, as the Bard said!"

Sebastian keeps moving, through the crowded lobby and back out the doors and into the snow. Once outside, he leans his head against the brick wall and takes in a deep breath of chilly air. Above him is the theatre's disused marquee, darkened, its remaining letters a meaningless jumble. The bouncer at the door, still checking IDs and handing out wristbands, glances over at him.

"Don't you fucking puke out here," the bouncer says.

Sebastian turns from the entrance and walks in the direction of the Le Centre Sheraton. It's snowing more heavily than before, and the flakes that fall upon him soak through his button-down. He realizes he's left his coat inside and that Harry has the coat-check token. But he doesn't want to have to face Harry's judging eyes, and the snow actually feels pleasant, a sharp coolness after the swirling fire of the club, and so Sebastian keeps walking, down the street and towards the distant skyscrapers. Their lights are a shimmering yellow against the dark-blue sky, and for a moment, in the misty haze of falling snow, Sebastian imagines he's still in the club.

A few taxis breeze by on his left, and across the street, a group of smokers lounge outside a bar, but otherwise the city is strangely empty for midnight on a Saturday. Snow collects atop the roofs of parked cars and on the stony eaves of buildings. Sebastian imagines that inside, behind each building's soundproof wall, lies the decadence of another club or bar, young people wearing thin dresses over leggings and dancing in heated rooms, their wet coats hanging in coat-check closets, their minds rooted firmly in the moment and in their artificial environments, oblivious to the snowy reality of the world outside. But as he walks the empty streets, his button-down soaked through now and a chill spreading across his skin, Sebastian wonders which is the real world and which is the stage.

He stops at the corner of Boulevard René Lévesque and Rue de La Cathédrale. Around him rises the glass and concrete of the business district. The gray-white building behind him has a neoclassical facade, complete with unnecessary Corinthian columns. To his left is a large park, empty at this hour like the rest of the district. Snow piles up on the benches and in the leafless branches of the trees and on the dead grass, while lampposts along the street cast a yellow glow across the park. In the center of the square is a statue of a man standing next to a rearing horse. When taken together with the columned building behind him and the French street signs, the statue makes Sebastian think of the parks in London and Paris filled with similar monuments to national heroes. Montreal is suddenly so distant from the rest of North America, a slice of Europe smuggled across the Atlantic, and from this vantage point, California and Berkeley are distant universes, too far away to matter or even be real.

Ahead of him, the light is red and the walk signal displays the large, red-orange hand. There are no cars in either direction, but Sebastian waits anyway. He pulls out his phone, his Motorola Razr (smartphones are slowly becoming more popular among college students, but Sebastian still refuses to conform to modernity and purchase one). The screen is cracked, a jagged spiderweb spreading out from one corner, but underneath it's still readable. The clock on his phone says 12:03 a.m., which means it's still early in Berkeley.

Sebastian pauses, takes in a breath, and calls Fatima. The phone rings just once before she picks up.

"Hey! I didn't expect you to call so early!"

Her voice is distant, the edges of it crackling like canvas being torn apart. He's rarely ever spoken to her on the phone and never actually called her himself. Like most members of his generation, Sebastian is a strictly face-to-face or text message person, and over the phone he's usually curt, anxious to get to the point and get back to the world, certainly not a fan of the prolonged conversations common in adolescent relationships where couples stay on the line while going about whatever task they have before them, as if the tenuous link provided by Verizon or AT&T will make up for their relationship's real world deficiencies. Now, however, he pauses, uncertain how to continue, uncertain why he's even called, a little taken aback by how strange it is to hear Fatima's voice floating on the waves in the air, completely disembodied, as if there's nothing about her that's at all physical.

"Is the party over already?" she asks.

"I left early," he says. "I wasn't really feeling it."

He thinks of Rosalind's body pressed against his in the musty closet, and the feel of her breath against his neck.

"What are you up to?" he asks.

"Just studying."

He tries to think of what Fatima looks like, the way she must be sitting right now, how her body would look angled in her office chair, how her hair would look pulled back in a ponytail or loose and scraggly around her ears. But the voice gives him none of this.

Across the street, the light turns green and the hand is replaced by a white walking figure, blurry against the falling snow. Sebastian, however, stays standing on the corner, unable to move.

"I went to the museum today," Sebastian says, after another silence.

"Oh yeah?"

He imagines Fatima glancing down at her economics textbook as they speak, her eyes tracing charts of data, graphs with colored bars and lines, bolded terms coined by former Reagan Administration officials in the last twenty-five years that were nonetheless intoned by her professors as if they were discovered in cuneiform on Sumerian tablets.

He imagines such tablets, sandy brown, engraved with the phrases "supply-side" and "trickle-down" (untranslated and in Sumerian, of course) and then tries to visualize his future with Fatima as clearly as he can those tablets. He looks up at the towering white building next to him and imagines its equivalent in San Francisco's Financial District. At the top would be where he works, a firm that does "creative consulting" or "design" or "marketing," some practical-ized version of a humanities degree, and behind a large glass window he would sit at a cubicle in a button-down and a tie, typing numbers into Excel spreadsheets, sending emails via Microsoft Outlook, glancing now and then at the clock and at the photo of Fatima next to it. After work he'd descend in the elevator, nod briefly to the doorman, and walk down to SOMA, to where he and Fatima lived, a faux-hipster apartment next door to other bourgeois couples who worked in the tech or financial industries and made enough money to afford high thread count bedsheets and $12 cocktails and all the other necessities of contemporary adult life. On weekends, meanwhile, he and Fatima would go down to the Embarcadero to drink their $5 Blue Bottle pour overs and eat their $5 cups of Three Twins ice cream and stare out across the Bay. Berkeley then would be barely visible over the fog that would shroud the Bay Bridge in a comforting embrace, and if ever Sebastian would have errant, nostalgic thoughts of wild parties in crumbling apartments, of plane rides with his Model UN team, of mornings spent four to a bed in a swanky hotel, sleeping off a night of drinking at an old theatre, the smell of lipstick and vodka hanging in the air against the fresh scent of clean towels, he'd only have to lean over and kiss Fatima and those thoughts would disappear like that other, vanished city across the Bay.

Isn't this future with Fatima real? Isn't that why he's called her? Isn't this why he left the party early, why he feels a gnawing guilt in his heart? But if so, why can't he smell the hardwood floors of his future apartment like he can the air of the theater's backstage? Why can't he taste the coffee he's made in his IKEA French press before he leaves for work the way he can the vodka he drank from the plastic cup earlier tonight? Why can't he feel Fatima's lips as she kisses him outside on the pier the way he can Rosalind's as she pulls him towards her in the storage closet? He tries, desperately, but already that vision is fading and he's back in Montreal, standing in the cold snow amidst the quiet buildings of the old world, listening to the breathing on the other end of the line, which sounds like static.

"I saw a painting that reminded me of you," he says to the phone. Fatima's breathing doesn't change at all. There is a brief silence as Sebastian waits for her to say something. When she doesn't, he continues on. "It was by James Tissot, called *Octobre*. A woman in black wandering through an orange forest, looking back at the viewer." Silence on the other end. Sebastian wonders whether the connection has been severed, if somehow the Montreal weather knocked down the signal as it tried to float up through the sky, burying it under a foot of snow. "You there?" he asks.

"I'm here," she says. "That's great. About the painting."

Another pause. The walk signal changes to a countdown, accompanied by the red-orange hand, now blinking. *Fifteen, fourteen, thirteen...*

"My interview didn't go well today," Fatima says.

Sebastian remembers she told him about an interview, with some company in San Francisco. She's been on so many lately, and he tries desperately to remember which company this one was for. The signal ahead continues: *nine, eight, seven...* Sebastian imagines the homeless man holding the signal and smiling at him from his bucket on Sproul Plaza. The actual countdown would now be at 168 DAYS TILL THE END (or maybe 167 already, if the homeless man is diligent and changes the number as soon as it's past midnight). Sebastian sees the days on the countdown flitting by as quickly as these red-orange numbers.

"How did it go?" Sebastian asks, in reference to the interview.

"I just said it went bad."

He can hear the edge creeping into Fatima's voice. He has to remind himself not to correct her grammar and tell her that it went *badly* and not *bad.*

"I'm sorry," he says. "I didn't hear you."

Five, four, three...

"On top of that," Fatima continues, "I found out I didn't get the Tesla job."

Two...

"I'm sorry," Sebastian repeats.

One. The light turns yellow, then red, and the hand freezes in place. It's red-orange is vivid against the white sheet of snow that blankets the sidewalk.

"I just don't know what I'm doing wrong!" Fatima says. "I have all the qualifications they're looking for, my GPA is perfect, I have rec letters from top professors, I've been doing internships across the Valley since high school, I'm a part of every computer club Berkeley has to offer. But when I go into these offices and talk to these men, it's like I know right then that I'm not who they're looking for. It's like, their applications say they're looking for one thing, but really they're looking for something completely different."

Sebastian thinks of the nights he's spent in Fatima's apartment, watching as she filled out those applications like a robot, copy-pasting the same cover letter into different forms, changing the addressee and the second line of the opening paragraph, where she always writes "one specific thing about the company itself to show that I have a personal interest in them." He's tried always to tell her that that's not how one gets a job, especially in a recession, but she simply says that "the tech industry is booming" and that "the recession only applies to people like you, who studied Art History." Sebastian wants to tell her that no, the recession doesn't apply to people like him because, recession or not, Art History majors will always have trouble finding jobs, since what they do isn't tied to the economy, and the reason they do it isn't tied to a financial motive, and that instead recessions hit people like her the hardest, those who from an early age have bought into the capitalist dream, believing that if they work hard and get their degree and have a good GPA and do a sufficient number of extracurriculars and dutifully ask professors for the requisite recommendation letters that they will be given the job they deserve by society.

"Maybe you're approaching it wrong," Sebastian says to the phone. "Interviewing is like acting. Or flirting. Your qualifications and your resume and all that don't really matter. It's the way you smile when you first step into the room, the way you shake their hand, the little joke you make, the way you look into their eyes…"

"Like you know anything about interviewing. Maybe you should go to one yourself before giving advice."

Her voice is harsh, and it's not just the static. Across the street, the light turns green again, and the walk signal returns. But Sebastian is once again paralyzed on the sidewalk. The snow starts falling more heavily around him, and he feels it streaking through his hair and down his face, melting in contact with his skin. He shivers and looks up at the dark sky above him, a vast void dotted with falling specks of white.

Fatima starts talking about the interview now, but Sebastian has stopped listening to her actual words. Instead he clings to the sound of her voice, and in the scratchy rhythmic droning he tries to grasp at some kind of melody, something that will pull him from the cold city, something more real than the snow falling around him, something warm like the theatre-club and like Rosalind's body and breath. But Fatima's voice has none of that. It emanates from the phone but the sound waves have no physical presence, and the voice may as well be one playing in his own head.

Sebastian feels his phone vibrate. He pulls it away from his ear and looks at it. Fatima's voice continues, now just a muffled spool of noise dissolving into the air as it unfurls. On his screen is a text message, from an unknown number: *Hey. I got your number from your friend Viola.*

Sebastian feels a thumping in his heart and suddenly he's no longer in the snowy air but in a club, the misty air thick with sweat and perfume, girls in dresses shimmering around him amidst flashing lights. An orange shape flickers in the peripheries of his vision. He feels warm breath against his neck and a wetness on the tips of his fingers. His phone vibrates again and another message appears under the first: *Interested in an encore?*

Fatima's voice continues, but Sebastian can barely hear it now. He can taste Rosalind's fruity lips and tongue. He answers the message: *Le Centre Sheraton, Room 651.* Then, he texts Viola: *I need the room. Can you and Harry stay out for another few hours?* Almost immediately, she responds: *Sure thing. Have fun. ;)*

Sebastian stares up at the sky. The snow continues to fall, the cold air swirls around him, and his shirt is soaked through, but he doesn't feel any of it. The city, the sky, and the weather are all as unreal as the voice on the other end of the phone, disembodied and a thousand miles away, from another world entirely.

"Hey," Sebastian says, interrupting the voice. "I need to get going. It's an expensive call."

"Oh, okay."

It's not entirely a lie, since Canada is in fact a different country, though Sebastian has of course never looked at a cell phone bill in his life, and it's his father who will pay it without giving the extra charges a second look.

Fatima's voice fades away, and when it does the whole city grows quiet. The snow continues to fall, but nothing makes a sound. It's as if the world has become a painting.

"I'll talk to you later," Sebastian says, to the silence on the other end of the line.

He hangs up and lets out a breath, which fogs up in the air before his face. The back of his throat is dry and cold, but his lips are warm, and with them he feels the soft skin of Rosalind's neck. The phone vibrates again: *On my way.*

Ahead of him, the light changes to green. Sebastian steps forward and crosses the street, towards the distant towers.

CHAPTER FIVE

A RAKE'S PROGRESS (1732-33)

She wears his sweater and nothing else and stands before his desk, tracing her fingers across the open art history textbook (Davies, Penelope J.E., et. al. *Janson's History of Art: The Western Tradition, Volume II (8th Edition)*. Upper Saddle River, NJ: Prentice Hall, 2010.). The pages show the eight panels of Hogarth's *A Rake's Progress*. Her blue eyes linger on the third panel, in which our rakish hero enjoys the delights of a brothel, and then on the fourth panel, in which he barely escapes the bailiffs who've come to haul him off to debtors' prison.

"We should get going," Sebastian says.

He tosses Juliet her underwear, which is still wet and smelling of her and which he pulled down her tanned legs only minutes earlier, when she was splayed on the bed, her shaggy mop of brown hair a mess across her face. She laughed as Sebastian buried his face between her thighs and as her long-fingered hands ran through his dark hair, and now Sebastian can still smell her, as if the air of his small room is permanently filled with that scent, stronger even than her perfume, a rosy musk that he also can't get out of his head. Sebastian wonders if, when Fatima returns from winter break a few days from now, she'll be able to smell either scent. He makes a mental note to wash the sheets.

Juliet slips on her underwear but keeps her eyes fixed on the book. From beyond her, daylight spills in through the blinds, which are pulled closed across Sebastian's small window. The room itself is tiny and narrow, with a desk built into an alcove in the wall, stacked with papers and books, a small, white IKEA bookcase (the Avdala) filled with a sea of black-spined Penguin Classics, and a twin bed with black and white sheets that takes up most of the rest of the carpeted floor. A mirrored door opens to a small closet, and a shiny metal light fixture in the contemporary, chic-minimalist style of the building hangs from the ceiling, incongruous with the light leather *Mad-Men*-style office chair below it. The walls are bare and decorated only with the museum postcards Sebastian has collected over the years, arranged in symmetrical rows by the years of his visit, a small timeline of his artistic education (the most recent postcard is of *Octobre*).

Sebastian pulls on his blazer and checks himself in the mirrored door, combing his tussled hair. Juliet looks at him with a rakish smile and steps towards him, covering the small distance across his apartment with two quick long-legged strides. She runs her fingers through his hair and reaches her other hand down to unzip his pants.

"We don't have time," Sebastian says.

"What's the rush? You said you don't have to be in the city until lunch."

Her French accent fills the room as much as her smell does, and Sebastian wonders if Fatima will be able to find traces of it too, the lilting echoes melted permanently into the walls. Her breath is stale, tasting of sleep and the morning coffee, which she brewed in Sebastian's kitchen earlier and which now sits precariously at the edge of his desk, steam rising from its still-warm surface. The coffee is a creamy, beige color, turned that way after Juliet poured in a dash of milk, and it matches the corduroy pants she was wearing the night before and which now lie in a crumbled pile by Sebastian's chair. Sebastian usually dislikes milky coffee, but right now he's enamored with Juliet's habits, which over the past three weeks he's grown accustomed to, the way she rises each morning around 8 a.m., slips on one of Sebastian's shirts or sweaters, smokes a cigarette out in the open air hallway, puts the espresso pot on the stove, and then comes back to bed for a quick fuck before returning to the finished coffee, pouring it into one of Sebastian's mugs, and carrying it carefully back into the room, where she sits on Sebastian's chair, still half-naked, and sips it while checking emails and social media accounts on her laptop. Today the mug Juliet drinks from is a touristy one from San Francisco, part of Fatima's Christmas gift. Fatima also gave him the espresso pot Juliet used to make the coffee, as well as the sweater she's currently wearing.

"Harry comes back from break today," Sebastian says, in reference to Juliet's desire not to rush. "I'd rather us not be here when he does."

Juliet looks at him with a fierce, faux-pouty face, which with her small eyes, mouse-like features, and messy hair, Sebastian finds thoroughly charming. It was this look that first drew him to her, back at the party at International House three weeks before.

"You're embarrassed by me?" she asks, mostly in jest.

"No, but when it comes to the mistress, a gentleman must be discreet, no?"

He means it as a joke, and he says it in his theatrical, affected voice. But Juliet looks offended by the word, and her faux-pout melts into a genuine frown. Sebastian immediately regrets what he said.

"I just don't want to have to explain it all to Harry," he says, his tone more honest now. "He's been very moralistic since Montreal."

"It's fine," Juliet says. "I understand."

She pulls on her corduroy pants, her legs disappearing into the fabric, and then pulls off his (Fatima's) sweater and picks up her white button-down. They're quiet for a moment as she turns to the mirror and adjusts her hair. Sebastian kneels to lace up his shoes. The smell of her underwear still hangs in the dusty air.

"I just thought you were going to tell Fatima about me anyway when she got back from break," Juliet says. "So what does it matter if your roommate finds out a few days before?"

Sebastian pulls his laces tighter than intended, and he feels the leather of his shoe pinch around his arch. He stands and puts a hand on her shoulder.

"It'll be a long conversation," he says. "I'd rather not rush through it."

Juliet is still upset, so Sebastian leans forward and kisses her on the tip of her nose. Despite everything, she can't help but break into a smile. The dimples on her face remind him of innocence and freshness, and he remembers that she's only nineteen and a sophomore (or rather a "second year" as she puts it, in that lovely accent of hers, which draws out the second syllable of "second."). Perhaps that's why the two of them so easily get along—Sebastian, in his heart, feels as young as she is.

The BART train is musty, the seats stained with coffee and other things, and the air smells faintly of farts and body odor. But all Sebastian focuses on is the rosy scent of Juliet's perfume. They sit next to each other, facing east and watching the Oakland suburbs recede, and though they don't hold hands or give any outward sign of their intimacy, it's clear from their body language, the way they're closer together than normal, the way her arm occasionally brushes his, the way their heads are angled towards each other even during silence, that they are some kind of couple. Fatima is in Southern California, spending winter break at her parents' place in Orange County, and it's unlikely that anyone who knows them both is on this train—and so Sebastian remains unworried about being seen with Juliet and ventures a warm smile in her direction and at one point, as the train passes into the tunnel and under the Bay, even reaches over and pushes a strand of unruly brown hair out of her eyes.

He met Juliet three weeks earlier, the very day Fatima left for break. After a tearful (on Fatima's part) farewell on the BART platform, in which he promised to call every day and assured that the three weeks would go by in a flash, Sebastian found himself breathing a sigh of exhilarated relief and texted all his friends to inquire about parties that evening. Since he returned from Montreal, life with Fatima had become increasingly unbearable, not because of any guilt or because Sebastian was on any kind of confessional verge, but because he felt like while he'd reached some kind of decision standing out on the street corner in Montreal listening to Fatima over the phone, she'd reached the opposite decision, as if she'd sensed what happened in the storage closet at the old theatre and on the hotel room bed in the Le Centre Sheraton (and then again in the shower) and was determined to pull Sebastian closer, to keep alive that future of hers, which as they rounded the halfway point of their senior year was becoming all the more real and inevitable. Sebastian still did find it comforting, especially when he passed that selfless, determined, homeless prophet still sitting on his bucket and broadcasting his warning (now at 133 DAYS TILL THE END), but only as long as long that future remained a future and never actually became a present. But every time Fatima filled out another application and went to another interview, every time she mapped out where her job might be and what apartment prices in SF looked like and pondered aloud whether it would be feasible to live in Oakland and commute or maybe even move farther out into the suburbs ("I mean, if we're eventually going to have kids, then buying a house in the suburbs now would be a good investment, since because of the recent crash, real estate prices are only going to go up."), and every time she urged Sebastian to apply for something and to start investing his money ("You should open a Roth IRA. Suze Orman recommends it.") instead of spending it on $4 coffees and lengthy $15 lunches at La Note, Sebastian felt a flutter in his heart and tried to cast his mind back to the musty smells of the old theatre, the flashing lights and the dancing girls, Rosalind's orange dress lying at the foot of his bed. And so when Fatima left, Sebastian was willing to accept any invitation to a party, even one from Imogen to a gathering that night with some of her political science friends at one of the apartments in International House.

Imogen was mostly interested in discussing the upcoming UC Berkeley Model UN Conference, of which she was now Secretary General (the previous Secretary General, Eric Lim, an overworked political science and economics double major, had a nervous breakdown and was recently hospitalized, and Imogen was called upon by Harry, Viola, and the rest of the Officer Board to step forward, something she did with eagerness).

She was speaking to Sebastian out on the apartment's balcony, seated on a metal chair. Exchange students clustered around them, smoking cigarettes in that casual European way, as if by sheer sangfroid they could avoid the pitfalls of lung cancer (Sebastian himself doesn't smoke— even he has one virtue).

"We've done quite well at away conferences this year—" Imogen said.

"You're welcome," Sebastian said.

"—and so we have quite the turnout expected. All our usual smaller schools plus UPenn, Harvard, and Chicago, of course, but also Columbia, Princeton—they have a small team, only three guys who look like extras from *Dead Poets Society*—and, wait for it…*Yale*."

Sebastian was less impressed than Imogen by the inclusion of George W. Bush's alma mater, and so she expressed his excitement for him, citing the incredible symbolic importance of having all the major Ivies attending their conference.

"Now, I'll need your help to make sure everything goes smoothly," she added. "I know it's still two months away, but a lot can go wrong, and Harry insists I have to use all the people Eric appointed as his deputies, even though they're all lazy fucks who care more about their own coursework and job applications than the conference—"

"The selfish pricks."

"—so I'm going to make you my Point Man. You'll help sweet-talk our sponsors and deal with the new hotel people, who are a little nervous about hosting a college conference—"

"We're not at the Union Square Grand Hyatt this year?"

"No. The Hilton, in the Financial District. The Hyatt refused to deal with us after that clusterfuck involving Raj and the pasta primavera last year."

In one of UCBMUN's more memorable incidents, a member named Raj Patel, after eating what he termed "the best fucking pasta primavera in the world" had a few too many shots (ten) of vodka and ended up puking the aforementioned meal all over the sixteenth-floor hallway (Raj was upset at losing such an exquisite dinner, but Sebastian assured him with Epicurean definitiveness that since he'd already tasted and enjoyed it, what did it matter whether it was down in the pipes of the city's sewage system or all over the carpeted floor of the Grand Hyatt?). Raj has since graduated and is now working as a consultant at Deloitte making six figures, though the incident remains soaked into the minds of the hotel staff, just like the vomit stain itself, which could never be fully removed from the carpet (something about the sauce used in the pasta primavera).

"Anyway," Imogen continued, "I'll need you by my side in case of any emergency shit that might come up—"

Imogen went on to inform Sebastian of his role at the conference, but Sebastian stopped listening as soon as his ear caught the sweet sounds of a French accent floating over from a nearby circle of smokers: "I never understood this American preoccupation with the future. Everyone here always asks me what I'm going to *do* with my degree, as if the only thing that matters is what happens after college and not the actual degree itself." (As with most continental Europeans, Juliet spoke English far better than any native Californian). "It's all very Puritan, no?"

Sebastian's eyes followed the floating voice over to a mousy girl with tousled brown hair who wore a striped shirt with sleeves that were a little too long and extended past her wrists so that only the tips of her long fingers poked through to delicately hold a clear plastic cup of white wine. Sebastian listened and watched as she expounded upon her theory regarding the hypocrisy of America's preoccupation with employment, and her voice, soft as it was, was strong enough to drown out even Imogen's grating, military cadence. Imogen, noticing Sebastian's wandering gaze, stopped talking and frowned and waited for Sebastian to remember she was there, and when he didn't, she leaned forward and snapped her fingers in front of his face.

"Hey, this is important."

"Important? It's a Model UN conference—"

"*Berkeley's* Model UN conference, which means Harvard, Princeton, and Yale will all judge us if it's not memorable—"

"But who cares? We'll be graduating soon, and in a year do you really think it'll matter whether you got a few Ivy League pricks hard for a weekend?" Imogen leaned back in her chair and her expression soured. Sebastian saw that he'd struck a nerve, and he felt the pain himself. Imogen hated to be reminded of the impending end of college as much as he did. "Anyway," Sebastian continued. "This is important too."

He gestured with his head towards Juliet.

"Another girl you're interested in? I can't think of anything less important."

"Maybe she won't just be another girl." Sebastian shrugged. "Maybe I'll marry this one."

Imogen rolled her eyes but grew serious at the word "marry." She stared at Sebastian for a moment before she spoke.

"How's Fatima?"

Sebastian frowned.

"She's fine."

Now, sitting next to Juliet on the BART train, Sebastian contemplates the last three weeks, a whirlwind of passionate sex and long conversations about Juliet's philosophy of the future. "I think the recession has actually been good for our generation," she said on one occasion. "Because of all the joblessness, people are rethinking their futures, wondering whether it's even necessary to immerse themselves completely in a corporate job, like they did before 2006. They slow down, they enjoy life, they travel the world. They're no longer in such a rush to settle down." And yet, how strange it is that in only three weeks, life with Juliet has developed a very "settled-down" quality, though of a kind far different from the monotonous monogamy Sebastian has with Fatima. Perhaps it's the presence of sex, which makes the routine of shared coffee and breakfast and holding hands in movie theaters all the more bearable. More likely, though, it's the thrill of adultery, the fact that he and Juliet know this little relationship, as settled as it seems in these three winter weeks, when the campus has emptied of all its folk and even the responsibilities of college have been put on hold, allowing Sebastian and Juliet to be like the lovers on Keats's urn, paused just at the precipice of fulfilling their desire, will all end soon, that Fatima will return and the world will resume and the countdown will continue and remind them that they're not just some "brede of marble men" and won't be "for ever panting and for ever young." Maybe it's that very temporality that makes their brief foray into domesticity all the more enchanting.

And then what of when it ends? In a moment of love-struck passion, Sebastian promised Juliet that he would tell Fatima and break it off, and now she's clinging to those words. For all her talk of not settling down, Juliet clearly wants to be more than just Sebastian's "mistress." Perhaps that would be for the best, though, replacing the unhappy, sexless arrangement he has with Fatima with this other more wild and frenzied version. Juliet will be going back to France at the end of the year, but maybe he can move there too, find a job in some bookstore, spend his mornings wandering the banks of the Seine and the halls of the Louvre, and then pop off to her Parisian apartment for a quick matinee before she has to rush off to her evening classes.

Sebastian has often woven fantasies about the girls he's been with, though in a few months such fantasies always inevitably dematerialize, and he knows that even with Juliet what is now breathtakingly fresh will become mundane, that the smell of her underwear will grow stale like the perfumes of all those previous women. And yet, it feels different now. Maybe it's the way this particular winter break acts as a last pause button before the final semester of his college life, or maybe it's that he met Juliet now, when his dreary, post-col-lege life with Fatima is becoming evermore a possibility. In a moment like this, the fantasy of living in Paris with a nine-teen-year-old sophomore and prolonging the carefree life of the past four years seems especially intriguing.

As the BART train hurtles through the darkness, Sebas-tian ponders his lovely Parisian dream while Juliet's perfume fills the air around him. In his mind he sees Hogarth's rake falling in love with one of the women in the brothel, marrying her, moving off to France, reforming his rakish ways, the artist's panels ending surprisingly early and with happiness for our hero.

❖

Sebastian's father is waiting for him outside Café de la Presse, leaning against the varnished wood paneling by the door, under the green sign with its crisp golden letters. As far as San Francisco establishments go, the place is very old-fashioned, the kind of restaurant with white tablecloths and properly folded napkins and world newspapers available at the front for its sports coat and khaki wearing clientele. It's his father's favorite, a short drive from the Kaiser where he works and not too far from his new house in Pacific Heights, and despite its relatively unhip vibe, Sebastian quite likes it too, not just for the French food but also for the traditional, European atmosphere, the spinning ceiling fans, the menus scrawled on chalkboards, the words "Breakfast," "Lunch," and "Dinner" written on the windows in Parisian cafe font, and the tables and wicker chairs set out on the sidewalk and always occupied, even during San Francisco's overcast and foggy winter weather.

Sebastian's father wears his standard tie-less button-down, loose-fitting black khakis, and dark-grey sweater, altogether modest enough. Looking closely, though, one can spot the subtle signifiers of his wealth and status, the expensive Omega watch on his wrist (brown leather bracelet, gold case, blue dial), the dark-framed Gucci eyeglasses, the way his hair is flecked with only the faintest linings of silver to suggest dignified aging, the way the skin of his face and around his eyes is too well preserved to be anything but upper-middle class, and above all the way he stands, hands in his pockets, leaning comfortably against the wall with that unique swagger borne of a life of relative privilege.

Sebastian's father is one of the rare breed of mixed-race first-generation Westerners, the son of an overeducated and underemployed engineer from Pakistan who immigrated to the United Kingdom in the 1950s, married a British woman, had a son (Sebastian's father), and then took his new family to America after the easing of immigration restrictions in 1965 to try his hand at the land of opportunity (ultimately succeeding so well that his son, and later his grandson, completely lost sight of the difficulties that first compelled him from his home in post-Partition Pakistan).

"Are you close with your father?" Juliet asked earlier, on the train.

"No."

"So you're a mama's boy, then."

"My mother's dead actually. Since I was twelve."

Juliet grew silent. Sebastian avoided her gaze and stared out at the houses flitting by and listened to the metallic skating sound of the train moving along the tracks, the occasional hiss and squeal of the brake as it slowed to bend around a curve.

"So you're not close to anyone then?" she asked.

"I guess not. Except maybe myself."

As they approach the restaurant, Sebastian notices that next to his father stands a tall woman with blond hair, his father's current girlfriend Megan, whom Sebastian recognizes from his Facebook profile (Sebastian's father is the type who created a Facebook account out of a desire to stay in tune with the trends of the young but who only updates it once a year, generally with a new picture of himself, relatively un-aged from the previous year, and his girlfriend-of-the-moment, always someone new, and generally younger). Megan wears the traditional semi-casual business attire of someone who works an office job somewhere in the city, pencil skirt, heels, white blouse, etc., and she is younger than Sebastian's father, though only enough to be fashionable among well-to-do men of Sebastian's father's age and ultimately old enough (late thirties) to avoid any suggestions of pedophilia (not that his father has that particular proclivity, though Sebastian does remember in his teenage years running into the occasional under-twenty waitress at breakfast).

"Should I leave now?" Juliet asks.

She intended only to accompany Sebastian to Union Square and then duck off to the nearby Asian Art Museum while Sebastian did his filial duty.

"You can say hi," Sebastian says. "He doesn't bite."

They reach the restaurant and slow their pace as Sebastian and his father meet each other's gaze. Sebastian's father steps forward.

"Sebastian."

"Father."

This formal mode of reference began as a joke when, after reading too many British novels from the nineteenth century, child-Sebastian took to calling his parents "Mother" and "Father." After Mother died, Sebastian never stopped referring to Father in this way. Now, Father and Son shake hands with practiced rigidity. Juliet and Megan wait in the wings and eye each other. Sebastian's father looks over Sebastian once or twice, as if surprised by something in his son's appearance (perhaps how much Sebastian is the spitting image of the old man's younger self), before turning to Juliet.

"Peter Khan," he says, shaking her hand. "You must be Fatima."

There is a brief, awkward pause in which, mid-handshake, Juliet looks over at Sebastian, and Sebastian looks over to his father, and his father looks back and forth a few times between Juliet and Sebastian, perhaps recognizing his error (after no doubt realizing that Juliet with her white skin and blue eyes couldn't possibly be the Pakistani-American Fatima Ahmed whom on previous occasions Sebastian indicated he was currently dating).

"No, no, this isn't her," Sebastian says. "This is Juliet. My friend."

Juliet shoots him another look now, full of enough venom that Sebastian's father immediately understands everything and gives his son a look full of parental disappointment, indignant but also somewhat amused. Luckily, Megan is oblivious to the nuances of the looks passed between the three and steps forward, inadvertently saving Sebastian from too prolonged an awkwardness.

"Hi! I'm Megan. It's great to finally meet you! Your dad talks about you all the time." She shakes hands with Sebastian and then fluidly turns to Juliet. "Are you joining us for lunch as well?"

Juliet looks uncertainly at Sebastian.

"I don't want to impose—"

"Nonsense, it's no imposition," Sebastian's father says, with a practiced smile that looks eerily like one of Sebastian's own. "We can always make room at the table for one of Sebastian's…friends."

Sebastian glares at his father, who meets the look with another smile. Then, with a theatrical wave of his hand, Sebastian's father gestures them inside.

❋

The ensuing lunch is as awkward as Sebastian expected. The restaurant is only faintly warmer than the street outside and more dimly lit. Most of the tables are empty, as it's almost 1 p.m., and the bankers and financial analysts who frequent the place have already returned to their cubicles, sufficiently nourished now for another afternoon's dreary toil. An older man sits with a newspaper and a café au lait (in a bowl, as the restaurant prides itself on its authenticity), and a young hipster couple, each with fedoras, peacoats, and hungover eyes, stares down at empty plates of what were minutes before ham and cheese omelettes and wonders how much judgment each will incur from the other if he or she orders another $12 omelette. The restaurant is largely silent, and the only sounds are the occasional clanging of dishes from the kitchen when the waiter steps through the swinging doors and the rustling of newspaper pages as the old man finishes a story and moves onto the next one.

Sebastian, his father, Megan, and Juliet sit in the center of the room, with empty tables on all sides. The waiter brings their coffees, espressos for Sebastian and his father and café au laits for Juliet and Megan. Sebastian sips his and looks across the table at his father, who relishes the awkward silence.

"So Julia," his father finally says.

"Juliet," she corrects.

"Sorry. How did you and Sebastian meet?"

"At an event at International House, a few weeks ago," she says.

"Only a few weeks? A recent friendship then."

"Yes," Sebastian says, the espresso cup rattling against the saucer as he sets it down with a little too much force.

"So you're from France?" Megan asks.

"Yes," Juliet says. "I'm studying abroad here for the year."

"Then this must feel so kitschy to you," Megan says, gesturing around. "We would have gone somewhere else if we'd known."

"No, no, it's not bad," Juliet says. "They do serve café au lait in a bowl."

"What do you study?" Sebastian's father asks.

"Literature," Juliet says. "Both French and English."

"Another humanities major," Megan says, laughing. "Don't get Peter started…"

"I have no problem with humanities majors," Sebastian's father says, looking directly at Sebastian. "I just think that *some* of them need to have a better plan for the future. They can't rely on their fathers to feed them their entire lives."

At that very moment, the water arrives with their food, setting down each plate and repeating each order aloud in a French accent (veal blanquette for Sebastian's father, smoked herring salad for Megan, a croque madame for Juliet, and a tuna tartare for Sebastian). The waiter then departs with a bow, and after a few moments of silent chewing, Sebastian's father turns back to Juliet.

"So what will you do with your major?" he asks.

"I don't know," Juliet says. "Maybe go to grad school eventually, in England, or here in the U.S. In the meantime probably travel, teach a little, do some freelance writing. Whatever comes my way, I guess."

"So you don't feel pressured to get a real, steady job?"

"No, not really." Juliet shrugs. "I mean, I'm only a second year so maybe I'll feel differently in two years. But right now, I don't see the point in worrying. Most of my friends who have graduated aren't getting hired no matter what degrees they have. So why bother trying? I'm perfectly happy putting all that off for a few years, taking it slow, easy, enjoying life rather than rushing towards some kind of predetermined end."

Sebastian watches Juliet and smiles through a bite of raw tuna. The way she talks, with practiced flippancy, is mesmerizing, as if these options for her future are things she's only just thought of and choosing something will be as simple as ordering lunch. It's so different from the bourgeois dream of Fatima, who would never let luck or fate or God or whatever force makes the world spin determine her future. Fatima would fight, struggle, force the world to spin the way she wanted, whereas Juliet was happy to sit back and let the earth's momentum carry her where it willed.

"I see no problem living in a small studio in Paris after college," she says, "doing whatever strikes my fancy, painting or writing or music, spending whatever money I make on plane tickets across the world."

"I'll live with you in your little studio," Sebastian says to her. "And we can travel the world together."

Sebastian doesn't really mean it, of course, and he says it mostly to irritate his father—but Juliet looks at him with sudden fondness. It's the first time Sebastian's outwardly acknowledged the possibility of a shared future.

Sebastian's father notices the look and shakes his head. "You'll need a real job, Sebastian. One that can pay for your...lifestyle."

"I'm sure I'll find something." He pauses mid-bite and watches as the waiter brings over a cheese charcuterie for the still-hungover hipster couple (who've by this point devoured their second set of $12 omelettes). "Do you think we can get one of those to share?"

Sebastian's father frowns but looks admiringly over at the varied cheeses and then asks the waiter how much it is.

"Twelve dollars, monsieur."

"We'll take one."

Sebastian smiles, and his father gives him a stern, disapproving look.

"You know, I did something similar after I graduated," Megan says to Juliet. "I studied history, at Berkeley in fact, and I didn't want to work, so I traveled for a while on my parents' money. Europe was cheap then, especially compared to the U.S."

"And your parents were fine supporting you?" Sebastian asks.

"Yeah, of course. My mom taught at a private school, and my father worked for Boeing, and I was their only child. As they put it, what else were they going to spend their money on except to make me happy?"

"I hope you were grateful," Sebastian's father says.

"Of course I was," Megan says. "And now I repay them by taking them on vacation to Europe each year. Last year we went to France."

"Oh really?" Juliet asks. "Which part?"

"Just Paris. The first time my dad had been."

"Did he like it?"

"Who doesn't?"

As they talk, Sebastian stares thoughtfully at his own father and wonders whether in twenty years the two of them would ever travel to Europe together. It seems inconceivable now, as Sebastian's father is perfectly capable of taking care of himself, and Sebastian doubts he would need or want his spendthrift son to accompany him. He was in Paris just last year, at a medical conference, and the Facebook photos he was tagged in (by one of the women he met there) made it clear that Sebastian was the farthest thing from his mind. Sebastian, for his part, finds the company of his father wearying and can't imagine vacationing with him. He endured enough of that in his teenage years, when his father and whatever woman he was with would drag him off to Europe—obviously, Sebastian appreciated the opportunity to go and the generous financial support he was given once there, but he would have preferred that his first visit to the Louvre wasn't supplemented with his father's surface level observations about the art ("I just don't understand what all the fuss is about," he said of the Mona Lisa. "She's not that pretty.")

"So how did you end up doing what you do?" Juliet asks Megan.

"I just sort of fell into it," Megan says. "I got a temp job in a hospital in New York, and then got promoted to full time. I did that for while, and then got married, and then divorced, and then decided to move back here. Once I got settled, I applied for hospital admin jobs, and with my experience I managed to land something easily. A few promotions later, and here I am."

Juliet is impressed by her nonchalance. The four continue eating for a silent moment.

"Do you have any kids?" Sebastian asks.

"I have a daughter, Laura. Why do you ask?"

"Just wondering if that was ever something you planned."

"I always wanted to have a kid at some point. But until

I got married, in my late twenties, I don't think I ever really thought about it seriously."

"How old is she?" Juliet asks.

"She's eight."

"And does she know what she wants to do with her life yet?" Sebastian asks, dryly.

Megan smiles. "Right now, she tells people she wants to be a doctor."

"Smart girl," Sebastian's father says.

❁

The waiter clears their plates and returns with the cheese charcuterie, which goes quickly, even though Megan cites lactose intolerance and declines to have any. Afterwards, she decides to order desert ("The salad wasn't very filling,"), and while she quizzes the waiter on which ones are dairy-free ("I'm sorry ma'am, I don't understand," the waiter says in his French accent), Sebastian's father rises to smoke a cigarette.

"Sebastian, come join me," he says.

"You know I don't smoke."

"Humor me this once."

Sebastian takes the hint and steps outside with his father, while Juliet assists Megan by speaking to the waiter in French ("I don't think they have anything dairy-free," she says to Megan. "In France, we don't really have the concept of dairy-free.").

Outside, the weather is colder than it was earlier. Black clouds have moved in above the street, and only a few stragglers remain seated at the tables outside. Sebastian's father leans back against the wood paneling where he was standing earlier and lights a cigarette, cupping his hand against the wind. He takes in a deep puff and then exhales slowly, evident relief passing across his narrowed eyes. Sebastian pulls his blazer tighter around him and wishes he brought a scarf.

"What the fuck are you doing, Sebastian?" his father asks.

"I'm standing out here with you, watching you slowly destroy your lungs."

"Don't be a smart-ass. I mean with fucking Amelie in there—"

"Juliet."

"Whatever."

"Since when have you taken an interest in my personal life?" Sebastian asks.

"I have no interest in your personal life, Sebastian. As far as I'm concerned, you can cheat as many times as you want on your supposedly serious, long-term girlfriend, as many times as it takes for you to feel like a real man—"

"*You're* going to lecture me? You of all people?"

"I'm your father, Sebastian—"

"How many times did you cheat on Mother?"

Sebastian's father grows quiet. The lit cigarette continues to burn, and he doesn't notice as the ashes fall onto his fine leather shoes.

"That was a long time ago," he says.

"Well, I still remember," Sebastian says. "So please don't try and get morally righteous about Fatima—"

"This isn't about Fatima. This is about that fairy tale you spun in there, about moving to Paris for some girl." Sebastian's father is leaning forward, jabbing his finger at the window of the restaurant, the cigarette still smoldering in his hand. "You're not the most responsible kid, nor the nicest or the most moral, but I never thought you'd be stupid too."

Sebastian feels his cheeks warming with indignation.

"I'm not stupid—"

"No? You think it's smart to fall in love with a French exchange student?"

"I'm not in love—"

"Oh really? Then why is it you're humoring her stupid, childish fantasy of traveling the world, living in Paris, and doing whatever 'strikes her fancy,' whatever the fuck that means? Is that what *you're* going to do?"

"Why not?" Sebastian asks, enjoying the anger now spreading across his father's face. "Maybe I will move to Paris after I graduate. She and I can live together while she finishes her degree, and I can do some writing, some traveling—"

"On whose money?"

There's silence. His father tosses the spent cigarette onto the sidewalk.

"She's still a child, Sebastian. I know girls like her, better than you think, and I guarantee you when she's your age, she won't be so relaxed about her future. And the last thing she'll want then is some sophomore year fling of hers who's still hanging around Paris believing himself to be in love."

Sebastian stares at his father in silence, arms folded across his chest. He looks at his feet and kicks at the remnants of the cigarette.

"Let's be real, Father," he says. "You know me better than anyone. Do you really think that in two years I'll still feel this way about her?"

Sebastian's father stares at his son and then smiles.

"No. I doubt you will."

He fishes in his pocket and pulls out another cigarette. After he lights it and takes a drag, Sebastian reaches out, and his father hands him the cigarette and watches as he takes a long puff. Afterwards, Sebastian returns the cigarette.

Suddenly, his father looks taller, the angular form, the broad chest, and the long arms all elegant and imposing— and as has happened many times before, Sebastian can't help but feel a strange admiration for him.

"I don't expect you to know what you want your future to be right now, Sebastian," his father says. "But I hope you understand that, whatever you're feeling for this girl, it will pass. It always does."

His father finishes the second cigarette, and then tosses it onto the sidewalk next to the remnants of the first. He crushes both with the heel of his shoe.

"Let's go back inside."

From overhead, Sebastian feels cold raindrops fall upon his head.

✳

On the BART ride back to Berkeley, later that afternoon, Juliet is smiling despite the fact that both she and Sebastian are drenched (the rain picked up on their walk back to the BART station, and neither had remembered to bring an umbrella). Now on the train, Sebastian smells the sharp scent of soggy clothing, which has completely dampened Juliet's perfume. His own hair is slick and dripping, and the back of his blazer is entirely soaked through so that he feels the slippery wetness as he leans back against the cloth seat. Below his feet, water puddles onto the train's metal floor.

Juliet leans her head against his shoulder. Her hair is wet and tickles his neck, and Sebastian flinches and pulls away from her. Juliet looks at him, surprised.

"What's up?" she asks.

He can see in her smiling face she's still thinking of Paris, perhaps of the things he hastily said at lunch. He thinks of his father, and the cigarette smoke mingling with the foggy weather. Juliet notices his troubled expression, and her smile fades.

"What is it, Sebastian?"

He lets out a steady breath. In the background, he hears the train whirring along the tracks. Outside the window, it's pitch black as they hurtle through the tunnel under the Bay and back towards Berkeley. He thinks of Hogarth's rake again and remembers the next panel, in which our hero has to marry an ugly, rich old maid to help him clear his debts, while his previous lover and young child look on in sadness.

"We need to talk," Sebastian says to Juliet.

CHAPTER SIX

PILGRIMAGE TO THE ISLE OF CYTHERA (1717)

She sits across from him, her black hair draped like a curtain across her face as she stares down at the menu in her hands. They are at Gather, a new bar/restaurant in Downtown Berkeley branding itself as "farm to table" American cuisine. The occasion is Sebastian's twenty-second birthday (January 29, 1989, Zodiac sign Aquarius), and Fatima insisted on taking him out to dinner. She originally proposed La Note, but Sebastian didn't think he could stomach French food after Juliet, so he suggested this as an alternative ("I know you don't like French food anyway," he said to Fatima).

The restaurant is large and open, with gray slate flooring, varnished wooden chairs and tables (which according to the menu are refurbished from discarded furniture and "found objects"), and soft lamps surrounded in wicker lampshades hanging from the ceiling. Large windows look out onto the corner of Oxford and Allston and across to the more humble Saturn Cafe, where students in hoodies binge on burgers, fries, and shakes with their laptops and textbooks spread open across the tables. By contrast, the clientele at

Gather is more refined and ultimately more Sebastian's type, well-dressed professionals, a few professors, students of course, but only the stylish, trendy kind who understand the importance of paying a few extra dollars to enjoy a fresher and more sophisticated meal, as well as the necessity of unwinding from a long day of studying with a $12 cocktail.

Sebastian and Fatima sit at a table in the center of the room. Around them circulates the characteristic babble of conversation and restaurant noise, the clanging of forks on plates, the clinking of glasses in toasts, the laughing and amiable chatter of various restaurant patrons enjoying this Saturday night, as well as the familiar smells of bourgeois cuisine, plates of steaming chicken (roasted not fried), salads doused with expensive dressings, garlic fries and their accompanying aiolis, mixed bouquets of red and white wine, and most prominent of all the post-industrial scent of polished wood and steel.

When the waiter arrives, Sebastian orders a Sazerac.

"May I see some ID please?" the waiter asks.

"Absolutely," Sebastian says, glad that at twenty-two, he still looks young enough to be carded.

"I'll have one too," Fatima says, handing the waiter her ID.

Sebastian looks surprised.

"Really? What will the temperance society say?"

"It's your birthday," Fatima says, shrugging. "I'll celebrate with you."

The waiter nods, hands back their IDs, and departs. Sebastian leans towards Fatima, as if seeing her in a new light. He wonders how she might change under the influence of alcohol, whether that furrowed brow will relax, whether the sharp eyes will grow softer, whether the anxious core will turn carefree.

As they wait for the waiter to return with their drinks, Sebastian feels a palpable uncertainty between them, not unlike the one that had pervaded the empty restaurant on their first date. Today, though, the restaurant is far from empty. Groups of people cluster by the large glass doors, waiting for a table, and the laughter and chatter reverberating off the walls gives the place a cafeteria-like atmosphere and makes Sebastian and Fatima's relative silence all the more pronounced.

"So," Fatima says finally. "How does it feel to be twenty-two?"

A few months before she would not have been the first to speak, and it would have been Sebastian who tried to fill the uncomfortable silence with lighthearted banter. But now she's making a greater effort, perhaps in response to Sebastian's increasing distance. Sebastian for his part has turned callous and indifferent since his talk with his father. His relationship with Fatima now feels even more mechanical, and though he goes through the motions of sitting down to another dinner, listening to her complain about another day, spending another passionless night with her in a twin bed, his mind is always elsewhere—on the girl in the black sweater in his Old English Literature class who flashed him a smile that morning, or the girl in the blue skirt on the couch across from him in the Morrison Reading Room who looked at him over her copy of *The Fairie Queene,* or the girl in yellow running shorts at the gym on the treadmill next to his who cast a quick glance towards at him as she wiped sweat from her brow, and he imagines kissing the first girl up against the blackboard, chalk dust smeared across the back of her black sweater, and he imagines lying on the couch with the girl in Morrison on top of him, her blue skirt pulled up and *The Fairie Queene* lying on the ground beside them (open to Book III, the one about Chastity), and he imagines himself in one of the locker-room showers with the girl at the gym, her yellow shorts hanging from the hook on the door and their sweaty bodies pressed together as they fuck against the tiled wall. And in the face of all these girls, who is Fatima? Someone who in one moment of melancholy he found himself drawn to and who now exists not as a physical being but only as a vague future?

And yet he is still here. Despite the dark feelings, despite the parade of girls who conjure fantasies in his mind, he is on his birthday seated with Fatima, now his girlfriend of eight months, having declined an invitation to get drinks with Viola and Harry ("I can invite my hot friend Jasmine," Viola said). Does that not mean that there is in fact a part of him, small though it may be, that wishes for everything with Fatima to work out?

"I'm not twenty-two yet," Sebastian says, in answer to her question. "Not till ten p.m."

"Holding onto every bit of youth," Fatima says, shaking her head. "Just embrace it."

Sebastian thinks of the homeless man's countdown, now at 112 DAYS TILL THE END. A server arrives with their drinks, and as her delicate, long-fingered hand places their Sazeracs down in front of them, Sebastian imagines that hand tracing its way down his body. Fatima takes a sip of her drink and grimaces.

"Ugh. I don't know how you can drink this stuff."

"I'll have yours if you don't want it."

Sebastian takes a sip of his own and feels himself relax at the pleasant tingle of the cognac and absinthe.

"So how'd the interview go?" Fatima asks.

She pushes her drink to the side and leans forward, elbows on the table. Sebastian avoids her wide-eyed gaze and stares at the bar in the corner of the room. The bartender, a young woman with dark hair, wearing a black button-down shirt, is making someone a drink, carefully pouring whiskey into a small glass in her hand. Sebastian imagines unbuttoning her black shirt and pouring that whiskey across her body and then slowly licking it off.

"I didn't do it," Sebastian says.

"What?"

"I took one look at the place and knew I didn't want to work there."

Fatima's face falls, looking surprised and then frustrated. Sebastian takes a long sip of his drink and remembers yesterday, walking into that office. The inside was generic, with bright fluorescent lighting, a few cubicles, and men of various ages in loose-fitting collared shirts and outmoded, wireframe glasses. Hanging above the door was a generic logo, a blue line curving around the company's name (Chiron Internet Solutions), which gave little indication as to what the company actually did. ("They build the infrastructure for wireless networks," Fatima told him earlier. "You know, like Chiron the boatman, transferring souls across the river Styx. Connecting people and all that."—"Okay, first of all, it's *Charon*, the boatman," Sebastian corrected. "Chiron was the centaur who tutored Achilles and helped the Argonauts. And anyway, even if they got the name right, the allusion doesn't make any sense. Are they implying that a good Wi-Fi connection is like being in the underworld? Is their company name intended to be a subtle comment on the way the internet is metaphorically *killing* us?"). The receptionist at the front desk (mid-twenties, blond hair, buttoned-up blouse, and pencil skirt) was the only appealing thing about the place (Sebastian imagined the two of them returning at night when the office was empty and fucking atop one of the desks, her blouse unbuttoned and her pencil skirt pushed up, while around them in the darkness the computers continued to hum).

"Do you know how hard it was for me to get you that interview?" Fatima says, leaning back in her chair.

"You said you just asked a friend who worked there to schedule me one."

"It's not like it's easy for her to do people favors!"

"I don't want to work at a tech company that builds wires—"

"Wireless infrastructure—"

"Whatever—"

"—and you wouldn't be building anything. You'd be in the marketing department, helping write their manuals and their sales pitches—"

"An art history degree put to good use. I guess I'd start with the logo."

But Fatima isn't laughing. The good humor she had only moments earlier has vanished. She takes another sip of her drink and grimaces and pushes it away.

"I don't understand," she says. "That job would have been perfect. It's right next to Pangea, and we could have found an apartment nearby in SOMA and walked to work together."

Pangea was where Fatima finally landed a job, as an intern (paid, at least, though the yearly salary of $22,000 would barely cover the expenses of living in San Francisco). The company did something in green technology that Sebastian didn't fully understand and must have used the same naming conventions as Chiron. It wasn't exactly Fatima's dream job, but after a grueling process of a long written application, four recommendation letters, two personal essays, and three interviews (one via Skype, two in person), Fatima felt a sense of accomplishment at having been accepted and convinced herself that the job must be worth it ("Maybe that's what they want you to think," Sebastian said.).

"What the hell did you do then?" Fatima asks. "You were in the city all day!"

Sebastian recalls walking out from the Chiron offices and up to Market Street, where he joined the crowds at the bus stop. Without thinking he boarded the 38, bound for the other side of the city, towards his favorite of San Francisco's museums, the Legion of Honor, tucked away into a park in the northwestern part of the city, near the quiet streets of Outer Richmond. It had been Sebastian's mother's favorite neighborhood, and he remembered weekends as a child strolling between the multicolored houses and walking down windswept Ocean Beach, watching the occasional car and cyclist pass, listening to the seagulls and the crashing waves.

The museum itself, located near the Lincoln Park Golf Course a few blocks from the ocean, was a neoclassical building from the early twentieth century, a replica of the French building of the same name built in the eighteenth century in Paris. The museum's collections were in line with Sebastian's tastes, art from before the twentieth century, mostly European. He knew the museum was hosting the touring exhibition on the fête galante style and that Watteau's famous *Pilgrimage to the Isle of Cythera* would be on display, on loan from the Louvre. Sebastian recalls seeing the painting during his freshman summer travels through Europe but feels that now, in the twilight of his college days, the frolicsome depiction of the fête galante might take on a different meaning. He had intended on going with Fatima, who'd agreed to go for Sebastian's sake, but yesterday he decided almost unconsciously to go alone. It was as if, in his mind, seeing a painting without her was as transgressive as any of the other things he'd done.

The girl at the counter handed him his ticket and told him he got a discount for riding the MUNI (she was tall and thin, with dark hair and pale lips, and Sebastian imagined them fucking atop a tarp in one of the under-construction galleries, entwined like figures in a Rodin sculpture). As he walked down the marble floors and towards the exhibition room, he passed by old familiar paintings from the permanent collection. There was Stanhope's pre-Raphaelite masterpiece, *Love and the Maiden,* depicting Cupid staring at a young woman who lay in a forest clearing, dressed in a flowing red and blue garment, while in the background other women danced in a circle among the trees (Sebastian imagined kissing the maiden while peeling off her clothing, layer by layer), and then the portrait by Élisabeth Vigée Le Brun of Hyacinthe Gabrielle Roland, looking seductively at the viewer, her red and black dress pulled down to bare her shoulder, her curly brown hair hanging coiled around her ears and neck (Sebastian imagined running his hand along that shoulder and then pulling that dress down just a little further), and finally Sebastian's favorite of the museum's collection, a little circular painting by Boucher entitled *Bacchantes*, of two blushing women sitting at the edge of a forest, playing a tambourine and a flute and dressed in eighteenth-century French attire, which they wore loose and bunched up around their thighs so their long white legs extended out from below (Sebastian imagined lying beside them in the grass, running his hands up those pale legs and under those flowing garments).

And then he reached Watteau's masterpiece. Though beautiful, the painting did not trigger the same wild racing of the blood. The pastel colors and rococo softness were soothing, and for a moment Sebastian felt as at peace as the depicted group of lovers who gathered on the hillside and stared at the trail of cherubs floating out towards the distant ocean, while the statue of Aphrodite, decked with a simple garland of flowers, looked on, blessing the group on their impending voyage to Cythera, her own birthplace and an island sacred to all lovers. But something about the painting was different from what Sebastian remembered. The colors were too light, too airy, too insubstantial. What he remembered as the glorious decadence of the fête galante was replaced by something nearing melancholy, a wistfulness in the way the two lovers in the corner leaned their heads against each other. Most troubling of all, Sebastian was struck with a new understanding of the piece, something he'd never noticed before: the lovers weren't departing for Cythera, despite what the misleading title suggested—they were leaving it. The island was not some insubstantial speck in the distance towards which the cherubs danced. It was here, this dreamy, faded landscape where everyone stood and from which everyone was about to depart. Sebastian was stunned by this sudden revelation and also by the fact that the painting looked nothing like the one in his memory. Did a few years of aging really change the world so thoroughly?

The truth, which Sebastian didn't realize at the time, was that this version of *Cythera* was not the one he'd seen before. It had been gone from the Louvre when he had visited, off on another exhibition tour, and the one he remembered was actually from the Charlottenburg Palace in Berlin, a copy that Watteau had painted for a private client, a brighter, more vivid, more decadent version of the same scene, with more figures and the mast of a ship rising up from the waters, and in which the lovers are happier and Aphrodite's statue is accompanied by a baby cupid, all in all a more innocent, joyous scene than his original.

In the restaurant, Sebastian feels a wave of melancholy at the memory.

"I went to the museum," he says after a moment, in answer to Fatima's question.

"The Legion of Honor?" Fatima asks. "To see that photo you wanted?"

"The painting. Yeah."

Fatima looks hurt.

"But I thought you wanted me to go with you..."

The waiter arrives with their food (a half-chicken for Sebastian and chickpea panelle for Fatima).

"Two more Sazeracs?" the waiter asks, noting the empty glasses.

"Yes, please," says Sebastian, having finished both.

Fatima stares down at her plate, her long lashes hanging low, and when the waiter leaves, she looks up, and Sebastian sees that her eyes are moist. He sets down his fork in frustration.

"Please don't cry." he says quietly. "It's just a painting."

The hot, buttery scent of the roast chicken rises up from the table. Sebastian's hands fidget, and he reaches for his drink before remembering it's empty.

"I just want to be a part of your life," Fatima says. She wipes her eyes with her napkin, but her voice continues to shake. "Model UN, art, your friends, the things you enjoy.

But I don't know what to do anymore. You've been so distant, Sebastian, no matter how hard I try. All I want is for us to feel together again, like we did in the summer."

Sebastian feels guilty then at the pain in her voice, and he reaches across the table to take her hand. "I'm sorry," he says. "Thank you for making an effort tonight." It's strange, but he realizes that he actually means what he says.

Fatima smiles and squeezes his hand. "Well, tonight's not over. There's one more thing I wanted us to do." She's stopped crying, and her voice has taken on a strange, sultry edge. "Something we'd have to go back to your apartment to do."

She tilts her head forward and bites her lip and gives him a look that Sebastian didn't think her capable of. He's taken aback and almost pulls his hand away—but Fatima holds onto it firmly. Her skin is surprisingly hot, as if there's a fire burning underneath.

"Are you sure?" Sebastian says.

"Yes," Fatima says, in a low, quiet voice.

Her whole body is leaning forward now, her pupils dilated, the vein visible in her neck, and suddenly, Sebastian imagines what it might be like to kiss *her* against a dusty chalkboard or lie with *her* on a couch in the Morrison Reading Room or have sex with *her* in a shower at the gym or in an office at night or on a tarp in an art gallery, to slow peel away the layers of *her* clothing, to run his hands along *her* bare shoulder and up *her* bare legs...

Sebastian leans forward too now, over his plate of forgotten chicken, so that his face is inches from hers.

"Is that really what you want?" he asks, his voice breathless.

"Yes," she says.

Under the lights, her lips shine, as if they were in a painting.

"Well then let's get out of here," he says.

❈

Despite Sebastian's dramatic pronouncement, they don't immediately "get out of [there]"—Fatima wants to finish her food ("This cost $18.") and so the intensity of the moment between them is dampened by their quietly and hurriedly finishing their meal. Nevertheless, the whole time Sebastian thinks only of Fatima, watching her lips close around her fork and noticing for the first time how big and red they are.

They are quiet as they leave the restaurant and walk back to Sebastian's apartment. Downtown Berkeley is as busy as ever, flashing lights, cars searching for parking, crowds gathered outside Jupiter and the movie theaters and the gelato places, but Sebastian and Fatima breeze through it all, hand in hand. Hers is warm in the cool night, and her pulse races in her wrist. In the elevator of his building, they stand for a moment after the doors close, still hand in hand, before Fatima turns and kisses Sebastian suddenly. Her lips are as warm as her hands, and she slips her tongue into Sebastian's mouth, something she's never done before. She smiles at him as the elevator doors ding open and then pulls him down the open-air hallway of the fifth floor and towards his room. Sebastian fumbles in his pocket for his keys, and his hands shake as he opens the door.

Inside, the lights are on, and down the long hallway, Sebastian hears movement and the clinking of glasses. Harry must be home. Sebastian's room is right by the door, and he may be able to enter with Fatima without having to see him—

"Sebastian!" It's Viola who pokes her head out around the hallway. "Didn't expect you back so soon!"

He is surprised to see Viola and, standing on the threshold of his room with Fatima, he feels a strange sensation of guilt, as if she's caught them in some sort of transgression. But Viola only smiles at Fatima too.

"Hey Fatima!"

"Hi."

"What are you doing here?" Sebastian asks.

"Harry and I were hanging out," Viola says, emerging from the kitchen with a handle of whiskey. "Come join us on the roof!"

Sebastian gives Fatima a brief look. Her eyes are narrowed and one of her hands is on the handle of the sliding door to Sebastian's room, while the other still grips Sebastian's.

"I think we're going to stay in tonight," Sebastian says to Viola.

"Just come for a second! Just say hi!" Viola pulls out her phone and furiously texts someone. "Harry wants to say happy birthday."

Sebastian has very little interest in seeing Harry now, as things between them are still tense, as they have been since Montreal. But Viola races down the hall and grabs Sebastian's other hand, pulling him towards the still open door.

"I'll talk to him tomorrow morning," Sebastian says.

"Two minutes, Sebastian!" Viola tugs his hand. "It'll be worth it, I promise."

Before he can do or say anything else, Viola pulls Sebastian out the door, one hand gripping Sebastian's, the other gripping the handle of whiskey. Fatima frowns but doesn't let go of Sebastian's other hand and follows them out the door, which closes behind her with a thud. All three of them are hand in hand now, and Viola pulls them through the door to the rooftop and up the quiet, darkened stairwell. Her hand is cool while Fatima's is still warm and pulsing rapidly with her heartbeat.

At the top, Viola pushes open the door. Sebastian steps out into the well-lit night, where it takes a moment for his eyes to adjust...

"SURPRISE!"

Standing before him are a sea of people, all with drinks in hand, their eyes wide, their faces filled with laughter:

Harry is there, as are Imogen, Nate, and everyone else from Model UN, along with causal friends of his from art history classes, old friends from his post-freshman-year summer abroad in Cambridge and his post-sophomore-year summer in Washington D.C., others he's met at various parties throughout college, and of course many whom he doesn't even remember meeting, a tapestry of four years of Berkeley spread across the concrete rooftop. The air smells of wine, whiskey, vodka, beer, and various fruit juice mixers, and on the table amidst the crowd sits a large plate of grapes and Trader Joe's cheeses. Overhead, the sky is a deep, navy blue, and despite it being January, the air has a strange warmth, as if all these bodies have conjured a collective fire, the kind that predates even Prometheus.

Sebastian gazes around, between the crowd and Viola, and feels indescribably moved.

Viola pours out a splash of whiskey into a clear plastic cup and hands it to Sebastian. He lets go of Fatima's hand to take it.

"Drink up, old man!" Viola says. "You turn twenty-two only once!"

Sebastian surveys the crowd and then raises his cup in a silent toast before tossing his head back and downing the drink in one long swig. The crowd bursts into applause, and Sebastian takes an exaggerated bow. After a moment, the applause dies down, and Harry flips his iPod on, and the ambient and now-familiar sound of a party settles across the rooftop.

Sebastian gives Viola a hug. She smells of cranberry and vodka and the scent is comforting and nostalgic.

"Thank you," he says. "This means a lot."

"Of course," Viola says. She pours Sebastian another helping of whiskey. "But don't get all sentimental. It's not like this is the last time I'll throw you a party."

Sebastian pictures himself living in Fatima's dream apartment in SOMA, paid for by their jobs at Pangea and

Chiron Internet Solutions. Would Viola still throw secret parties for him then? She is such a figure of the present that Sebastian can't even imagine what her future may look like. He'd be more surprised to learn that she ended up working some corporate job than that she simply dematerialized after she stepped off the stage at graduation, her atoms returning to their original forms to mingle with the Berkeley air forever.

Sebastian glances over his shoulder to Fatima, who hasn't moved from the door. Her arms are crossed over her chest. The desire he felt earlier is still there, but it's faded, and he feels torn. He can still see the slope of her neck and the curve of her lips, but he can also hear the sounds of the party behind him, and the rush of cool air that sweeps across the rooftop is exhilarating and brings with it an emotional swell far deeper than even desire.

"Do you mind if we stay up here for a bit?" Sebastian asks.

Fatima's eyes shrink, and her lips quiver.

"Sure. Whatever you want."

Sebastian touches her shoulder and gives her a heartfelt look.

"We'll go back down soon," he says, in a low whisper. "I promise."

Before he can say more, though, he feels a tugging on his own shoulder. Nate is there, reaching out his fat-fingered hand.

"Congratulations!" Nate says, as if by turning twenty-two Sebastian has accomplished something particularly difficult. "Like Viola said, you're an old man now!"

Nate laughs as if he's told a joke, and Sebastian notices what looks to be a triple shot of whiskey in his hand. He's already looking sloppy, slurring his words and swaying in place.

Behind Nate is Imogen, a large drink in her hand too, her hair uncharacteristically frazzled and her eyes red from a lack of sleep (planning a Model UN conference is no easy task).

"Happy birthday," Imogen says, clinking her plastic cup against Sebastian's.

"Thank you."

She downs her drink and then refills all their glasses with a fifth of whiskey.

"You drinking, Fatima?" Imogen asks.

"I don't drink," Fatima says.

"You should. It's nice."

Imogen downs half of her second shot.

"Are you alright?" Sebastian asks.

"Just stressed," Imogen says. "I got an email from the Hilton people warning us that they'll call the cops if our Saturday evening party gets too rowdy."

Since the beginning of the new semester, Imogen has been treating Sebastian as her Point Man without his officially having agreed to the job, though so far, the only thing he's actually done is convince the Hilton to let them host the Saturday evening party in the hotel's ballroom and include a limited cash bar.

"Anyway," Imogen continues, "I might call you late at night any time from now till the conference itself, in case the hotel tries to fuck us. Sorry, Fatima. You'll have to share him."

Imogen says this without intending any double meaning, but Sebastian still feels uncomfortable.

"That's fine," Fatima says. "I understand."

Nevertheless, she gives Sebastian a sad and frustrated look. Her eyes beckon him, and she gestures her head towards the door. She slips her hand into his and squeezes it, and he can feel her pounding pulse.

"Well, if you'll excuse us," Sebastian says to Nate and Imogen.

Sebastian and Fatima step away from the group and towards the rooftop door. Before they can leave, though,

Harry and Viola appear before them, Viola with a fifth of vodka and cheeks flushed red. She sways with drunkenness too, but her sprightliness helps her pull off a gracefulness that Nate could not. Harry meanwhile holds his drink with a stately dignity, and he betrays no hint of intoxication.

"Vodka?" Viola asks, holding up the fifth.

"Not right now," Sebastian says.

"It's your birthday, Sebastian!"

"And I want to remember it. I've already had a lot at dinner."

"How was dinner?" Harry asks.

"It was good," Sebastian says, glancing at Fatima.

Fatima smiles and squeezes his hand again. Harry glances approvingly at their entwined fingers, and Sebastian feels relieved, since lately Harry's been looking at him with the dreary solemnity of a monk reprimanding a young novice caught masturbating in the vestry (something Sebastian knows most monks certainly overlooked, in a "'don't ask, don't tell' sort of thing," as Viola would have put it). Even now, though, Sebastian can see in Harry's eyes a brewing storm of unease, his moral imperatives fighting against his friendly nature, as if seeing Fatima and Sebastian together, while comforting in the moment, only reminds him of all the times he's seen Sebastian staring off across parties at a different girl.

"Well, happy birthday, Sebastian," Harry says, stiffly.

He extends his hand, and Sebastian shakes it with rigid formality. He can feel Fatima's own hand burning by his side. With another curt nod to Harry and a smile to Viola, Sebastian turns and leads Fatima through the door and back into the stairwell.

As the door closes behind them, he hears Viola say, with surprise, "Are they going to fuck?!"—the last word partially cut off as the door muffles the sound of the party. Sebastian looks at Fatima and attempts an awkward laugh, but she doesn't reciprocate. Her pulse is wild, and her hand tense.

Slowly, they make their way down the stairs. The stairwell is cold and musty, as it was before. The sounds of the party emanate through the concrete and stucco walls, Viola's wild laughter most prominently. Sebastian suddenly longs to be back up there, in his comfortable, familiar world, where the night air is warm from all those bodies and scented with alcohol.

When they reach his door this time, he remembers it's unlocked and doesn't fumble for his keys but opens it with mechanical precision, his heart no longer beating furiously. The lights in the kitchen are still on (Viola is notoriously bad with turning lights off), and their steady, quiet hum is the apartment's only sound. Sebastian can't hear the party at all from here and wonders if it's vanished entirely, the fifty or so people disappearing like a dream. He has a brief, wild thought that he should run back up and check.

He slides open his bedroom door, and he and Fatima enter slowly. The room is the same one they've been in at least a hundred times (and the same room where he lived for three weeks with Juliet), the same twin bed, the mirrored sliding doors to his closet, the alcove with the desk, the white bookshelf, the vintage office chair, a few dirty clothes scattered on the ground, and the rows of postcards lining the walls. But now it feels like they're entering together for the first time. Sebastian closes the door slowly and locks the latch with a metal click. Fatima looks around uncertainly for a moment before setting her purse down by the door and putting her jacket on the chair. It falls off the first time, and she has to do it again.

The sight of the room makes Sebastian think of Juliet, the smell of her underwear and her French accent bouncing off the walls, but he pushes that smell and that voice away and turns to face Fatima. He reaches out and touches her neck. Her pulse is still wild, and he wonders if her vein will burst from the pressure. Her eyes have contracted, and she looks up at him with fear. He tries to be gentle as he bends down to kiss her, but he can feel her recoiling in his grasp. Her lips are still warm, but she doesn't open them like she did in the elevator, and the kiss is dry and tasteless.

"Do you really want this?" Sebastian asks, placing his hands around her shoulders.

"Yes," Fatima whispers. "I do."

She kisses him back, but her lips are dry. Her hands tremble as she tries to push Sebastian's blazer back and off his shoulders, and he has to stop her and do it himself. His bare arms feel cold in the room, and he shivers. Fatima's shirt is still on, and he wonders if he should take it off.

"Are you cold?" Sebastian asks.

"A little," she says.

"I'll turn on the heater."

Sebastian pulls the space heater from under his desk and turns it on, but the air doesn't get any warmer. He shivers and stares at Fatima. She waits, uncertain how to proceed. He steps towards her and runs a hand through her hair. His fingers must be cold, though, because she jumps at his touch.

"Sorry," she says. "Sorry."

"It's okay."

He puts his hands under her shirt and pulls it up and over her head. Underneath, her bra is white and simple. Her shoulders hunch forward and push out a roll of skin at the top of her stomach. She isn't fat by any means, but something about her body is lethargic, flabby, even though he knows she goes to the gym regularly. Sebastian reaches behind her and unclips her bra. He lets it fall to the floor, but Fatima catches it and places it on the chair, over her jacket, where it looks strange. Her breasts are perky, brown like the rest of her, and her areolas are even darker. This is the first time Sebastian has seen her topless, and he should be excited. But he isn't. Her breasts hang limply off her body. Fatima seems to sense his judgmental gaze and pulls her arms instinctively back and around her chest. Sebastian stops her and pushes her arms away and then bends down and gently kisses her breasts. Once again, he can feel her recoil at his touch.

He kneels and starts to unbutton Fatima's pants, but her hands instinctively move down to stop him.

"What's wrong?" he asks.

"Not so fast," she says.

Sebastian stands, uncertain what to do. Fatima stares back at him, with shrunken pupils and a furrowed brow. He strokes her cheek and kisses her again. She seems to relax a little and even closes her eyes. Sebastian lifts up his own shirt and pulls it off. She reaches out her hand and rests it on his chest. The hand feels cold and clammy and shakes. Sebastian reaches behind Fatima and cups his hand around her ass and pulls her towards him, pressing her body against his. The skin on her breasts is cold too, and her arms are crushed awkwardly now against his chest.

He kisses her again, fiercely, trying to inject some life into her. She barely kisses him back, her lips not moving, not opening, still cold and dry. He grabs the back of her head and pushes her face into his. He takes one of her hands and slowly brings it down, towards his pants. He places it right above the zipper and button, hoping she'll do the rest, but when she doesn't, he decides to do it himself, unbuttoning and unzipping his pants, taking her hand and placing it on his underwear, hoping the contact will stir something inside him—

"You're going too fast," Fatima says, pulling her hand back.

Sebastian lets out a breath and drops his hands to his side.

"What?" Fatima asks. "What's wrong?"

"Nothing's wrong," Sebastian says quickly.

Fatima is shivering, and her arms are clutched at her side and bent at the elbows like a chicken's. Sebastian realizes he feels nothing at all. He tries to recall what he felt in the restaurant, to bring himself and Fatima back to the museum, to the paintings, to the Bacchantes with their long legs in the field of grass—but it doesn't work. He can't imagine Fatima anywhere else but here.

Sebastian wonders then if Fatima herself feels anything when she looks at him. Does she get excited at all seeing him like this, shirtless, pants unzipped, slight bulge visible in his underwear (smallish as of now, though Sebastian is a "grower, not a shower," to a maximum length of about seven inches, what a girl once described as "ideal")? Does she even get wet at all, like Rosalind or Juliet? He thinks of them now, the way they tasted when he buried his face between their legs, the way their pubic hair clung to their skin after he licked it, the way Juliet smelled stronger but Rosalind tasted sharper. In the room of the Le Centre Sheraton, after Rosalind knocked on the door, it took less than two minutes for them to be on the bed, his shirt off, his pants down, her underwear pulled to the side, his fingers wet from being inside her, his tongue all over her mouth and working its way down her neck, shoulders, breasts, stomach, while here in this very room he sat naked on that chair where Fatima's jacket and bra now hang while Juliet, wearing the sweater Fatima had given him, sat in his lap and rocked slowly back and forth, the inside of her warm and wet and the chair's leather creaking rhythmically until she finished with a sharp, warm-breathed exhale into his neck.

Sebastian turns away, letting out another frustrated breath. He wants now for Fatima to be gone. He wants to think of Rosalind and Juliet and masturbate to an amalgam of the two, imagining them both here, fucking him at the same time with wild abandon while the space heater whirs nearby. But the room is cold, and there's only Fatima, standing awkwardly.

Sebastian sits down at the edge of the bed and stares at the ground. He's still wearing his leather shoes, and they are dark against the gray, faded carpet.

"What's wrong?" Fatima asks again, stepping towards him.

She tentatively takes his hand in hers, but he feels nothing.

"I don't think I want to right now," Sebastian says.

His voice is hoarse, and he barely hears it above the whirring of the heater. Fatima looks down at the ground and pulls her hand back. She is about to cry. Sebastian considers reaching out to give her a reassuring squeeze on the shoulder but decides not to.

Fatima puts her bra and shirt back on. Sebastian watches her and stays seated on the end of the bed. When she's fully dressed again, she looks at him. For some reason, he expects her to be crying, but she's not.

"I think I'm going to go home," she says.

Her voice is flat and hollow, and it seems to die in the air as it leaves her mouth.

"Okay," Sebastian says.

Fatima picks up her purse and exits his room. Sebastian waits until he hears the apartment door close before he stands to put on his shirt.

CHAPTER SEVEN

MARRIAGE A-LA-MODE (1743-45)

She lies on the hotel bed, naked and on her iPhone, atop the crisp white bedsheets, which cascade around her like flower petals. Her legs extend towards Sebastian, who sits at the end of the bed, also naked, and her black hair streams across the piled pillows in all directions, reminding him of John Everett Millais's *Ophelia* drowning in a pool of flowers. On the nightstand, the clock reads 6:01 a.m.

The hotel room is poorly lit (surprising considering that rooms at the Hilton run over $200 a night) even with the lamp on the nightstand, the floor lamp in the corner, and the light in the entryway all flipped on. The off-white curtain is pulled closed over the window, and though early-morning light from the cloudy skies outside filters through around its edges, it feels only appropriate to keep the curtains closed and thus seal the room and everything inside it in secrecy. The air smells of cleaning products, recently vacuumed carpeting, and sex. Two discarded condoms lie on the beige carpeting by the side of the bed, and another few lie unopened on the dresser, though Sebastian has to rest at least a few hours before they'll be needed.

"This one?" Imogen asks.

She shows Sebastian the screen of her phone. He takes it and scrolls through the panels of Hogarth's *Marriage A-la-Mode*.

"That's the one."

"On the wall in your room?"

"Yeah."

Imogen frowns.

"It would be too crowded. I like the way it is now."

Sebastian looks back down at the paintings. The satirical pieces together tell of the tragic arranged marriage of the Viscount Squanderfield (Hogarth's naming conventions are as subtle as those of Charles Dickens), a bankrupt young aristocrat who weds the daughter of a wealthy merchant for financial reasons, and then not only contracts syphilis from a prostitute but also discovers his wife in a bathhouse having an affair with Silvertongue, the lawyer who helped arrange the marriage. The men fight, and Squanderfield is mortally wounded and dies somewhere offscreen. Silvertongue is then hanged, and the lady and her child (Silvertongue's most likely) both fall into poverty.

Sebastian is struck in particular by the second panel, *The Tête à Tête*, in which the unhappy couple sits in their luxurious house. The wife's legs are open (a common sign of sexual promiscuity in eighteenth-century art) and her eyes contain a sly look, while the husband sits haggard and disheveled (perhaps from a recent trip to the brothel himself). Sebastian imagines waking up each day and finding on his walls next to his mirrored doors this image of Squanderfield, the sad young man with his locks of curly hair, his fair skin, his fine clothing, all not enough to mask the despair in the way he slouches and the deep despondency in his eyes.

"Besides, why do you need them on your walls?" Imogen asks.

"A reminder not to get married?"

"Something tells me you of all people don't have to

worry about that. Though I suppose you did come close." She leans forward and takes the phone from him. Sebastian notices how her hair comes down to just above her breasts. "Did Fatima take it well?"

Imogen says this casually, but Sebastian can tell that she really wants to know.

"I don't want to talk about it," he says.

He rises and begins dressing, avoiding Imogen's gaze. She has light brown eyes, small yet fierce, and Sebastian is afraid that if he stares directly into them he'll reveal to her the truth, that despite what he's told her, he hasn't actually broken up with Fatima.

He recalls the night he and Imogen first slept together, less than a week ago, back in Berkeley. He was at her studio, reviewing last minute plans for the conference, and he'd brought a bottle of wine, which they'd finished in half an hour, and it was only after they'd been making out for ten minutes on Imogen's couch (with Imogen on top, of course) that she asked him if he and Fatima were still together.

"I heard rumors you two were having problems back on your birthday," she said. "We all thought you were having an intimate couple's moment down there, but then you came back up looking like someone had chopped off your balls—"

"I remember."

"My point is, I don't want to be the other woman. So I need to know. Are you and Fatima still seeing each other?"

She was straddling his waist and looking down at him imperiously, her face set like a mosaic of a Byzantine empress, her lips and tongue glossy-red from the wine, her hair hanging in waves around her face, one hand resting tentatively on his belt buckle. And so he said the only thing that seemed appropriate ("No, we're not seeing each other."), and Imogen promptly began unbuttoning his pants. He tried to sit up, to kiss her and to roll on top of her, but she held him down with one hand while with the other she pulled out a condom, which she ripped open with her teeth. Sebastian wasn't used to being the submissive one, and so even after she put the condom on him and pulled him inside her, he tried to take charge and roll himself on top. But Imogen was stronger than he was, and she pinned his arms down and then eventually wrapped one of her hands around his throat and held it there, digging her nails into his skin until he came with such exhilarating force that he thought his semen might burst through the condom's latex like water through a poorly built dam.

As Sebastian soon discovered, sex with Imogen was always like this, a war that ended with one of them on top holding the other down by the throat (earlier this morning in the Hilton bed, Sebastian was the victorious one, holding Imogen's arms down and then gently squeezing her throat until she came in one sharp, sudden, breathless convulsion). Yet even after a whole week of nights like these, Sebastian can't bring himself to end things with Fatima. After all, Fatima represents something no other woman can. Since she's landed her new job and is planning her (their) move to San Francisco, she is more and more a world beyond college, a concrete (or rather, glass, steel, and stucco) future, a life after the homeless man's countdown (currently at 85 DAYS TILL THE END) will reach zero, and Sebastian needs the comfort that the idea of this future brings just as much as he needs the wet release he gets nightly from Imogen.

"So, why is it you only put up European art?" Imogen asks from the bed.

He's standing at the mirror, combing his hair, and can see Imogen looking at him in the reflection. She's sitting up now, her legs slightly open, and his eyes are drawn to the patch of dark hair between them.

"What else would I put up?" Sebastian asks.

"I don't know. Mughal miniatures?"

"You know I'm only half-Pakistani, right?"

"So put up half a Mughal miniature then."

Sebastian frowns. "I prefer European art."

"Of course you do. There aren't any white women in Mughal paintings."

He feels himself growing irritated. "You know a lot about Mughal paintings, do you?"

"I do actually. My dad and his brothers all have lots of prints of Persian miniatures hanging in their houses. It's a similar style to Mughal art, right? Just older?"

"I think so," Sebastian says. He actually knows very little about non-Western art.

"Did your parents have a lot of art hanging around your house when you were growing up?" Imogen asks.

"My father hates art."

"What about your mom?"

Sebastian tenses. "No. I know she liked art, but as far as I remember, she never had any prints."

An uneasy silence falls across the room. The clock now reads 6:06 a.m. Imogen looks at it and lets out a sigh.

"Well, I better get ready. Conferences don't run themselves."

She rises and begins getting dressed. Sebastian checks his phone and glances at the date: Friday, February 26. He hadn't forgotten, but the reference to his mother brought it to the forefront of his mind, and he thinks now of what he has to do today.

It's strange that another whole year has passed. He felt like he was just there, standing before her grave under the cloudy skies, his father stiff and formal by his side. Today, his father is away, at a medical conference on the East Coast, and Sebastian wonders if he'll have the decency, today of all days, to abstain from his usual conference frivolities. He's technically still seeing Megan, but Sebastian knows that around an open bar and a flock of overworked female nurses and doctors eager to unwind, his father won't be able to help himself simply for the sake of a yearlong relationship. Megan in fact texted Sebastian, asking if he needed someone to accompany him to the cemetery since his father wouldn't be there. There was no malice in the offer, and she was only being thoughtful, but Sebastian felt her presence, even in a text message, to be an intrusion. He politely declined and told her he'd be fine alone.

The journey to the cemetery in Hayward takes over an hour, first on a BART train down to the South Hayward station, and then on a bus, which smells of piss and creaks and hisses as if it runs on an old Industrial-Revolution-era steam engine. Sebastian eventually disembarks at the Chapel of the Chimes Park and walks up to the cemetery's main mausoleum, a circular, contemporary structure, clearly intended to be comforting (the circles no doubt meant to represent the cyclical nature of life and death) but which for Sebastian mostly invokes post-Cold-War bureaucracy and has all the charm of a middle school multipurpose room. The building in fact has always reminded Sebastian of the multipurpose room of his own middle school in San Ramon, the building where Sebastian was told of his mother's car accident, and since then that style of building, no matter how circular, can never be comforting. Sebastian, of course, insists that the connections he draws between the cemetery's mausoleum and his middle school multipurpose room are based solely on their aesthetic similarities and not any emotional trauma he's associated with the 1990s beige stucco style.

Fatima is waiting for him on one of the wooden benches outside the mausoleum. She's on her phone and wears a business suit and black heels (Pangea called her in for another "follow-up" interview earlier that day, "just to clarify a few things," the assistant assured). In the way she sits, her legs crossed and her straightened hair falling like a sheet before her face, she looks nothing like a college student but instead like an actual adult. Suddenly, the idea of Imogen in her pencil skirt and blouse rushing through the Hilton halls with a laminated "Secretary General" badge around her neck seems to Sebastian extremely childish, like someone playing dress-up.

He never told Imogen that Fatima would be here. In fact, he never intended for Fatima to be here at all until she asked him yesterday if she could come with him. No one except his father ever accompanied him to the grave, not even Viola or Harry, and for ten years it was a very solitary ritual in Sebastian's life. But when Fatima asked, he realized he wanted her there with him. Her serious demeanor, often so inappropriate for college and its frivolities, was perfect for this moment, and he knew she would bring to the cemetery the comforting maturity of the adult world.

She looks up from her phone and smiles when she sees him.

"Hey."

She kisses him hello. It's a closed-lip peck, not wet like the open-lipped kiss Imogen gave him when he left the hotel room, but right now it's what he wants. In fact, there's a thrill to kissing Fatima like this, a thrill that's eluded him for their entire relationship. He tells himself that perhaps it comes from some increased maturity, that on a day like this, when he's thinking of his mother and the ending of things, he longs for something more than just the wet spot between a girl's legs, and that Fatima, mature, wise, competent, and polished, gives him all that. Of course, the truth, which he doesn't want to admit, is that he feels this thrill only because this clandestine meeting with Fatima has, by his decision to keep it secret from Imogen, taken on the air of infidelity, and that by telling Imogen that he and Fatima have broken up, Sebastian has unwittingly injected passion into every meeting between them, because now he's not just spending time with his girlfriend (as un-passionate an encounter as there ever was) but in fact cheating on his mistress. The sad truth is that the thrill Sebastian feels in kissing Fatima is nothing more than the same thrill he's felt with every other girl these past nine months. But it's the anniversary of his mother's death, and so even Sebastian can be allowed a small delusion.

Sebastian takes Fatima's hand, and they walk down the concrete path towards the graves. February in the Bay Area is cold and rainy, and while the skies are clear today, the grass around them is green and wet and smells of a recent rainfall. A cold wind rustles the bare branches of the ordered trees. The cemetery looks and feels the same as it does every year, and while Sebastian understands that this consistency exists because he comes every year on the same day, the repetitiveness has become jarring. In ten years Sebastian has grown from a boy to a man (or at least a man-child), but his mother's new world has stayed exactly the same. Is that what it takes for time to stop? Is death the only true Fountain of Youth? After all, his mother, who died when she was thirty-five, is still thirty-five and will always be.

They reach the cemetery's Muslim section, the Garden of Noor. Ornamentalism and ostentation are discouraged on Muslim graves, and so the stones lie flat on the ground, rectangular slabs with only brief inscriptions. This sparseness gives the cemetery a natural, undisturbed look, and if it weren't for the flowers laid carefully on the grass, from a certain angle, it may appear that there are no stones at all and that the cemetery is just a grassy field stretching out towards a distant hill.

Sebastian's mother is in the middle of the tenth row. The graves on either side of her have flowers, but Sebastian didn't want to bring any and told Fatima not to do so. The idea of commemorating death with something as transient as flowers always seemed to him a mockery. His father always brought them, but right now his father isn't here.

Sebastian and Fatima stop before the stone, still holding hands. Sebastian's eyes trace their way across the familiar inscription: *Amina Khan—June 8, 1965 - February 26, 2001.*

Below is a simple Arabic phrase: بِسْمِ اللهِ الرَّحْمٰنِ الرَّحِيْمِ—Bismillah ir-Rahman ir-Rahim. In the name of God, the most gracious, the most merciful.

Sebastian's father had to fight with the board of the San Ramon Islamic Center about the inscription. Technical Islamic law (of which his father knew close to nothing) stipulates that graves must remain unadorned, and even Qur'anic phrases are discouraged. But Sebastian's father was insistent. Perhaps it was the guilt he felt for all the things he did to his wife, or perhaps it was a deeper, more spiritual, and ultimately selfish guilt, guilt at having abandoned the religion of his own father, guilt at his own multitude of sins, the inscription on the headstone a way of atoning to God for everything all at once. If that was the case, Sebastian felt it was an insufficient recompense.

Sebastian kneels before the grave, something he's rarely done. Usually his father is the demonstrative one, a form of theatrics Sebastian finds callous, considering that while his mother was alive, his father was never so emotionally sensitive. But today, with his father absent and the weight of his senior year on his shoulders, Sebastian wants to be close to his mother, to return to the comfort of when he was eleven, to the warm smile and the dark hair colored with red highlights (as was fashionable in some circles of Pakistani immigrants at that time), which always made him think of shooting stars sailing through space, and to the way she would, after his father reprimanded him for some small transgression, come into his room and stroke the back of his head and whisper comforting Urdu phrases until he felt better. Sebastian thinks of this and runs his own hands through the grass. It's wet and cold. He digs his fingers into the dirt, as if that may bring him closer to her, to that old warmth.

Fatima kneels next to him and holds his arm.

"Tell me about her," she says. "You've never told me anything about her."

"What's there to say?"

"Where did she work?"

Sebastian laughs. Fatima would, of course, define a person's life by their occupation. And yet, it's comforting to think about his mother in this way, to remind himself that she was an ordinary person, with daily struggles and hopes, a job she went to and came home from, a paycheck she received every month, bills she had to pay, a life in the real world she was able to live, even for a little bit.

"She was a teacher," he said. "Middle school history."

Sebastian was always grateful as a child that she had the job she did, because it meant that, all through elementary school, she could be there after school to pick him up, leaning with casual grace against her silver Honda Civic, and that for three hours after school before his father returned she would make him a snack (something sophisticated, like a tuna and alfalfa sprout sandwich, and not the haphazard peanut butter and jellies that were his father's creations) and then sit with him and prep for class or grade papers while he read. She was more relaxed in those hours, more ultimately herself than after his father came home. And even when he didn't come home, she wasn't the same in the evenings, when she'd wait expectantly, wondering if at any moment he might breeze through the door with a jingle of car keys, or if this was one of those nights when he had a "work emergency" and had to stay late at the hospital.

Sebastian clutches the grass and the dirt more tightly and starts to cry. It's more a wetting of the eyes than anything else, moisture seeping out between his eyelashes, but it's enough that Fatima notices and takes his hand in hers.

"Do you think I'd be a better person?" Sebastian asks, clutching Fatima's hand. "If she were still alive?"

Fatima pulls him close in a warm embrace.

"Don't say that," she says. "You are a good person, Sebastian."

Sebastian rests his cheek on Fatima's shoulder. The polyester of her jacket is scratchy, but her body is warm, and he feels her heart beating. She strokes the back of his head and runs her hands through his hair, saying the words again and again like a divine incantation, "You're a good person, Sebastian. You're a good person, Sebastian," as if through repetition, they'll come true.

✦

Later they sit inside a Starbucks not far from the cemetery. Fatima is halfway through a sugary, milky drink. Sebastian is drinking an espresso, but he finds it too watery and sweet, and he wants nothing more than a strong double shot of Lavazza or Illy, a caffeinated slap across the face to wake him from his emotional stupor.

"Are you okay?" Fatima asks.

She grasps his hand. Her touch feels colder now than it did outside, perhaps because of the overly air-conditioned atmosphere of the Starbucks.

"I'm fine," Sebastian says, attempting a smile.

Being inside a Starbucks always makes him feel uneasy. Each one looks eerily the same, with shiny fake-wood tables and industrial coffee makers humming mechanically in the background, the smell of sugar and Lysol hanging in the air while overweight customers ask the beleaguered baristas if they can make their chocolate Frappucinos with lowfat whipped cream.

Sebastian glances at his watch, which reads 1:45 p.m.

"I should get back soon," he says. "Imogen will need help setting up for the party."

Fatima nods but looks disappointed. Her eyes are fixed on him, as if searching for the person she saw back in the cemetery.

"Listen," she says. "I know things haven't been great between us lately."

Sebastian nods, though internally he dislikes the relationship cliché. Fatima takes a deep breath and continues.

"But I was thinking about something today. Well, to be honest, I've been thinking about it for a while."

Her brow is furrowed, and she's biting her lip. Has she found out about one of the girls? If so, Sebastian realizes suddenly that he'll be incredibly disappointed. Will it really end on this day of all days, when he feels closest to her?

Fatima lets out another breath before speaking in a rushed torrent of syllables.

"Have you ever thought about getting married?"

Sebastian stares at her. Behind him, the barista is explaining to a middle-aged lady that soy milk is not nonfat and actually has only marginally fewer calories than regular milk. ("Really?" the lady says, horrified. "But I've always ordered soy instead of regular!").

"With me, I mean," Fatima says, laughing to try to ease the tension (ultimately unsuccessfully). "It's just, it's the end of the year, and I feel like people in relationships are thinking about that. My roommate Jane from last year, she and her boyfriend just got engaged."

"Are you proposing to me?" Sebastian asks.

"No! No, I'm just…I'm just asking if it's something you've thought about. If it's something you'd want to do."

She looks at him expectantly. Sebastian lets out a breath. The air is cold, and he smells a whiff of soy milk floating over to him from the counter (the middle-aged woman looking resigned as she waits for her drink).

"I love you, Sebastian," Fatima says, leaning forward. "I know it's been hard lately, and it maybe feels like I've been uncertain, but I'm not. I love you, even though you don't think about the future or plan things out like I do. But none of that matters, because, I know you can change, and I know I can help you change. You're smart, Sebastian, and I know that one day you'll find a job that pays well, and I want to be there for you, to help you become the person I know you can be. I know I haven't dated as many people as you have, but I've never felt this way about anyone else, and

I…I want to spend my life with you."

Fatima is earnest, oh so earnest, and yet all Sebastian can think is how pathetic this monologue feels, a proposal in a Starbucks, delivered with more generic relationship platitudes than a made-for-TV romcom. If it isn't for the fact that he's just been kneeling by his mother's grave, hand in hand with Fatima, crying, thinking about his childhood, Sebastian would laugh in her face, would tell Fatima no, that he doesn't want to get married, not to her and not to anyone. He would finally be able to say to her all the things he's always felt, would realize in a flash that a post-college, married life with Fatima, no matter how stable it may seem in the face of the end of the world, is actually the last thing he wants.

But instead, Sebastian stares at Fatima and thinks of his mother and the line of graves on every side of her, and he wonders, why not marry Fatima? His mother after all married someone imperfect, someone she wasn't fully compatible with, and straight out of college too, when she was only twenty-two herself, and she dealt with her choice and extracted from her brief life all the happiness she could. Wasn't it selfish of Sebastian to reject all that and to imagine there was something else? College would be over in less than three months (eight-five days), and perhaps it was time for him to say goodbye to this charmed life, to move from youth to manhood, to stand before an imam and pledge himself to Fatima.

"You don't have to say anything now," Fatima says, bowing her head in the face of Sebastian's silence. "Just think about it. Okay?"

Fatima offers to drive Sebastian back to his hotel in the city ("The Hilton in the Financial District, right?"), but Sebastian tells her he'll take BART. She drops him off at the

South Hayward station and gives him a lingering kiss. She doesn't say anything, but her eyes remind him of what she asked.

On the train back to the city, he gets a text message from Imogen (*Conference emergency. You on your way back?*). Yet Sebastian's mind is far from the possible "emergencies" of a Model UN Conference. Instead he thinks of his parents' marriage. They rarely spoke of their wedding, and the only evidence that it even took place was a small photo album, laminated and with a red cover, one which Sebastian remembers finding in a cabinet when he was a child, with photos that were faded and glossy in that '80s way. Sebastian's father wore a big, baggy black suit, a large brown tie, and an off-white button-down, and Sebastian's mother, still innocent and childlike at twenty-two, was bedecked in extravagant Pakistani attire, a baggy, multicolored shalwar kameez, a dupatta around her head, her face painted pure white and her cheeks covered with red dots. Their respective families, meanwhile, gathered around them, the Pakistani women in shalwar kameez, the British and American women in dresses, the men on both sides in equally dandyish suits. The wedding was technically Islamic (no alcohol was served), though as the photos suggested it was a diverse affair, a mix of white and brown skin tones, Western and South Asian styles. Sebastian remembers everyone dancing, laughing, intermingling, all together poster children for multiculturalism. Even as a child, though, Sebastian was struck by how resigned his mother looked amidst all the gaiety. The marriage was an arranged one, organized by their families via local Bay Area mosques, and they'd met for the first time just two days before the wedding. In all the photos, Sebastian's father seemed completely fine with it, perhaps knowing even then he'd never fully commit himself to his marriage vows anyway—but his mother always looked melancholy, in every single photo, her eyes downcast and far away, even when she was smiling for the camera, perhaps thinking of all her possible futures about to disappear.

❁

"There you are!" Imogen says, as Sebastian enters the hotel. "I thought you'd be back earlier."

"Something came up."

She is standing in the lobby, on her phone, looking frazzled. The entrance is filled with Model UN delegates, dressed in suits, carrying placards and folders, and talking excitedly about their committees and about the impending evening party. Sebastian finds the gathering surprisingly juvenile, the faces far too innocent and carefree, with none of the sadness his mother carried at twenty-two.

"Well, something's come up here too," Imogen says. "The hotel staff changed their mind and now won't even let us have a cash bar for the party."

Imogen glares over at the reception desk, where a few older hotel employees (in their late twenties and early thirties) in official Hilton uniforms stare icily across the lobby at the congregation of college-aged children. Imogen looks back at Sebastian, her eyes searching his for an acknowledgement of how serious the problem is.

"Show me the ballroom," Sebastian says, doing his best not to let his disinterest show.

Imogen leads him past a throng of delegates and through a set of double doors. The ballroom is a large space, carpeted and with a stage at one end, never intended for anything other than formal dinners and corporate functions and certainly not as a space for college students to party. Imogen's people, though, are doing the best they can with the room, and the DJ they've "hired" (a friend of Harry's, whom he convinced to work for "exposure" instead of money) is currently overseeing a group of UCBMUN members who clumsily work to set up and test the sound system.

"There were supposed to be two bars on either side," Imogen says, gesturing to the walls. "Now we're really fucked. They'll be riots worse than the Arab Spring if people can't drink at an MUN party."

Sebastian glances across the room and spots a small storage room to the side of the stage.

"There," he says, nodding.

He walks towards it, and Imogen follows, her heels soundless on the carpeted floor. Sebastian opens the door and gazes inside. The room is small, but there is a long table that will suffice.

"We can make our own cash bar," he says. "Send some people to buy a bunch of alcohol, set it up in here, and then spread the word. Charge five dollars a drink, whether it's a glass of wine, a beer, or a mixed drink. We'll make a profit."

"The hotel won't agree."

"We're not going to tell the hotel. It'll be a speakeasy, so to speak."

Imogen looks for another moment at the room and then back at Sebastian and lets out a relieved breath.

"Thank you. I should have thought of this."

She sends out a few texts. Sebastian watches her, feeling like this morning in her hotel room was a lifetime ago. Even standing here with her now, in this enclosed space, her sharp perfume encircling him, all he thinks of is the smell of fresh grass, the feel of dirt under his fingernails, Fatima's eyes as she leaned forward across the fake wood and proposed.

Imogen finishes, puts her phone away, and smiles.

"Sebastian Khan, to the rescue," she says. She steps towards him, a seductive gleam surfacing in her eyes. "I think I have another emergency I need your help with…"

She grabs him by the neck and kisses him and then takes his hand and slips it down her skirt. She is surprisingly, unpleasantly wet, and Sebastian, without intending to, recoils and pulls his hand away.

Imogen frowns. "What is it?"

"Sorry," Sebastian says. "I'm just not in the mood right now."

Imogen's frown softens, but not completely. To Sebastian, her pouting looks childish, and he turns away.

"I'm going to change for the party," he says. "I'll see you in an hour or so."

Without looking back at her, he steps back out into the ballroom. The DJ is testing out his set, and eardrum-splitting electronic music blasts periodically from the speakers before cutting out abruptly so the DJ can give instructions on fixing the volume ("Just a little louder, I think!"). But Sebastian doesn't notice. His mind is far from the ballroom, out amidst gravestones lining green fields, back in the past in a laminated photo album, dancing with his mother at her wedding.

The party that night begins as smoothly as anyone could have hoped, Sebastian's speakeasy working for the most part marvelously, the only flaw being that the drivers sent out to get alcohol forgot to buy mixers for the hard liquor, meaning the only drink options are beer, wine, or shots (which Sebastian tells the bartenders, commandeered from UCBMUN's underclass members, to price at $3 instead of $5). At first, some of the more pretentious delegates (the sweater-vested ones from Princeton in particular) object to this ("What is this, a high school party?"), but after about an hour and a few reluctantly taken rounds of $3 shots, even those sweater-vested three are happily throwing down a twenty for a round of 6 (the extra $2 a much-appreciated tip for the already-overworked bartenders).

Sebastian, however, spends the evening in a melancholy mood and stands at the edge of the party, leaning against a wall. The DJ's music fills the ballroom, a generic blend of hipster rock and electronic beats, and the air still smells of hotel carpeting, though layered on top is the hard liquor the speakeasy is liberally dispensing. But even the familiar smells of a college party aren't enough to keep Sebastian in the moment. Instead he thinks of Fatima's proposal and wonders how the others would react. Imogen, who's in the crowd, dancing and trying to unwind, would say no in a heartbeat and cite a myriad of reasons why women shouldn't get married in their twenties, from statistics about how unmarried women make more money and get more promotions to more philosophical arguments about the importance of independence for the contemporary working woman. Harry, who's standing and chatting with one of the sweater vests about the ethics of not voting ("Our liberal democracy is built upon the Enlightenment principles of individual freedom, and so the decision to abstain is as fundamental as any other right."), would only say yes if he knew the girl was "the one," whatever the fuck that meant. Nate, who last Sebastian saw was ogling another poor girl, would probably say yes to anyone who asked. And as for Viola, Sebastian can't imagine a world in which she would ever consider the idea. Her opposition to marriage is so much more fundamental than that of Imogen, who may eventually consider getting married sometime in her thirties, when she's living in an apartment and making six figures. Viola, though, is the kind of girl who Sebastian knows will never get married, stubbornly living an independent and free life all the way to the grave (Sebastian, in a morbid mood, imagines Viola's tombstone, which, of course, she'd insist on writing herself: "Here lies Viola, who truly lived.").

As if on cue, Viola emerges from the darkness.

"There you are! I haven't seen you all night!"

She leans against the wall next to him. As always, her blond hair is a wild mess across her face and her breath smells of whiskey, rum, and vodka. But when she sees Sebastian's melancholy posturing, she tones down her drunken energy, and her eyes soften.

"You saw your mother today, didn't you?" she asks.

Sebastian nods. Viola's eyes narrow, though, as if she

recognizes there's something more to Sebastian's sadness than just another annual visit.

"Everything okay?"

Sebastian knows he'll never be able to hide the truth from her.

"Fatima asked me to marry her."

Viola reacts calmly, taking another sip of whiskey and nodding as if Sebastian said nothing more extraordinary than that he was considering dropping a class.

"I'm surprised it took her this long," she says.

The understated reaction is initially jarring but also, Sebastian realizes, exactly what he needs to hear. It pulls him from his grave pondering and reminds him that, to an objective ear, Fatima's proposal is nothing more than an inevitability.

"You didn't say yes, did you?" Viola adds, momentarily worried.

"No. But I told her I'd think about it."

"What the fuck is there to think about? You obviously don't want to get married straight out of college, and even if you did, she's obviously not 'the one,' as Harry would say."

"I know but…"

Sebastian shakes his head. Viola leans closer, disbelief in her bright eyes.

"What's the matter with you? The Sebastian I know would never think twice about something like this!"

"I've just been wondering—"

"About what?"

"About my mother. About marriage. About how much she sacrificed in marrying my dad. You know she was twenty-two when they got married?"

"So? It was also The Eighties, and the world was a different place. And anyway, even if she did sacrifice a lot, she didn't do it so you could make the same mistake she did!" Her voice has gone up in pitch and is piercing to

Sebastian's ears. "Honestly, what are you even going to do if you say yes to Fatima? Are you going to have a fucking *wedding?*"

"Sure, why not? You can come if you want. There'll probably be an open bar—"

"Are you going to stop cheating on her?"

Viola's gaze is a cold dagger to his chest, and when he remains silent, she laughs.

"I know you, Sebastian," she says. "Even at your wedding you won't be able to take your eyes off the brides-maids, and you'll probably end up fucking her maid of honor in the bathroom before rushing to the altar to say your vows."

"I can change—"

"So you're going to stop fucking Imogen then?"

Sebastian grows irritated.

"How do you—"

"Oh please. It's obvious from the way you two have been inseparable the past week. I'm not judging by the way, good going. She's probably great in bed. All that anger and militant energy…"

Sebastian recalls the way Imogen pinned him down and the force of her hand and nails around his throat. "Yeah," he says. "Yeah, she's pretty good…"

"And you want to throw that all away for *Fatima?* She'll probably still be scared of your dick come the wedding night and won't even know where to put it. I'll have to check the sheets for blood to make sure the marriage has been fully consummated—"

"Stop it."

"Why? I'm not wrong."

Sebastian looks away, back out to the party. The crowd on the dance floor has grown, and Sebastian sees Imogen floating among them, dancing like she's underwater, her hair pulled down from its bun, the flowery tresses flowing around her like they were that morning on the hotel bed.

"You've been dating Fatima for nine months now," Viola says. "And you've cheated on her how many times?"

Sebastian tries to ignore her, but Viola's voice rises above even the DJ's music, with a discordant melody of its own.

"Trust yourself, Sebastian. If you really wanted to be with her, you wouldn't have fucked all those other girls, and you wouldn't be still fucking Imogen now."

Sebastian watches Imogen dancing, her hips swaying left and right, her hair whirlpooling around her head and neck like waves.

"Go fuck her," Viola says, a voice over his left shoulder. "Forget Fatima and go fuck Imogen, right now, like I know you want to."

And suddenly Sebastian finds himself moving, out across the carpeted ballroom floor, through the sea of dancing bodies and towards Imogen's bobbing form. The music pulsates, so loud it drowns out his thoughts, and the air smells so much of alcohol that his nose stings. He's not drunk, but he no longer feels in full control of his actions, as if he's caught in an oceanic current.

"There you are!" Imogen says, her eyes brightening when she sees him.

Without speaking, Sebastian grabs her and pulls her away from the dance floor and over towards the speakeasy. She's surprised but doesn't protest, especially when he reaches down and squeezes her ass.

"I want you," he whispers. "Right now."

He presses himself against her and feels her body perk up. His heart beats faster and faster as his legs carry him to the corner of the room. They jostle through the line of people waiting to buy drinks and enter the speakeasy. Inside, the UCBMUN-members-turned-bartenders (all completely sober) look up.

"We need the room," Sebastian says.

The bartenders wordlessly file out, grateful for the reprieve, though the guy at the front of the line (one of the sweater-vested Princetonians) is indignant.

"Hey, what about my drinks!"

Sebastian looks down at the boxes of alcohol stacked by the door.

"Take whatever you want," he says. "On the house. Put it outside."

The Princetonian looks like he's just won the lottery and at first is too stunned to move. Sebastian looks at his watch.

"I'm closing the door in five seconds," he says.

The Princetonian and the other delegates in line behind him move quickly. Sebastian is impressed by how much alcohol an under-pressure group of committed college students can transport from one room to another. When the alcohol is all outside, he closes the door and turns to Imogen. The sounds from the ballroom grow muffled, and the room is quiet save for the walls, which rattle from the residual sound of the DJ's pounding electronica, and Sebastian and Imogen's heavy, rapid breathing. Sebastian stares at Imogen, his blood racing with a determined lust, like waves crashing against a cliffside. Imogen is wearing her usual conference attire, a gray pencil skirt, heels, and a white blouse, though she's undone the blouse's top button, revealing her long throat. Sebastian traces his eyes up to her lips and cheeks, both flushed red and in sharp, vivid contrast to her dark flowing hair. Once again, he has the impression of her being underwater—or perhaps it's him, and she's the one standing on shore.

He steps towards her, and she grabs the back of his neck, and they kiss furiously. He takes her by the waist and tries to maneuver her towards the nearest wall, but she's faster and stronger and spins him around and slams him against it, and he feels a sharp but energizing jolt of pain in his back. He tries to move, but Imogen has pressed herself firmly against him. As they kiss, she begins undoing his belt.

"Does it turn you on that I'm a bad person?" Sebastian asks.

"What?"

Her hands pause on the button of his pants.

"You know I've cheated on Fatima five times."

Imogen frowns. "I didn't know it was that many."

He can smell her breath, a mix of different alcohols all swirled together.

"It is," Sebastian says. "But you're turned on by it, aren't you?"

He stares at her breasts, which rise and fall like buoys on the ocean.

"Why are you saying this?" Imogen asks.

"Tell me you like it," Sebastian says, breathlessly. "Tell me you like that I'm a bad person."

"Sebastian—"

"Tell me you like it, Imogen. Tell me it turns you on, tell me it makes you wet, tell me that you wouldn't want me any other way…"

He's dizzy from the alcohol, and he imagines that he's lying down and that Imogen's on top of him, pinning him into the ocean floor like an anchor—

"I like it," Imogen whispers, her lips glistening with his saliva. "I like that you're a bad person."

Sebastian grabs her by the back of the neck and presses his lips against hers, shoving his tongue into her mouth like a diver plunging into undersea darkness. She bites his lip, and he feels the skin break, the sharp twang of pain, the blood dribbling down his chin. He kisses her again, tasting blood now mixed with the alcohol on her tongue. With one hand, she unbuttons his pants and reaches her hand inside his underwear, and with the other, she grips his throat, digging her nails into his skin. Sebastian closes his eyes and Imogen squeezes both hands harder, and as his blood races downwards and his heart beats faster, he feels his senses blur together—

"Sebastian?"

His eyes flash open. The voice is wrong, out of place.

He knows it, but he can't place it. He turns to face the door and finds that it's open. He stares at the face looking back at him, and suddenly, his senses come flooding back, like he's come up to the surface for a breath. He can hear the thudding bass shaking the walls of the room, he can smell the sweat and the alcohol, he can feel the warmth in the air—and he can see Fatima, standing in the doorway, with a horrified expression.

Sebastian can't understand. It's impossible that she's here now. She's not supposed to be here. She's not supposed to be at a Model UN party. She's supposed to be in Berkeley, in her apartment, studying for her economics tests. She's supposed to be in the cemetery, kneeling with him next to his mother's grave. She's supposed to be in some distant future, in a glass and steel apartment in SOMA, years after college is over.

Imogen pulls both her hands away, and a confused expression spreads over her face too. Sebastian still struggles to catch his breath, but he hurriedly buttons up his pants and looks back and forth between Fatima and Imogen, who stare at each other and then at Sebastian. Imogen's confusion melts into anger as she beings to understand. She glares at Sebastian and wants to say something but can't because Fatima is crying now, her hand against the wall, and the sudden, punctuated sound of sobbing jars them both from their thoughts.

"Fatima," Imogen says, her voice quivering. "I'm so sorry. I thought…"

But she trails off because it doesn't matter now, because it's clear Fatima can't hear a word she's saying and can't even see because her face is buried into her arm and she's leaning against the wall, her body spasming with each fresh sob.

"Fatima," Sebastian says quietly.

"I wanted to surprise you!" she says, through tears. "I wanted to show you I cared!"

Sebastian feels like he'll drown in her tears if she doesn't stop. He reaches forward and places his hand on her arm, to try and stop her from crying. But when his fingers barely graze her shirt, she whirls towards him and snarls.

"Don't touch me!"

Her eyebrows are narrowed and her hand is up, having batted Sebastian's away. There's a fury to her expression, a fire Sebastian has never before seen, and it frightens him. Before he can recover, though, Harry bursts into the room.

"There you are!" he says, looking between Sebastian and Imogen.

He's breathing rapidly, and he barely registers Fatima's presence.

"What?" Imogen asks.

"There's an emergency," Harry says. "The hotel staff found out about the alcohol. They've called the cops."

"Fuck," Imogen says.

She rushes out the door, shouldering her way past Sebastian and Fatima, Harry right behind her. Sebastian wants to say more to Fatima, but he hears the growing commotion outside, sounds of fear and surprise overtaking the crowd. The DJ's music shuts off abruptly, and the walls of the room stop shaking. Lights come on through the door, accompanying a chorus of indignant voices.

Sebastian gives Fatima one last, anguished look. Her eyes are cold, hollow, and unresponsive, as if she's no longer present, no longer looking at Sebastian but through him, back through their past. She's leaning against the wall, and Sebastian knows there's nothing he can say to fix this, and so he leaves her and exits the room.

Outside, his eyes take a moment to adjust to the brightness. The students are still clustered together in front of the stage, looking as dazed as Fatima as they stare around the ballroom. On the stage, the DJ is indignant but then, after a moment, humble. Sebastian follows his gaze and sees a group of cops streaming in through the open double doors. There are only about five of them, but they dominate the room with their dark blue uniforms and their service weapons hanging casually from their belts. The drunk students look suddenly like children, caught by their parents breaking curfew.

One of the cops has a megaphone. When she speaks, it amplifies her voice with a sharp, reverberating edge that sends spikes of pain through Sebastian's ears.

"Who's in charge here?" the cop asks.

Sebastian looks over at Imogen. She's at first paralyzed and in shock but after a moment collects herself and steps slowly forward. She pulls her hair back up into a bun and buttons the top button of her blouse, but she can't hide the drunken glaze over her eyes or the way her cheeks are flushed and her lips still smeared with traces of Sebastian's blood. Sebastian feels the bite on his lip now, as well as the pain around his throat, a throbbing that sends jolts spearing through the bottom half of his face. His head aches too, and though he hasn't drunk much at all, he can feel the hangover rushing to meet him. He feels thirsty, and longs for a glass of water. He thinks of Hogarth's despondent young man, the Viscount Squanderfield, sitting in his chair in his luxurious house, with the dazed look of a man who only a moment ago realized he's been drowning.

CHAPTER EIGHT

BEATA BEATRIX (1871-72) / PORTRAIT OF A YOUNG MAN (1513-14)

She stands in line about a block ahead of them, under the neon martini glass that marks the entrance to the club. The sign's yellow light falls upon her like a halo, illuminating the red hair she has pulled back into a bun and turning it a shade of orange that shimmers each time she moves her head. Her hands are buried in the pockets of her peacoat, and underneath she wears a sweater, as white as freshly fallen snow. What draws Sebastian to her, though, is that she carries herself like an adult, with nonchalant poise and aristocratic disdain, her gaze pointed up at the starless city sky and projecting power and confidence, as if the vast black canvas belongs entirely to her.

Chicago in the early springtime is cold and windy, and the dry air smells of gasoline. Foul-smelling gusts whip at Sebastian's face and neck and turn his skin red and raw. Beside him, Viola and Harry are bundled up in scarves and gloves and long double-breasted jackets and look vaguely like a pair of spies in a John Le Carré novel, waiting on a bridge in East Berlin to meet their Russian informants.

Their vacant, distant eyes and thoughtful expressions certainly contribute to this impression. Harry looks particularly severe, with his lips pulled in a thin line and a stoic resolve in the way he stands upright against the howling wind. Only Nate standing behind them ruins the image, his jacket too small for him and his fat face comically red from the wind.

In reality, their mission has none of the glamour and danger of Cold War espionage, and they are instead standing in line for a club, in this case one rented out by the University of Chicago's Model UN team for their Saturday evening party. None of them, though, are thrilled about the prospect (except Nate who keeps talking loudly about the "hot girl from committee" whom he hopes to find in the club), and they're only here because Harry insisted they have to "network" with their chairs to make sure they win awards. Viola suggested they just buy some alcohol from Trader Joe's and drink it in their hotel (The Comstock Inn, a cheap family-owned place where the Berkeley delegation always stays, built in the 1920s, with a ghostly white exterior, carpeting reminiscent of *The Shining*, and rooms likely haunted by the ghosts of dead bootleggers), and even Sebastian wasn't at all excited about journeying out to a party, feeling too much like an empty wine bottle someone kept overturning in the hopes that a splash still remained at the bottom. He's here now simply because according to the homeless man, there are only 56 DAYS TILL THE END and because this will be his last Model UN conference party.

It's only the sight of the girl, Helena (Canada from his committee), that fills him with life again—although calling her a "girl" feels utterly inadequate, since she's like no girl Sebastian has seen before. He knows she's a student at NYU, but she looks like she works at an investment bank or a management consultancy firm and belongs not in a chalk-smeared classroom sitting on a flimsy, blue plastic chair but in a boardroom or a corner office overlooking a glass city, or in an upscale hotel bar, sipping $15 cocktails served on monogrammed napkins. He stares at her now as she stands haloed under the neon light, and he feels the old familiar thrill, the slight increase in his heartbeat, the blood racing through his veins, and that swelling down below—though he also feels something beyond simple sexual desire, because in her maturity she reminds him of Fatima, and he imagines that sleeping with her might grant him passage into the adult world.

"Is it her this time?" Harry asks.

His voice is as bitter as the wind, and the words come out like spit. Sebastian meets Harry's gaze, which is full of malice. Viola gives Sebastian an apologetic look but doesn't speak.

"Another white girl," Harry says. "You're consistent at least."

Sebastian wants to remind him that Rosalind was likely mixed race and that Imogen only looked white and was as much a person of color as Harry himself, and that obviously Fatima wasn't white in any way. But he stays quiet, knowing that Harry the artistic philistine would never understand. For Sebastian it isn't about the race of the women, about whiteness as a Platonic ideal, but instead about aesthetic whiteness, whiteness as a literal color, the beauty in the contrast between dark hair and pale skin, no matter what its racial source. Harry would simply see it as self-hatred (which was ironic, Sebastian thought, given that "Harry" still grew embarrassed anytime anyone called him "Hari").

Harry's irritation, though, is reasonable tonight, considering the dire straits of the club over which he presides. The cops, thankfully, didn't arrest anyone that night in San Francisco, though they talked with Imogen for over an hour in one of the hotel's offices. Afterwards she went straight to her room and didn't respond to any of their texts or calls. Worse was the hotel itself, which fined the club for violating the contract and reported them directly to the University.

Ultimately, the conference lost UCBMUN a considerable amount of money (which would have to come out of the University's yearly budget for extracurricular activities), and Imogen and Harry were called into the ASUC offices and told that the club would have to be disbanded, and it was only because Harry protested fervently (with all the rhetorical skills Model UN had taught him) that he was able to wrangle a deal: the club would have to prove its worth in the final conference of the year at the University of Chicago, and only if it won Best Small Delegation would the University consider not disbanding it. It was a lifeline that Harry graciously accepted, but one that meant that the club needed a renewed sense of purpose and that the club's Head Delegate, Sebastian Khan, would need to step up. But while Sebastian was perfectly happy stepping up (in fact, he looked forward to it, since after his breakup with Fatima, he was willing to distract himself with anything), Harry felt Sebastian was the wrong person to lead the travel team in a moment like this (he blamed him for the incident with the cops, since the speakeasy was Sebastian's idea)—and so he corralled the UCBMUN Officer Board to strip Sebastian of his title.

It was a devastating evening sitting in Cafe Milano, with lukewarm lattes and over-dressed salads spread across their table and students nearby chattering away about trivialities like final exams, and watching in silence as the other officers slowly raised their hands in what was an almost unanimous vote (Sebastian obviously voted "no", and Imogen, who'd stopped showing up to meetings since the conference, was put down as an "abstain"). The biggest blow, though, was watching Viola raise her hand with all the others.

"Harry asked me to," she told him later, after everyone had left. "And I didn't want to fight him on it. He's just trying to do what's best for the club."

In the end, Harry appointed himself Interim Head Delegate, which Sebastian would have considered a Machiavellian political maneuver, except that he didn't see what benefit it would actually bring Harry. Viola said it was about duty, that Harry, the dictionary definition of a good guy, didn't want the club to be disbanded and future students to be deprived of Model UN (but also, more selfishly, probably didn't want to be remembered as president of the administration that oversaw the collapse of the county's oldest Model UN club). But Sebastian believed there was something more. Like all college seniors, Harry too was afraid of post-college life, and his obsession with Model UN was likely just a desperate attempt to find meaning in something, however irrelevant it would soon be. It was pathetic, but Sebastian understood.

The line now shifts forward, and Sebastian watches as Helena steps out of the neon martini halo and up to the bouncer on the threshold. The bouncer scans her ID and then waves her in, and her shimmering red-orange hair disappears into the darkness.

"Do you even know her?" Harry asks.

"She's in my committee."

"Did you actually talk to her, or just stare at her across the room?"

"We went to the museum together," Sebastian says, with irritation. "This afternoon."

Harry frowns. "During committee?"

"Yes."

The committee in question is UNESCO, and the issue the delegates have been spending two and a half days discussing is Organized Crime in Art and Antiquities. The topic should theoretically interest Sebastian, and Harry, despite their animosity, assigned him the committee for that very reason (Harry himself is off on the Future Security Council as India, debating the rise of religiously-inspired cyberterrorism, while Viola is in the fourteenth century on the Council of the Florentine Republic as Archbishop Iacopo Palladini, discussing the Guelph-Ghibelline conflict). But since the loss of his title, Sebastian's interest in Model UN has dwindled, and instead of throwing himself into his part with the gusto of an actor giving one final, grand performance, he's chosen to wile away the weekend's hours in a tragic anticlimax.

"Sebastian, I told you that you need to take this seriously!" Harry says. "Every one of us needs to win an award to have a chance at Best Small Delegation! You can't just wander out of committee like that!"

Harry glares at Sebastian, like a priest lecturing a wayward member of his flock. Viola looks away and whistles a tune in a very forced attempt to appear disinterested.

"I'm not going to win, Harry," Sebastian says. "I'm sorry, but I just don't care enough."

His tone has enough finality that there's nothing left for Harry to say, and instead they stand in bitter silence. Ahead of them, the bouncer lets another group of students into the club. Sebastian imagines Helena somewhere inside, still silhouetted in the angelic neon glow of the martini sign.

When they met in committee, she was seated to his right at one of the long tables, one black-legginged leg crossed casually over the other, her hair shimmering even under the fluorescent lights of the Hyatt conference room. At the front, giving a poorly written speech was Malaysia, a small, chubby girl, not entirely unattractive, but certainly not with the blistering confidence of someone like Helena. Nate, though, seated on Sebastian's left, was staring at Malaysia as if she were Helen of Troy, his mouth hanging partially open with his characteristically dumbfounded expression. Sebastian would normally have elbowed him to keep him from looking too obviously creepy, but he was distracted by Helena, who was looking up ticket prices for the Chicago Art Institute on her phone (an iPhone 4, the newest model, so common now among college students that even Viola gave in and got one, leaving only Luddite-Sebastian stubbornly pre-Information Age with his cracked Motorola

Razr flip phone), and after watching her thumb linger over an image of Edward Hopper's *Nighthawks*, Sebastian leaned towards her and jotted down in her notebook, *Shall we ditch committee and go?* Helena looked at the message and smiled and then up at Sebastian and smiled again. Her brown eyes and her snow-white sweater were luminous. *Sure*, she wrote, below Sebastian's proposal.

They disappeared after break, leaving only their placards to mark their empty seats. The weather was cold but cloudless, and pale sunlight reflected off the city's tall glass buildings, shrouding the sky in a yellow glow. Helena walked beside Sebastian, her shoes clipping on the sidewalk and strands of her red-orange hair swinging like a pendulum against her face.

It was twenty minutes from the Hyatt to the Art Institute, and in that time Sebastian learned that Helena was a senior at NYU and that she also studied Art History but that, unlike him, she took it seriously and already had a job lined up after college, a year-long paid internship at the Metropolitan Museum of Art, and that in a few years she'd apply to graduate school ("I want to go to Columbia, since it means I get to stay in New York, which is where I eventually want to live and work, but I'd make do at any of the Ivies, or even Berkeley I suppose...") and that ultimately she had ambitions to be a museum curator. She delivered all this information in an articulate, passionate monologue, and left Sebastian reeling with admiration and envy. To him, that kind of life planning was for scientists and engineers, and he never imagined he'd find it in a humanities major, and certainly not an Art History major like himself. It made him think of Fatima.

"What about you?" she asked, as they walked along the tree-lined edge of Millennium Park. "Are you also interested in curating?"

"I don't know," Sebastian said, taken aback by the question. "I haven't really thought about it."

"Or is academia more your thing? Become a professor and teach old paintings to young kids?"

"Maybe. It would be nice to stay in college the rest of my life."

Helena laughed, and Sebastian felt his heart stirred by the musical sound, the fading notes carried upward by the wind.

They soon reached the museum, a Beaux-Arts style building of sand-colored stone, with two bronze lions flanking the main entrance. Before going inside, Sebastian ran his hand across one of their manes but retracted it quickly when the cold metal stung his skin.

Inside, they bought their tickets from a hipster-clad guy working at the front desk and then moved towards the galleries. The air was heated and pleasant, a sanctuary against the bitterness of outside. Helena wanted to see the twentieth-century rooms, and Sebastian didn't object. Here, in the museum halls, she was something divine, an angel gliding down the staircases and across the wooden thresholds, casting her benevolent eyes on the paintings left and right, explaining to Sebastian in a soothing voice what each one meant and why it spoke to her. She could have stayed silent, though, as far as Sebastian was concerned, since he was content simply to watch her, to worship the image of her slightly upturned head and the way the pale light that streamed in through the broad windows haloed her shining hair. She was a savior to him, especially as they drifted through the increasingly jarring and oppressive post-modern galleries, and when he came face-to-face with the bewildering colors and shapes of Roy Lichtenstein's *Woman III,* he simply turned back to Helena and her comforting and divine grace.

They eventually did make their way back to the nineteenth century, in the last of the museum's open hours. Back at the Hyatt, the committee's afternoon session would likewise be winding to a close, but Sebastian wasn't thinking anymore of Model UN. As the sun dipped behind the buildings and the sky grew grayer and darker, he and Helena lingered in the timeless space of the museum's marble halls.

"Tell me about this one," Helena said.

They were standing before Rossetti's *Beata Beatrix* (1871-1872), a large portrait of a red-haired woman kneeling with her hands clasped in prayer, her eyes closed and her head tilted upward, while a red dove with white poppies in its beak floated down towards her. The painting had the classic Pre-Raphaelite sensuality, the vivid red and green of the woman's dress, the softness of the background where two robed figures stood in some kind of grassy, rustic environment, while a sundial gave symbolic import to the passage of time. Below the actual painting was a smaller perdella that depicted the same woman standing before a man whose arms were stretched out to her in amazement, while behind her were clustered a gaggle of awed onlookers. The gilded frame of the painting bore several Latin inscriptions, as well as the name of the work, just above the perdella.

As with *Cythera*, there were several versions of the piece, and this one was a replica, made by Rossetti for a patron. The original hung in the Tate, though it didn't have the Latin frame or the perdella below. Sebastian remembered the original from his trip with Viola, but this time it was his memory that was hazier than the version before him. In his mind, the painting was murkier, gloomier, a more obvious rumination on Beatrice's impending death. But here before him was something altogether more positive, not so much about her mortality but about the inevitability of her rebirth in Paradise.

"Rossetti was a Pre-Raphaelite," Sebastian said, in answer to Helena. "They rejected the classical ideals of the Renaissance and looked back to Italian art of the fourteenth century—"

"I know who the Pre-Raphaelites are," Helena said, with an amused smile. "Tell me about the painting itself."

Sebastian remembered then that Helena wasn't just another attractive girl whose only exposure to the nineteenth century was having watched *Moulin Rouge*, but someone who knew everything he did, and in all likelihood far more.

"It's a painting of Beatrice," Sebastian said. "Dante's Beatrice."

"Ah."

Helena turned back to the painting, as if with new eyes. Sebastian felt his heart beat faster.

"Have you read Dante?" he asked.

"No. I'm a Modernist through and through."

"Well, in the *Divine Comedy*, Beatrice appears as Dante's guide into Paradise, the symbol of a pure and divine kind of love, leading him ultimately to his transcendent vision. She was also the inspiration for his love poem *La Vita Nuova*. She died while he was writing it, though, so he left it unfinished."

"So she was a real person then?"

"Of course. Why wouldn't she be?"

"I don't know. Maybe Dante made her up."

Sebastian felt uneasy, having never considered this before. He turned away from Helena to look back at the painting.

"How old was she when she died?" Helena asked, after a long silence.

"Young. Twenty-four I think."

"How sad."

Sebastian turned back to Helena, who was staring up now at Beatrice's ageless face.

"There's a happy ending, though," Sebastian said after a moment. "The perdella at the bottom is of Dante and Beatrice reuniting in Paradise."

Helena smiled but didn't turn from the painting. Sebastian stared at her profile, the way her head tilted upwards like Beatrice's own, to take in the full height of the picture. He imagined replacing her black leggings, white sweater, and gray scarf with Beatrice's dress. He imagined her with her eyes closed in beatific prayer.

"What does the Latin say?" Helena asked.

Sebastian turned back to the frame. He'd taken a few introductory Latin courses and did his best to try and translate (luckily, he also recognized the phrase from *Brideshead Revisited*).

"Quomodo sedate sola civitas," he said. "How lonely the city stands."

The two stood in silence as the phrase settled around them. Despite its melancholy, Sebastian felt only joy staring at this painting, something he hadn't felt wandering through the misshapen modernist images and the jagged lines of color. What the painters of the nineteenth century and before understood was that art was not just a formal exercise. Art was first and foremost about beauty, and no one knew that as much as Dante Gabriel Rossetti, who like Sebastian also must have felt he was born in the wrong era and no doubt longed for the pre-mechanized, pre-Renaissance, Medieval world of courtly love (sanitized, of course, of disease, serfdom, and everything else that would have made the Middle Ages a hell), so much so that he used his middle name as his first to honor the great poet of that age. In *Beata Beatrix*, Rossetti painted with pure emotion, as if it was his own love who prematurely died and he who saw her again in Paradise.

"I'll admit, it is quite beautiful," Helena said.

Beautiful. The word repeated in Sebastian's mind, in Helena's calm, comforting voice. He felt that in that one word was contained everything he'd been seeking this past year in college. For a year, since he'd seen the homeless man, he'd been afraid of the end of college and what lay ahead for him, and he'd tried for nine months to quell that fear with Fatima simply because she offered him a stable future. And even when both his body and mind rebelled against that future, even when he was drawn to other women and repelled by

Fatima, he clung to it, redefining it as a sacrifice, in defiance of his father, in honor of his mother. But now, when that future was gone, the glass and steel building in SOMA shattered in one disastrous night, what was left? What was there that could give him meaning after college? Wasn't there ultimately only this one word, "beautiful?" Wasn't that all that mattered? Even Helena, the modernist, trained to be wary of such pure aestheticism, could recognize the power of beauty. In the end, this was what Sebastian cared about the most, this image of the beautiful Beata Beatrix, divine, drawn with Pre-Raphaelite perfection. He realized in that moment that even when college ended, when Berkeley would be a distant memory, this painting and all the others that had stirred his heart would still exist, and with them there would always be a Helena, a girl whose angelic presence could guide him through the halls to Paradise and then stand with him and gaze upon the face of pure beauty, a girl in whose own face he could see that same beauty mirrored back.

Now, in the bitter cold of the present moment, as the line outside the club shifts forward, and he, Nate, Harry, and Viola stand a few steps away from the threshold, Sebastian imagines entering and searching for her divine light somewhere in the darkness.

❋

The club is modern, and insistently so. Even from the coat check line, Sebastian can hear the pounding bass and the electronica, which only gets louder after they've moved farther inside, through the slate-floored hallways and out into the main room. Here, everything is made of metal or particle board, from the bar's countertop to the frame around the mirror that hangs behind the liquor bottles to the staircase that leads up to a special VIP section guarded by its own bouncer and a red velvet rope and reserved only for University of Chicago club members (and anyone they've allowed in, as evidenced by the disproportionate number of attractive girls that crowd around the section's white leather couches). Purple mood lighting floods the whole room, and large speakers at the far end, past the bar and the crowded dance floor, pound out loud electronic music. Unlike most clubs, the air doesn't smell of sweat or booze, as if secret purifiers line the insides of the walls and keep the atmosphere cool and odorless. Sebastian finds it all too clean, a sinister utopia, a futurist's wet dream of a club, scrubbed and polished of all life and heart, and he longs for the grimy walls of the old theatre in Montreal, where dust hung in the air and the walls told stories of years of human presence. If this club had any previous life before its current incarnation, there is no sign of it anywhere. The walls are as white as blank pages and reflect only purple light and the shadows of dancing students.

"We should find our chairs and schmooze a bit," Harry says. "I might be able to get us into that VIP section up there."

Harry moves off in the direction of the metal staircase, and Nate disappears into the crowd after announcing his intention to "find Malaysia," like a fat Renaissance explorer sailing east to seek out the Indies. Viola and Sebastian, meanwhile, step up to the bar to buy drinks.

"Harry means well," Viola says.

"I'm sure he does."

The bartender turns to them. Viola orders a vodka and tonic. Sebastian, feeling irritated and anxious, orders two double shots of vodka. He downs one as soon as it arrives and takes the other one to sip on.

"Are you okay?" Viola asks.

She's leaning towards him, her blue eyes narrowed with concern through the tangle of her blond hair. Sebastian feels the double shot taking hold, and she seems at once very distant and very close. His chest and arms tingle as the vodka rushes to his head.

"I'm fine," Sebastian says. "I just need to find someone."

He turns away from her and steps into the crowd. His head spins from the vodka, and with it spins the room, but the buzz he feels is far from the deliriousness of UCSB earlier in the year, when he chased Lorelei's red hair through the Isla Vista streets. Instead, it's a dull throbbing where his head meets his neck, an expanding and contracting of his vision, a pressure in his ear that reduces the individual conversations around him and the music from the speakers into one uniform, indistinguishable drone. Helena must be somewhere in this dancing mass of people. He saw her enter not long before him, and he remembered her peacoat hanging in the closet behind the coat check desk (there were several black peacoats, it being a common color and style among the fashionable youth of 2011, but Sebastian felt certain that this particular one was hers). Still, he feels like he's losing track of time, and after a moment, he's not sure how long he's been looking for her. The purple lights glow brighter, reflecting off the bare skin of the dancing students, and the music grows louder too, pounding from the speakers hanging ominously from the ceiling, giant black boxes looking indifferently down upon the gathered crowds. There's no DJ in sight, the club no doubt having realized that paying a DJ to play pre-recorded music is a waste of money and that if there's enough alcohol, people will dance to anything. Sebastian still can't smell either alcohol or sweat, even though the bodies thronged around him glisten like extras in a Gatorade commercial. He wonders if the vodka has dulled his senses, or whether he's not had enough yet. He downs the double shot in his hand and blanches at the sharp taste. He doesn't remember vodka being so unpleasant. He looks around for a place to throw away his empty plastic cup but can't find a trashcan here on the dance floor. On his left is a circle of awkward guys, standing while two girls dance wildly between them (in a moment, the two girls leave suddenly to get a drink, and the guys are left awkwardly staring at each other for a few seconds before they wordlessly leave as well). On his right two people from his committee (Czech Republic and Namibia) grind on each other and vigorously make out, only a few buttons and a pair of underwear away from fucking right then and there. But whereas before, when he was searching for Lorelei or Rosalind, such unbridled sexuality would have fueled his roving eyes, he now finds this open display of lust distasteful, a reminder of the basest level of desire from which he knows Helena is separate. She isn't just a body like these two, craving carnal pleasure. She doesn't sweat. She glides down museum halls and speaks in calm, comforting tones about art. She glows with divine light.

Sebastian weaves his way through the crowd towards the far wall but doesn't find her there, and so he turns back around and surveys the club. His head pounds from the four shots of vodka, and he feels a lurching in his stomach. The faces in the crowd now all look the same, laughing with one voice. In the distance are Viola, Harry, and Nate, leaning against the railing of the VIP section. But they too have the same face as the dancers in the crowd, and Sebastian wants them all to disappear. In fact, he wants everyone in Chicago to disappear, everyone except Helena, so they can walk the empty city together, as if it's their own museum.

Sebastian finds himself back on the other side of the crowd. He sees a trashcan, but the plastic cup he was holding is gone, dropped somewhere out on the dance floor, though he doesn't remember doing so. He thinks he sees Helena's white sweater at the bar, but when he fights his way through the irritated students waiting in line, he realizes it's a different girl, and the white of her sweater fades. He orders two more double shots from the bartender, downs them both, and then steadies himself against the particle board, which is irritatingly smooth. He puts his hand to his mouth, and the girl who isn't Helena looks worried and pulls her drink closer to her, as if she's afraid he'll somehow puke inside it. He closes his eyes, but even then he still sees the purple light and the dancing bodies.

Sebastian opens his eyes and lurches over towards the metal staircase to the VIP section. The bouncer at the velvet rope frowns and holds up his hand.

"I'm with him!" Sebastian shouts, louder than necessary.

He points up at Harry, who stands by the railing at the top of the stairs, holding a drink and talking to a group of University of Chicago students and looking particularly presidential. Harry sees Sebastian and frowns but then nods to the bouncer. Reluctantly, the bouncer lets Sebastian past the red rope.

At the top of the stairs, Sebastian ignores Harry and glances across the VIP section. It's quieter up here, but Sebastian's ears still ring and his head pounds. Students lounge across white leather couches around small metal tables, drinking (slightly) nicer vodka served in glasses instead of plastic cups. It's darker than down on the dance floor, and Sebastian can barely make out people's faces.

"Dude, where've you been?" Harry asks, grabbing Sebastian's shoulder.

His grip is strong. Sebastian pushes back at him, but then stumbles and has to catch himself on Harry's arm.

"I'm looking for someone," Sebastian says, his words one long slur.

"Don't embarrass us!" Harry says, lowering his voice to a hiss.

Harry's grip is painful now, and Sebastian struggles to break free. He considers punching Harry in his smug face and breaking his glasses, or else stomping on his leather shoes and fracturing a toe.

"I'm fine," Sebastian says to Harry. "Just let me go."

Harry looks at him warily but releases his grip. Sebastian's arm throbs in pain, and he wants another drink. There's a bar here, in the corner, and he makes his way towards it, steadying himself on each leather couch he passes and ignoring the students who glance up at him in judgment.

He reaches the bar and leans against the particle board, which is cool against the burning skin of his palms. The bartender looks at him, eyes narrowed.

"Double vodka shot, please," Sebastian says.

His tongue feels parched and his throat dry. His head pounds to the electronic beat. He still sees flashes of purple in the peripheries of his vision, but his eyes have adjusted to the dark, and now he looks around the room, which is decorated differently from the rest of the club. Bulbs hang from small metal chandeliers in the ceiling, though the pale white light they cast is barely visible against the purple flashing from over by the railing. The floor is a jarring zebra pattern, and the walls are decorated with generic contemporary art. The couches meanwhile are an ugly off-white, aggressively modern, all sharp angles and thin metal legs, and clearly uncomfortable to sit on.

But then Sebastian sees her in the center of the room, spotlit from above by one of the metal chandeliers, seated on one of the white couches with the confidence of someone who belongs there, leaning casually back, legs crossed, one arm resting on the top edge of the couch, and her red-orange hair glowing. She's sitting with others from their committee, next to The United States (a white guy in a white V-neck) and across from Nate and Malaysia. Helena's attention, though, is directed primarily at The United States, the two of them angled towards each other, his large hand resting just next to her leg, the white of his skin a vivid contrast to her black legging.

Sebastian moves towards them, taking a sip of his double shot of vodka and trying to appear as sober as possible.

"Hi," he says, putting his hand on Helena's couch.

Helena stares up at him.

"Hi!" she says, looking surprised to see him.

The United States gives Sebastian a brief, amused glance.

"May I join you?" Sebastian asks.

"Be my guest," Helena says, gesturing to the couch across from her.

Sebastian hoped to sit next to Helena, but he doesn't want to appear overeager, so he takes a seat next to Malaysia, who smiles at him and scooches to make room. Nate's bulk takes up most of the couch, and Sebastian finds himself pressed against Malaysia, her hand placed gently on his leg. In other circumstances he would be aroused, but now he feels nothing, as Malaysia, with her cherubic face and skin-tight jeans, looks like a high-school student compared to Helena reclining across from them with elegant noncha-lance, her mixed drink sitting casually before her, the black straw sticking upward from the ice. Sebastian holds his own drink awkwardly, and the condensation drips from the outside onto his pants. He wants to put it down on the table, but the surface is so small and there's so little room left he's afraid he'll spill it across the zebra floor. Under him, the leather couch squeaks loudly each time he moves.

Helena and The United States are talking, but it takes Sebastian a moment to focus on the conversation and push away the noise of the club.

"It is a strange topic," The United States says. "I just don't see the value in devoting so many UN resources to a few pieces of stolen art."

He's a tall, well-built guy, attractive in the modern way (chiseled jaw, big biceps), and the V-neck shirt he wears emphasizes his arms and chest. When Helena leans towards him, the white of her sweater blurs with his shirt.

"Oh come on," Helena says to him, with a hint of playfulness. "You know the art has value. Historical value. Cultural value. Why else do you think the Nazis worked so hard to destroy it?"

"I guess people do pay millions for it," The United

States admitted. "But still, it's an inflated market. The art doesn't have any intrinsic value. It's only valuable because people say it is."

Sebastian is annoyed but senses a way to draw Helena back towards him.

"Of course art has an intrinsic value," he says, leaning forward.

The United States smirks. "Are you an art history major too?"

"Yes," Sebastian says.

"But he only studies the nineteenth century," Helena says quickly. "The Pre-Raphaelites."

She pronounces the name emphatically, as if it's a joke. Sebastian feels hurt by her unexpected dismissiveness.

"What's wrong with the Pre-Raphaelites?" he asks.

"You mean besides the fact that their entire movement is just one big male-gaze circle-jerk?"

The United States laughs, even though Sebastian doubts he knows who the Pre-Raphaelites are. Sebastian meanwhile feels stunned. He thought Helena liked Rossetti's Beatrice. Didn't she call it beautiful?

"And I'm sorry," Helena continues, "but I have to say it's hard to take *Beata Beatrix* seriously when you consider that by the time Rossetti painted it in 1870, the Impressionists were already meeting and would soon be revolutionizing art. I'll admit, of course, that today the Impressionists are very tedious and bourgeois, but at least they played an important role in the trajectory of art history, whereas the Pre-Raphaelites were just some anachronistic aberration of Romanticism, fifty years too late, leading to nothing but Aestheticism, which is of course the great dead end of culture. Honestly, I feel like people only like the Pre-Raphaelites because they're so easy to like, beauty that ignores any possible ideological complications, history airbrushed of everything but maidens in castles. It's just the nostalgia of people on the verge of growing up who want to rush back to a comforting and idealized version of childhood."

Her words shatter Sebastian, like a mirror into a thousand shards. He stares at her, dumbstruck and overwhelmed with emotion. In a flash, her divine light disappears, the white glow of her sweater and the remnants of the neon martini halo from outside blinking out in an instant, as if someone has pulled the plug. All that's left is the blinding purple light, reflecting off her sweater and surrounding her in a sinister halo.

On his right, Malaysia leans towards him.

"I like the Pre-Raphaelites," she says, in her high-pitched voice.

She gives his thigh a squeeze. Across from them, Helena smirks and takes a sip from her drink.

"Alright," The United States says, turning his body towards Helena. "I'll admit you're right. The art has some value, even from an economic perspective, since you can monetize the historical and cultural importance and approach it as a supply and demand issue—"

"It's not just about the fucking economics!" Sebastian says.

He speaks louder than he intends, the words "monetize" and "supply and demand" having passed through his brain like knives ripping through canvas. Helena's smirk falls away, and she and The United States look surprised at Sebastian's anger.

"Is that all you can think of?" he continues, staring at The United States. "Is that all art is to you? Just a fucking wad of cash, a line item in a budget, a pending transaction on your Bank of America account—"

"Oh calm the fuck down," Helena says. Her eyes flash like shards of glass, and Sebastian recoils at the coldness of her voice. "Art has always had an economic side. Do you think Renaissance artists painted and sculpted whatever they wanted? They did what their patrons told them to do, what bankers like the Medicis paid them to do. You can wish all you want that art be freed from commerce, but even your Pre-Raphaelites had to pay the goddamn bills."

"But that's not where the value comes from!" Sebastian says, his blood racing. He doesn't care anymore about impressing Helena—he wants only to defend his artistic ideal against the onslaught of her disillusioning modernism. "The art the Nazis looted isn't just valuable because some collector might pay hundreds of millions for it, or even because it's associated with a historical period or cultural movement. It's valuable because of what it is!" Sebastian is still drunk, but he's speaking now with surprising clarity, even as his heart beats faster and faster. "I mean, have you seen that missing painting of Raphael's that we talked about in committee, *Portrait of a Young Man,* his self portrait, the one stolen by the Nazis? When we lost that painting, we lost more than just *money* or even some representative work from some historical period, since it's not like we're lacking in art from the Renaissance. No, that painting had value because of its individual artistic merits, its individual *aesthetic* merits—" (here he uses a word that he knows will annoy her), "—and so when we lost that painting, first and foremost we lost those specific colors and that specific canvas and that specific image of that specific young man—"

"You mean this young man?" The United States asks.

He holds up his iPhone, which displays the painting, via its Wikipedia page. Raphael's face stares back at Sebastian, the long brown hair, the black hat, the fur draped over the body, the puffy folds of the white shirt underneath, the pink, sandy wall behind him, and the distant Italian landscape beyond.

"Doesn't look missing to me," The United States says.

"It's not the same," Sebastian says. "It's just a photo."

"I think they referenced it in a Simpson's episode," Nate says.

"But why isn't it the same?" The United States asks, staring at the painting on his phone. "Why is the original so valuable? Why have we wasted so much capital—" (Sebastian bristles at the word) "—trying to recover it?"

"Because it's a unique cultural artifact—"

"Unique?" Helena asks, laughing. "I agree it's valuable, but it's not as if we don't already have a hundred portraits of young men."

"But they're not all the same!" Sebastian says, a wild edge creeping into his voice. "Each young man is different—"

"Okay," The United States says, "but then why couldn't someone just print out a high quality version of this photo, frame it, and claim it's the original? Why would it matter if it wasn't?"

"But it wouldn't be real!" Sebastian says.

He's desperate now to make this V-necked asshole understand, but desperate also to assuage his own fears, because, though he won't admit it, when he stares at that painting reproduced in pixelated perfection on the screen of the iPhone, he wonders whether The United States isn't right. The truth is, Sebastian wouldn't be able to tell the difference between that photo and the original. He's never even seen the original. To him, Raphael's self-portrait exists only as a reproduction, and yet still he's moved by it each time he sees it. Doesn't that call into question every piece of art he's ever seen? In a museum, he's never been as compelled by a painting he sees for the first time as he is by the ones he's sought out himself after seeing them first in an art history textbook. So is he really moved by the painting itself, or just a memory of a reproduction? Does it really matter to him then if this is actually the canvas that Raphael's brush touched or just an iPhone screen touched by some douchebag in a V-neck? When he thinks of *Beata Beatrix*, does he imagine the one hanging in the marble halls of the museum or the one reflected back at him from his laptop? Does he think of Dante's original or the second version with the perdella? And even then, does it matter, since either way, when he thinks about any piece of art, it's not actually the physical image he sees before him, but just a memory, a reproduction in his own head, which, no matter what, is already one step removed from reality? If that's the case, does the physicality of anything even actually matter? Was the idealized Helena he constructed in his brain and believed wanted to fuck him any more unreal than the real Rosalind he fucked in the storage closet? And is the real Helena sitting before him now who he knows now will never fuck him any more real than the red-haired Lorelei who he doesn't actually remember fucking? Weren't they all just as unreal as the faux-Madeline he conjured up in Viola's apartment?

He stares down at the zebra floor and feels his head spin. When he looks back up, Helena and The United States are kissing, her hands on his chest and neck, his bicep around her shoulder. Sebastian feels woozy and wonders how much time has passed since their conversation about art. The United States' iPhone lies on the table, next to their drinks, the portrait of Raphael still staring out into the world.

Sebastian turns to his right to find Malaysia facing him. Behind her looms Nate, who since they sat down has inched closer and closer to her, leaving a large empty space on the other side of the couch. Sebastian is on the verge of falling off his end and onto the dizzying zebra floor, and he has to place his arm around Malaysia to keep himself seated. Malaysia doesn't seem to mind and leans into him, both hands on his thigh now. Her pupils are dilated and her lips curved into a smile. Her breath smells putrid, a mix of beer, vodka, and cranberries.

"I didn't get your name," Sebastian says.

"Elena," she says.

Elena. How ridiculous. A lesser version of Helena. But ultimately wasn't one as good as the other? Her jeans and T-shirt were the farthest thing from Helena's black and white elegance, but that elegance was currently intertwined on the white leather couch with The United States' torso and arms, and Elena was right here, and if she didn't speak, and he closed his eyes, couldn't he just pretend that she was Helena? Would it really be all that different?

A minute later, Sebastian finds himself in one of the bathrooms, the door locked and his tongue in Elena's mouth. She tastes of day-old alcohol, and her lips are extremely dry. The bathroom is made completely of metal, the sink, the walls, the urinal, the stall, and even, bizarrely, the floor. The air smells of chemical soaps and cleaning products. Sebastian doesn't remember the journey here from the leather couches, or what he said, or how upset Nate was, or whether Helena noticed. His hand moves mechanically to Elena's jeans, unbuttoning them and slipping itself inside and into her underwear. She's as wet down there as her mouth is dry. Her lips make splotchy sounds as she sucks at his face. He tries not to look at her while they kiss, but every wall of the bathroom is like a blurry mirror reflecting the bright fluorescent lights. Above them, a fan whirs, and outside Sebastian can still hear the faint beat of the music.

Elena kneels on the floor, unzips Sebastian's pants, and yanks them down. The metal bathroom wall is shockingly cold against the skin of his ass. Elena's hands are warm though, and she places one against his thigh and grabs his penis with the other, and then beings to suck on it. Her mouth is warm too, but the feeling isn't pleasant. Her lips, too dry just a few moments ago, are suddenly too wet, and spit dribbles into Sebastian's pubic hair. Her tongue isn't really moving and just lies at the bottom of her mouth, occasionally brushing against his shaft or the skin around his scrotum. Most importantly, he's not hard, and can't seem to get hard, and his penis hangs limply in the swamp of her mouth.

Sebastian closes his eyes and tries to imagine she's Helena. But he can't imagine Helena kneeling like this, dirtying her black leggings even on this immaculate metal floor. He also can't imagine Helena ever condescending to give a guy a blowjob. No, she would demand the guy be on his knees, while she sits up on the metal sink, her legs spread open while her hand holds his head down until all he can taste is her clitoris…

The thought briefly revives Sebastian and he feels himself growing hard, but when he opens his eyes to see the top of Elena's head jerking back and forth furiously like a bobblehead toy, he feels himself go soft again. He pushes at Elena's head to get her to stop.

"What's wrong?" she asks, looking up.

There's spittle running down her chin and a strand of his pubic hair hanging off the end of her lip.

"I'm just not feeling it," Sebastian says.

He buttons up his pants. His penis is still wet and the dampness in his underwear makes him feel like he's pissed himself. Elena looks sad and stares up at him from the bathroom floor.

"I'm sorry," Sebastian says, shaking his head.

He turns and stumbles out the metal bathroom door without looking back. Outside in the VIP section, purple light assaults his vision once again and electronic music pounds at his ears. The club teeters like an unsteady seascape, and the leather couches bob like lifeboats, glowing a taunting angelic white. Sebastian's stomach churns violently, and he turns and vomits all over the full-length mirror beside the bathroom door. It leaves a watery mess that drips steadily to the floor and a yellow and beige streak slashing diagonally across his reflection, like an abstract painting. His nostrils begin to tingle from the smell.

Before he can orient himself or wipe the lingering vomit from his lips, he feels a strong set of hands grab him by the shoulders.

"That's enough," the bouncer says. "You're done here."

Sebastian feels himself dragged away, the zebra floor moving under his stumbling feet and the bulbs in the metal chandeliers burning brightly overhead. He tries to protest, but his throat is too dry. He looks across the couches but doesn't see Helena's red-orange hair anywhere. He feels a sharp pain in his head, and he closes his eyes, but even the darkness seems made of purple light.

"He's with me," a familiar voice says.

"He needs to go," the bouncer says. "Now."

"Okay. I'll take him."

Sebastian feels his weight transferred to another set of arms, thinner and lankier, and he opens his eyes and finds himself being helped down the stairs by Harry. Sebastian instinctively tries to pull away, but Harry holds on firmly until they've crossed the slate floor and passed coat-check and are back outside in the cold. When Harry lets go, Sebastian feels his muscles sag, and he has to lean over and put his hands on his knees to keep himself upright.

The bouncer at the threshold stares at him warily.

"If you're going to puke, do it in the alley," he says.

Sebastian doesn't puke, but he remains bent over, his vision still unsteady, while Harry calls a taxi. Afterwards, Harry looks at Sebastian with resignation.

"What?" Sebastian asks, looking up, his hands still on his knees.

"I just can't believe you," Harry says, shaking his head. "I ask you for one thing, to give this conference your best effort so that we don't lose the club. But all you care about is trying to fuck another white girl."

Sebastian feels himself tremble with rage, and he does his best to stand up straight.

"Oh, you're one to fucking talk!" he says, spitting out the words. "*Hari* Kumar!"

The name makes Harry flinch, and Sebastian feels a surge of pleasure.

"Tell me, *Hari*," he continues, his voice rising with drunken energy. "Do you ever tell any of the white girls you try and flirt with your real name? Or do you always pretend to be half-white, like me?" He's smiling now, amused at

Harry's discomfort. "That's what you've always wanted, isn't it? To be like me?"

Harry stares back at him, and his eyes narrow.

"Maybe once, Sebastian," he says. "But not anymore. Not after seeing what you did to Fatima."

Harry turns back to the club, and the bouncer lets him back in. Sebastian wants to say something, to defend himself, to have the last word—but he's utterly speechless, like a Model UN delegate with no arguments left to make. All he can do is stare at Harry's retreating form until it disappears into the darkness.

❁

Sebastian doesn't wait for the taxi Harry called and decides instead to walk back to The Comstock Inn, even though he doesn't know the way. The wind whips at his hair and face and pulls his shirt against his body, but he doesn't feel the chill, even as the skin of his hands turns red. Instead the air feels hot, and sweat pours down his face. Overhead, a gibbous moon hangs low in the cloudless sky, casting a strange orange light that makes the city look ablaze, like a hellscape, an inferno, but with no angel to guide him through.

It's early for a Saturday night, only midnight, and the sidewalks are still filled with crowds that Sebastian has to shoulder his way through, mostly young people standing in line for clubs or smoking in shivering clusters outside bars, a few middle-aged people stepping out of fancy hotels to hail taxis, an old homeless man begging outside the stairs of an L station. Occasionally Sebastian passes under a set of Chicago's multilevel streets, which rise above him like a sinister Tower of Babel, the rusted steel beams shaking each time a car passes overhead and the howling wind like the cry of a man who's just thrown himself from the top. Roving yellow headlights fill the dark streets ahead of him, but to

Sebastian, none of them appear angelic, just dirty rays illuminating the grime streaking the weathered buildings and the potholes scarring the roads. He stumbles through a crosswalk, and a car honks and swerves behind him. His heart beats in steady rhythm with each of his thudding footfalls, and the world around him spins in slow motion.

Eventually, he enters the business district, where the streets grow quiet. A few lights illuminate the upper floors of the glass buildings, and doormen stand solemnly in front of luxury apartment towers, but very few cars pass by. With no yellow headlights to balance its glow, the orange moon is brighter than before, and it drowns the towers in fiery light, which reflects off every window. For a moment the city looks unreal, like a painting by Hieronymus Bosch or Pieter Bruegel the Elder prophesying the end of the world, the homeless man's countdown in visual form. But then Sebastian smells the foul wind, a mix of gasoline and rotting garbage, and feels the sweat all over his body, and he knows that the city is unmistakably real, not a painting in some museum, not a flickering phantom in a snowscape. Each glass tower and each still-lit window speaks of the real world, of people working, of life after college, and overlaid atop it all he suddenly hears Fatima's voice, not crackling and distant over a phone like in Montreal but in his head and in the sky, booming like the voice of God:

"You're a horrible person, Sebastian, the worst kind of person, not just a cheater, but a liar too! How on earth can you go from holding my hand and crying at your mother's grave to having sex with one of your Model UN whores on the same fucking day? The same fucking day! How can any good person do that?" They're the words she spoke to him a month ago, when, after their breakup, she came to his apartment to collect her toothbrush and spare clothes. But tonight he feels like he's hearing them for the first time. "I proposed to you, Sebastian! I was vulnerable! I was honest! I opened myself up to you! But you just lied to me, like it was nothing! Like I was nothing! I got Harry to admit by the way that it wasn't even the first time, that you had sex with a bunch of girls this year—and so I just don't understand! Cheating is one thing, but you made me think you actually cared about me! That you loved me! That you wanted to spend your life with me! I thought we were going to live in the city together, get married, maybe even have kids. But you were lying to me this whole time! Like a fucking sociopath!" He can hear Fatima crying, and each sob tears at his heart. "I don't know what you're looking for in all these girls, Sebastian, but I hope you never find it! Never, never, NEVER!"

Sebastian soon reaches the glittering water of the Chicago River and one of its many bridges. The surface shimmers under the orange moon and the yellow lights, and he feels dizzy, as if he were underneath and trying to swim to the surface. Across the water, past the bridge's red metal railings, rises the glass tower of the Hyatt, where only this afternoon he and Helena sat in committee. Had it really been less than a day? To his left the river empties into the black mass of the lake, and to his right the river plunges into the city under more bridges, with grand buildings looming over it on either side. The river looks small and powerless against the city, as if it's the buildings that are guiding its course, and Sebastian feels a wave of sadness as he imagines it winding its way through a sea of metal and glass, lost and lonely, in search of whatever it is that rivers seek.

On each side of the bridge rise two stone bridge houses, each with a sculpture of a scene from Chicago's history. Sebastian stares at the sculpture before him and tries to bring his blurry vision into focus. After a moment, he sees that the sculpture depicts an explorer in seventeenth-century garb, standing tall and proud and staring off into the distance. Behind the explorer stands a Jesuit priest, his hand on the explorer's arm, while around them crowd several Native Americans, some kneeling, some standing, all clearly subservient to the great White Men. Above them is a magisterial woman, holding a torch and a shield, most likely the personification of some abstract virtue. An inscription below the sculpture reads:

> *The Discoverers—Jolliet, Father Marquette, La Salle, and Tonti will live in American history as fearless explorers who made their way through the Great Lakes and across this watershed to the Mississippi in the late seventeenth century and typify the spirit of brave adventure which has always been firmly planted in the character of the middle west. Presented to the city by William Wrigley Jr., 1928.*

It's the kind of art Sebastian is supposed to like, grand, romantic, symbolic. But here it's a joke. The inscription makes it seem as though Tonti is an equal participant in this fearless act of exploration, whereas the sculpture clearly puts him in an inferior position relative to Jolliet and Marquette. And then there is the woman-angel, the greatest of the sculpture's lies. Sebastian knows now that in life there are no angels guiding people towards discoveries. The reality of Jolliet's expedition must have been quite different than the image here. Mud-soaked, tired, wary of attacks from neighboring Native Americans, he probably never believed in any kind of Manifest Destiny. To him, the lakeside that would become Chicago would have been no different than the rest of the continent, cold, windy, green only sometimes, surrounded on all sides by people hostile to his colonizing presence.

In the lie of this sculpture, Sebastian sees the lie in all art, and especially the art he loves, the art that Helena so derided, the art of the Pre-Raphaelites. Those paintings of beautiful women aren't mirrors of reality. They are only comforting illusions that tell Sebastian what he wants to see. That mantra of John Keats on which Sebastian has based his life, that beauty and truth are one and the same, is in fact a lie. In truth, Beatrice might never have been a divine, graceful presence, kneeling in a ruined city while symbolic doves fluttered to her hands. Perhaps she never loved Dante at all. Perhaps Dante's poetry and Rossetti's painting are lies like this sculpture. Perhaps that hoped-for reunion in Paradise, when Beatrice will throw herself into Dante's open arms, is nothing more than yet another fantasy of deluded men.

Sebastian feels a sudden chill as a cold wind sweeps along the river. He realizes he left his coat in the club's coat check. Shivering, he stumbles away from the bridge but trips on the sidewalk and almost falls over the railing and into the river. The water churns below him, a dark, undulating mass, and the orange moon shimmers on its surface, bobbing like something that's slipped from his grasp, Helena's glowing head of hair disappearing gradually into the black depths. Sebastian imagines diving for it and trying to reach it as it recedes before him, following the glow until he's far below the Earth's surface and is falling through Dante's hell, not stopping until he reaches the center, passing the lustful in the second circle and the Epicureans in the sixth circle and even the fraudulent in the eighth circle until he's down in the deepest level of the ninth circle with the traitors and the oathbreakers, swallowed up in one of the mouths of Satan—

Sebastian backs away from the water, shaking from the cold and feeling unsteady on his feet. He spins around, trying to make sense of where he is, but the buildings blur together into one giant glass mass, and he doesn't remember whether he's already crossed the bridge or not. He looks for the Hyatt but all the lights and the moon fuse together into one orange glow. The air smells of gasoline, even though he can't see a car in either direction. There's a street sign nearby, but it's too dark and his vision is too blurry, and so it might as well say "Purgatorio."

Sebastian turns around and around, wondering desperately what to do. His Motorola Razr doesn't have wifi, and so he can't just pull up Google Maps and navigate his way back to The Comstock, though even if he did have an iPhone, he's far too drunk to figure out how to use it. He feels simultaneously hot and cold, the air chilly but his face and body covered in sweat, which soaks through his shirt. In frustration, he tears off his blazer and throws it to the ground. He stumbles as he does and has to catch himself on the bridge house sculpture.

Breathing hard, he stares down at the crumbled blazer lying on the sidewalk. The blue looks black in the darkness, but Sebastian imagines that the right kind of light will reveal all the times he's ever stained it, all the whiskey, vodka, gin, beer, wine (and semen) he's spilled or spit onto it, somehow still there, preserved despite all the dry-cleaning, a canvas of all his misdeeds. He wants to burn the blazer and scatter its ashes out among the high-rises. But he has no lighter or source of fire, and instead the thought of flames make him feel cold, and so he picks it up and slips it back on.

He takes out his phone and scrolls through his recent calls, trying to read the names beneath the cracked screen. He doesn't want to endure the shame of asking Harry for help, and he doesn't think Nate will be willing after the Malaysia incident—but when he reaches Viola's name he stops. After a moment, he presses the green button and puts the phone to his ear and waits.

"Hello?"

Her voice is groggy and half-asleep but also comforting and familiar.

"Viola! Viola, I need your help…"

"Sebastian?"

"I'm…I'm lost. I don't know where I am."

There's a pause. He can hear Viola's breathing and some shuffling.

"Viola, please!" he says again, louder this time. "I need help! I don't know which way to go!"

"Okay, okay, calm down Sebastian, calm down. Where are you?"

"I don't…I don't know. There are buildings. Glass buildings, lights everywhere. It's really cold, but I keep sweating."

"It's okay, you've just had too much to drink. Tell me what the cross streets are."

"I don't know. I'm at a river and bridge. There's an ugly, racist sculpture."

"What?"

"It's got Indians kneeling and white people looking into the distance and an angel in the sky…it's so ugly, Viola, it's so fucking ugly!"

"Okay, Sebastian. Give me a minute."

There's a crushing, awful silence. Sebastian spins in place. All directions look the same. He sees the Hyatt across the river, and his eyes trace their way upward, up the windows along the side, all the way into the cloudless black overhead. If there are stars up there, he can't see them, though several of the windows of the hotel shine far more brightly. He wonders if Helena and The United States are up in one of those rooms.

"Viola. Are you there?"

"I'm here, Sebastian."

"Please don't leave."

"I'm not going anywhere. I think I've found the sculpture you're looking at. Is it called The Discoverers?"

"Yes! Yes!"

"Okay. You're on the Michigan Avenue Bridge. You're not far. Which direction are you facing?"

"I don't know. I have no idea where anything is."

"It's okay. The sculpture is on the north side of the bridge. The Hyatt should be across the river. You need to walk across the bridge towards it."

"How far?"

"Just walk, and when you get to the other side, I'll tell you where to go."

Sebastian walks quickly, trying not to look over the railing at the water below. He can hear Viola's steady breathing on the other end of the phone. He clings to it and wishes she would speak again, just so he could hear her voice. Even the memory of it from moments ago is soothing, cooling his sweating brow, warming his chilly body.

He reaches the other side of the bridge and looks up at the Hyatt. The street looks familiar now, and he remembers leaving the lobby this afternoon with Helena.

"I've crossed," he says.

"Okay. Keep walking, down this street."

He does what Viola says, feeling lighter on his feet. After a few blocks, the glass skyscrapers disappear on his left and he can see the full canvas of the sky stretching above Millennium Park. The orange moon is somewhere behind him, hidden behind an old stone building. The air still smells of gasoline, but he no longer feels so cold, and the sweat on his brow is drying.

Viola continues guiding him from street to street, her voice soft and soothing as she tells him each new turn. Eventually, he sees a familiar set of high-rises and between them the square white roof and red awning of The Comstock Inn.

"I see it," he says. "I see it!"

His head spins as he rushes forward into the street.

"I'm out front," Viola's voice says. "I think I see you."

She's there, standing under the awning. Her blond hair, though disheveled from sleep, is angelic and whips gently in the wind. She's wearing jeans and a T-shirt, and her eyes look tired.

Sebastian has never been happier to see anyone in his life, and he stumbles across the grass towards her.

"Viola!"

She catches him before he falls on the concrete. He can smell her body, a warm, human smell. Her voice still echoes in his ears, drowning out the unpleasant silence. He leans his weight against her with relief.

"Thank you!" he says. "Thank you so much!"

"Hey, don't worry about it," Viola says. "I knew you wouldn't be that far away."

"I thought I was lost…"

"You're fine now. You're fine."

She leads him tenderly to the door of the hotel. He smells the grass under his feet, freshly watered earlier that night. The wooden door is old and takes a moment to open. Inside, the small lobby is dark and the reception desk closed. Old floral-patterned sofas line the common room and remind Sebastian of ones he saw in old photographs of his grandmother's house in Pakistan. They give off a musty odor, which Sebastian inhales with pleasure.

Viola leads him down the narrow hallway to one of the club's shared rooms. He's comforted by the peeling wallpaper and the overhead light, which flickers with each step they take. Viola uses an old-fashioned metal key to open the door, which creaks as they enter. She leads Sebastian across the brown carpeting. Above, an old ceiling fan gently spins. The bathroom door is slightly ajar, and inside Sebastian sees the chipped toilet and the dirty tiles and hears the drip of the shower.

"I puked," he says, turning to Viola.

"It's okay," she says.

She leads him into the bathroom and pulls the chain for the light. After a moment, it flickers on. Viola closes the door while Sebastian leans against the sink. He stares at himself in the mirror. Vomit streaks his lip and chin, and his blazer is a dirty and disheveled mess. His glasses are slightly askew, and his eyes are glazed over, the pupils so dilated that nothing seems to remain of the irises, as if Sebastian's eyes are lifeless and someone has already placed small black coins over them for his passage to the underworld, the payment for Charon to ferry him across the river Styx.

Viola takes a towel and wipes Sebastian's chin and then hands him a cup of water. As he rinses his mouth, she applies paste to his toothbrush and then watches as he brushes. She smiles, and their eyes meet through the mirror.

Afterwards, Viola gives him a Tylenol for his headache. She switches off the light as they leave the bathroom. Sebastian stares across the small room with its double beds. Nate is in one, sprawled across it, still in his clothes, snoring. Two sophomore members of their club sleep in the other. Harry and the rest of their delegation are in a different room.

Viola pulls Sebastian down to the floor, where she's laid out a blanket for herself. She takes off his glasses, sets them on the nearby table, and pulls off his blazer. She slips off her own jeans and gets under the blanket, while Sebastian changes out of his clothes and into a T-shirt. He's meant to sleep next to Nate, but the last thing Sebastian wants is to be squeezed onto the edge of the bed like he was on the couch in the club. Instead, Sebastian snuggles up next to Viola, who puts her arm comfortingly around him. Her body is warm, and he can feel her beating heart.

"Are you okay?" she asks.

She speaks in a whisper, but even in the faint syllables, Sebastian can hear traces of the earlier melodies that guided him through the darkness. Her mouth is inches from his own. Her breath smells of toothpaste and sleep, and he can feel it blowing against his lips.

"No," he whispers back. "I'm not okay. I'm all fucked up…"

"You'll be fine," she says, holding him close. "You'll be fine."

He closes his eyes and rests his head next to hers. The skin of their foreheads touch. As he falls asleep, he feels her body against his, rising and falling with each breath, and he listens to her heart and his beating in tandem.

CHAPTER NINE

THE EVE OF ST. AGNES (1848)

She walks across Memorial Glade, blond hair swishing across the shoulders of her blue blazer, the warm, late-spring wind ruffling the hem of her black skirt. Over one shoulder is slung her leather messenger bag, and as she vaults the steps to Doe Library, her black boots clicking a jaunty beat against the stones, the bag swings in rhythm with her hair. Sebastian sees her from his spot on the glade, where he sits reading *Beowulf* and thinking about his final paper on mortality in Old English poetry. He wants to call to her but she's too far away, and he can only listen as her clicking steps disappear under the bust of Athena.

It's surprising to see Viola like this, out in the open air of campus, alone. Since that night in their Chicago hotel, he's seen her plenty of times, first on stage for the conference's closing ceremony where she accepted her award for Best Delegate and where the entire Berkeley team posed for a photo after winning Best Small Delegation (with a beaming Harry standing front and center), then at the final UCBMUN meeting a week ago where she clapped with the rest of them as Harry proudly announced that due to their victory in Chicago the ASUC had agreed to continue funding the club, and then most recently at the final UCBMUN party on Sebastian and Harry's rooftop where she celebrated like everyone else in a final bout of Dionysian revelry and congratulated next year's President and Officer Board (among them Nate, who managed to win his election as Vice President after giving an eloquent speech in which he cited "everything [he's] learned this past year from traveling conference to conference with the club's graduating members, especially Sebastian Khan."). Yet each time, Sebastian and Viola never had a moment alone together. Now everything is ending, and he doesn't know if he'll get another chance to see her. Today is the last official day of instruction, and in a few hours Sebastian will have his final undergraduate lecture, on Byzantine History. Meanwhile the homeless man's countdown reads 15 DAYS TILL THE END, two weeks that will flit by with a few exams, two final papers, and, of course, graduation itself. Sebastian has already picked up his cap and gown from the table on Sproul Plaza, and the white box now sits at the foot of his bed, and every morning Sebastian stares mournfully down at it, as if it contains the shift of a condemned man set to be executed. And yet, despite all these signs of endings towering around him like the campus's shadowy buildings, he still can't help but think of the personal, of Viola lying next to him in the cozy room of the Comstock, the warm scent of her body, the feel of it against his own, her blond hair and blue eyes, her troubadour's voice singing him to sleep.

He stands and puts *Beowulf* away and walks over to Doe Library, up the stone steps and over to the benches. He stares up at the long windows of the North Reading Room and wonders if Viola will enter and sit at the end of the table, crossing her legs and waving down at him with her black boots.

He pulls out his broken phone and types out a text

to Viola: *Hey—I feel like I haven't seen you in forever. Grab a drink tonight?* He hesitates, surprised at how unsure he feels. Before he can change his mind, though, he pushes "send" and closes his phone.

He sits down on one of the stone benches across from the window. Students breeze in and out under the bust of Athena. A professor stands by the entrance and smokes a cigarette. A girl at the other end of the bench chatters away on the phone to what sound like her parents. Inside the reading room, the tables are filled with students, who sit with headphones in their ears and books open, cramming for their impending finals. There's not a space anywhere open for Viola, but Sebastian waits nonetheless, hoping that she'll stroll casually down the aisle and that a chair will materialize for her at the end of the table. If so, when she sits she'll be framed perfectly within the lattices of the window, and the light from inside that filters out to him will shroud her in a bronze glow and give her a historical aura, casting her as some sculptured goddess from antiquity.

He thinks of when he first saw Viola, almost four years ago now. He was in an unfamiliar apartment on Telegraph, a building built in a kitschy style with two faux-Corinthian columns flanking the entrance, and he was staring around at a group of people he'd only just met at his first Model UN meeting the previous week and holding in his hand a red cup with a mixed drink (a few shots of vodka with just a splash of diet coke) that one of the seniors had made for him. Sebastian was unfamiliar then with the Berkeley party atmosphere, the chorus of shouts and laughter that drifted out the partially open window and greeted him as he pushed open the gate, the sharp scent of alcohol that stung his nose as he entered the apartment, the warm and stuffy feel of over fifty bodies piled across IKEA furniture, and so even he was nervous and tentative that night, wondering if perhaps he shouldn't have come and whether, after an hour of shaking a few hands and exchanging a few "what-do-you-study"'s, he should have another vodka or just leave. That was when he spotted her, leaning against the distant wall, near the balcony doors, gently sipping from a red cup. She wore jeans, a plain black shirt, and what Sebastian would come to know as her classic blue blazer, much the same as his own, rolled up at the sleeves to reveal the lining underneath. The red of her cup stood out in vivid contrast to her blond hair, and behind her, the stone balcony's iron railings looked like something straight out of the past, and if it wasn't for her very modern attire, she could have been standing in a painting from the nineteenth century.

She noticed Sebastian from across the room and smiled at him first. He was flustered, still off balance from the unfamiliar world of college, but he did smile back and watch as she approached him, weaving her way through the crowd of laughing bodies, her steps in sync with the hipster-rock playing from the small speakers by the host's MacBook Pro.

"Hi," she said. "Are you new here too?"

"I am," he said.

"Nice to meet you. I'm Viola."

"Sebastian."

They shook hands. Her skin was cool in contrast to the warm air around them. He noticed her eyes, pale blue, brought out by the apartment's dim, dusky light.

Back in the present, he stares up at the window, for a full half an hour, thinking of that day in the past, waiting for her now to enter and take her seat at the far end of the table, toying with his phone in case it vibrates with a response. But it never does, and she never comes, and soon the bells of the Campanile ring out 1 p.m. It's that vibration and not his phone's that floods the campus, traveling through the air and down Sebastian's spine, and it feels to him as if all of Berkeley is ringing with that mournful note.

❋

Professor Walter is seated at his desk, legs crossed, leaning back in his chair. The room around him is entirely unchanged from the beginning of the year, with the same posters on the wall, the same books, the same bust of Epicurus holding down a stack of papers. The air still smells of old paper and leather, but whereas once Sebastian found the smell comforting, now it seems stale and makes the room feel claustrophobic. Walter is as equally unchanged as his office, still dressed in baggy slacks and a loose dress shirt, the gray in his hair in exactly the same place, not a single strand of his mustache altered since their last meeting.

"*Beowulf,* is it? Not a bad way to finish, ending at the beginning. Do you know what you're writing about?"

"Sort of," Sebastian says.

"And have you finished classes?"

"One more, in an hour. Byzantine History."

"Oh, exciting! I always found the Byzantines the most *tragic* of collapsed empires. There's a unique melancholy one feels wandering through the ruins of the Theodosian Walls just outside central Istanbul."

"I might skip it."

Walter's eyes narrow in uncharacteristic disappointment.

"Now why on earth would you do that?" he asks.

"Does it even matter?" Sebastian says. "I already did the reading. I know what happens. The Ottomans win. Constantinople falls. Constantine XI dies. The Byzantine Empire goes the way of all empires before it."

"Well, that's history. But it's worth studying, even if it's inevitable."

"I don't see how attending a lecture on the last days of the Byzantine Empire will help me in the future."

"The future? Since when have *you* cared about the future?"

"Isn't that what college is for? To prepare us for the future? To help us get jobs and careers?"

He says this in a voice dripping with disdain, as a bold challenge to everything he knows Walter stands for. As expected, Walter looks aghast, as if Sebastian has announced he'll do something horrifying, like kill someone or burn every known copy of the collected works of John Keats.

"That's not what college is for!" Walter says. "College is about *learning* things. Not about getting a *job!* Do you think the university is some kind of factory, where you put in your hours, and after four years they hand you a job at your graduation ceremony along with your diploma, like a paycheck? A job, a career, those are things you get *after* college, after you've stumbled through the world for five, ten, fifteen years!" Walter's expression then softens. "It may not give you the answers about the future, Sebastian, but perhaps reflecting on the end of a thousand-year-old civilization is the kind of distance you need."

Sebastian sighs and leans back in his chair, silent for a long moment. He thinks of the fall of Constantinople, of Constantine XI fleeing in terror from a line of charging Ottoman sipahis.

"You know what I've realized?" he finally says. "About *Beowulf,* and really Anglo-Saxon poetry as a whole. It's all about failure."

Walter pauses and stares at Sebastian, looking entirely unconvinced.

"Do elaborate."

"Well, in reading *Beowulf* again, I can't help but think about the ending. Beowulf dies and is buried in some earthen mound. And that gives everything this melancholy cast, and suddenly, I'm seeing images of death everywhere in the poem. The poet will describe the glorious hall of Heorot but then also foreshadow its ultimate destruction. He'll tell of how great the Danes and the Geats are, but then remind us that they will one day be wiped out. And we ourselves know that their Pagan culture won't withstand the oncoming tide of Christianity. Then of course there's the

Dragon-hoard where the dragon that Beowulf fights lives, a hoard that was described as once being the barrow of an old King whose name has been forgotten. So, in the end, when Beowulf is buried in a similar barrow, how are we not meant to see it as an image of failure? Beowulf is dead and soon his barrow will become a dragon-hoard and his name will also be forgotten."

"But you're forgetting one thing," Walter says. "Beowulf isn't forgotten. And as far as I know, there's no sequel to the poem in which his barrow becomes the home of a dragon some future king will fight. No, Beowulf's name still lives on, over a thousand years later, bandied about by university intellectuals. The *poem* is his true barrow, and it's preserved him, made him immortal—"

"I'm tired of that argument," Sebastian says. "Every intellectual keeps falling back on that idea, that somehow in existing, art preserves its subjects forever, that it's some kind of Fountain of Youth—"

"But you *yourself* made that argument!" Walter pulls open a drawer and rifles through it, and after a moment, he produces a stapled set of papers, which he tosses before Sebastian, next to the bust of Epicurus. "In your essay on *The Eve of St. Agnes!*"

"I remember—"

"You said that the poem is Keats's declaration that art immortalizes, the same declaration he made in *Ode on a Grecian Urn*. Prophyro and Madeline and all their sensory experiences are preserved in those lines even after the beadsman has counted his rosary and died—"

"But maybe I was wrong. Maybe I was just young, and that's why I read everything that way. Maybe Keats wasn't trying to say that art preserves youth but that even the young grow old. Maybe Keats didn't see himself as Prophyro and Madeline but as the beadsman, bookending this fairy-tale romance, imagining unreal tales of immortal love while he himself grows old—"

"Keats was twenty-three when he wrote that poem, so I hardly think he was afraid of aging—"

"Why not? You don't think twenty-three-year-olds are afraid of getting old?" Sebastian is standing now, leaning over the desk, his passionately gesticulating hand inches away from accidentally sending the bust of Epicurus flying against the far wall. "I'm only twenty-two and that's *all* I fucking think about!"

Sebastian stops and hears his own wild breathing and his heart beating frantically in his chest, and suddenly he's aware how quiet the room is. He closes his eyes and feels a wave of embarrassment.

"I'm sorry," he says, sitting back down.

"It's alright." Walter looks at him sympathetically. "I understand."

Sebastian opens his eyes and stares at his essay and at the name "Madeline." He thinks of the poem, and of the various Pre-Raphaelite paintings of its scenes (a favorite subject among the nineteenth-century Victorians), of John Everett Millais's stoic Madeline, standing in her blue dress and about to disrobe, of Daniel Maclise's more sensual Madeline, unfurling her hair just after prayer, her dress already slipping down to reveal the curve of a shoulder, of William Holman Hunt's more humble Madeline, about to flee with Porphyro past the passed-out revelers who lie asleep across the stony ground. But in the faces of these Madelines, Sebastian sees only Viola. He imagines taking her hand and fleeing with her out into the storm, past the beadsman and into immortality.

"There's something else that's changed," Sebastian says. "I think I'm in love."

Walter looks at him, surprised.

"Are you sure?"

Sebastian nods.

"I think I've been in love this whole time without realizing it."

Walter frowns.

"You know, it's moments like these when people start making *rash* decisions, decisions they may later regret. I knew many friends who thought they were in love in their final year of college and staked their futures on that belief. Most of them are now divorced, and the rest are all unhappy."

"This is different," Sebastian says, with the kind of certainty that can only come from youth. "She's different from all the girls I've been with. She's like me. When I look at her, I feel like I'm looking into a mirror."

"That's not love," Walter says. "That's narcissism."

But in his heart, Sebastian doesn't agree. Viola's resemblance to him is deeper than Walter can know. She's *spiritually* like him. The two of them, they share a worldview that no one else he's ever come across has had. He stares down at his essay while visions of Viola in Pre-Raphaelite paintings dance before his eyes. He feels like he's there, in Keats's castle, tasting the exotic spices, feeling the warmth of the fire and the torches, listening to the gentle strumming of Porphyro's lute.

"I'm going to tell her," he says. "I'm going to tell her I love her."

"Sebastian, wait," Walter says. "Don't rush into something. It may be that you're feeling this way because all around you, you see signs of endings. The Byzantines, Beowulf, the beadsman…but what might seem like an ending to you now might years from now become something different. From where I sit, the end of college was anything but an *end.* Your graduation ceremony is called a *commencement!* It's meant to symbolize a beginning, the beginning of your first steps into the real world. So ask yourself, is this girl *really* the one you want to spend your future with? Or is she really only a mirror, as you say, just the embodiment of a college self that you're afraid of losing, a symbol only of the *past?* Do you actually even *know* her, Sebastian? Do you know who she *really* is? What she *wants?* What her *dreams* are? You might think you do, but take it from me, those aren't things you can learn from a *mirror*."

Sebastian resents Walter's paternalistic tone, and he suddenly wonders if this whole time he's been mistaken about his mentor figure. Perhaps Walter was never the glorious image of rebellious adulthood Sebastian believed him to be, but just a sad old man, unmarried, lonely, nostalgic for his youth and trying to justify the decisions that led him to his present state by compelling Sebastian to make those same decisions, not the classic wiser adult vicariously righting his own failures through a protégé, but instead a delusional old man-child, desperate only to people the world with mirror images of his younger self.

Sebastian's phone vibrates. It's Viola, answering his text: *Yeah that sounds great! Jupiter at 8?* He feels a swell of elation in his chest, and he texts back a confirmation and then quickly stands. He can hear his heart racing, and he wonders if Walter can too.

"I should go," Sebastian says.

Walter simply nods, though his eyes are narrowed with worry.

"Well, thanks for visiting," he says. "Keep me posted on whatever you end up doing. And remember: don't do anything you'll regret."

Sebastian departs Walter's office (leaving the door partially ajar for the nervous-looking freshman girl who stands outside, holding the familiar brown and green copy of the Modern Library edition of the collected works of John Keats) and walks down the third-floor hallway of Wheeler, past other offices and towards the stairwell. The sound of his footsteps against the floor makes him think of Viola's boots clicking across the stone steps outside Doe Library. His mind follows those echoing footfalls, back through college and to that building on Telegraph, between the Corinthian columns and into the crowded apartment, where freshman Viola stands in the murky light.

❀

At Jupiter, Sebastian and Viola manage to get a table in the corner of the main room. Though crowded with students keen to celebrate the end of the year, the setting is strangely romantic, with a lit candle flickering between them in a red glass candleholder and dark wood paneling on each of the walls. They have to lean their heads close to hear each other over the din of the bar, and their hands rest only inches apart. Viola's blue eyes are luminous in the dim light, like the only stars in a vast, dark sky. The air smells of mozzarella and hops, though to Sebastian these aromas are no match for Viola's own unique scent, which since that night in Chicago has never left his mind.

"Did you hear about Imogen?" Viola asks. "She got into the UN's internship program. It's unpaid, but still, she gets to live in Geneva."

Sebastian feels a tinge of jealousy. He and Viola traveled through Geneva on their trip through Europe at the end of their summer abroad in Cambridge, and he remembers the city fondly, the clean, manicured streets of cobblestone, the statues of obscure Swiss political heroes, the grand stone building which once housed the League of Nations and now serves as the headquarters for the UN's Geneva offices. He imagines Imogen, in a crisp pencil skirt, hair up in her characteristic bun, walking purposefully through those halls, her high heels clipping a diligent pace down the marble, a stack of important documents tucked under her arm.

"And Harry got a job in the Governor's office in Sacramento," Viola adds. "Nothing glamorous, but I think he's actually getting paid."

Sebastian has never been to Sacramento, but he imagines Harry in a suit and tie in the halls of the capitol, his languid stride taking him in and out of meetings, a legal pad filled with notes in his leather satchel, and as with Imogen his Model UN skills actually put to good use. With the end of Model UN, Sebastian no longer sees Harry at all, as the latter is out of the apartment before Sebastian gets up and asleep by the time he gets home. It's as if Harry's already up in Sacramento, having graduated early and ascended to a higher plane.

A silence falls across the table. Sebastian feels the unspoken question lingering in the air between them, even before Viola asks it.

"Do you know what you're going to do after college?"

Sebastian stares at the flickering candle flame. The wax shimmers in the overhanging light. It looks like a pool of water and the candle flame like a person on the verge of drowning.

"Do you?" he asks.

"I think so," she says, leaning back into her chair. "I'm going to travel. Go on some kind of middle-class grand tour, like the great writers of old, except with less money."

"Where?"

"Anywhere. I don't know. But I should be able to afford it. I've applied to a bunch of freelance writing jobs, and one of them is this content mill where you get paid twenty-five dollars a piece to write shitty, five-hundred-word articles. It's dull but easy, and it takes me half an hour to write each piece, which means if I work for three hours a day, five days a week, I'll make three thousand a month, which should be more than enough to cover hostels, train fair, and food during the journey."

"Don't forget taxes," Sebastian says. "And airfare."

"I'll have airfare covered," Viola says. "I got another job that's just for the summer, teaching SAT prep to privileged high schoolers at some private summer school down in Southern California. I'll make almost six thousand after two months of full-time work, which is more than enough for a plane flight and some emergency cash."

She smiles and takes a long, smug sip of her beer.

"Not bad for a humanities major, huh?" she asks.

Sebastian stares at her, a little in shock. She still speaks with her musical voice, but he's never heard her use so many numbers in so short a conversation. It's unnerving and reminds him of Fatima and her penchant for budgeting, but it also makes him think of what Walter said, about whether he truly *knows* Viola. He didn't expect her, of all people, the perpetual freshman who always seemed to him to do nothing but go to class or drink, to have everything so fully together. Yet here she is, with two jobs, and what is actually quite an enviable plan for at least the immediate future. Sebastian feels more than a little jealous as he imagines her traversing Europe in an old train or crossing South America on a rented motorcycle or hitchhiking down Tibetan highways as she follows the path of the ancient Silk Road. He wonders if perhaps she'll want company on her journey across the world.

The thought lingers in his mind as he finishes his beer and stares at her across the candle. Her blond hair stands out against the dark wood behind her. He feels tension circling them, and he wonders if she feels it too, if she can see the way he feels about her reflected in his eyes.

"Shall we go elsewhere?" he asks, gesturing to their empty beers.

"I think I have an old bottle of wine in my apartment," Viola says. "Want to go there?"

They leave Jupiter and walk down Shattuck towards the north side of campus. The street is swirling with that strange mix of Berkeley nightlife, students who are over twenty-one (and those with fake IDs) and the various yuppies who call Berkeley their home, walking in groups or arm in arm as couples, holding half-eaten cups of gelato, gathering outside the movie theaters, lingering outside bourgeois bars to smoke. As they walk, Sebastian can feel Viola's body next to his, even though there's a foot of space between them. She radiates warmth and vitality, and he wants to hold her to him, to put his arm around her waist, to have her rest her head against his shoulder and sigh contentedly like all the couples he sees around them.

After they walk for about fifteen minutes, the moderate bustling of downtown gives way to quiet residential streets, apartments of students alternating with charming old houses of longtime residents. Lights are flicked on in most buildings, giving the night a comforting glow. Crickets chirp in the darkness, and Viola and Sebastian's feet tread a joint rhythm down the sidewalk. Sebastian's heart races as he watches her walk, noting the swish of her black skirt against her bare legs.

They reach Viola's apartment and enter the creaking gate quietly, like two teenagers sneaking in after curfew. Part of the building's staircase is still damp from a recent rainfall and smells of wet wood and chipped paint. The scent reminds Sebastian of all the previous times he's climbed these stairs, the nights of partying, the quiet nights of studying, the nights, more precious now in retrospect, when it was just the two of them, sitting together on her navy blue IKEA sofa, drinking wine and talking about Medieval history or French literature or European art, about anything but the present and the future.

Inside, though, the apartment is not as he remembers. The posters have been pulled from the walls, and the spaces where they once hung, hidden from view for these past three years, now stand out as a series of eerie white rectangles, cleaner than the dirty walls around them. Boxes cover the hardwood floor, packed with all of Viola's things. The space against the far wall, where Viola's roommate Sarah's desk once stood, is empty too, and dust collects at the boundary of where it used to be. Of the original furniture, only Viola's desk and the IKEA Solsta remain.

"Sarah had no finals, so she moved out yesterday," Viola says. "She's back in her parents' place down in Cupertino. The apartment looked super weird without her stuff, so I started packing mine."

"You're not leaving any time soon, though, right?"

"I don't know. I have my Ottoman History final next week. History department graduation isn't for a few weeks, but I might skip it and just get my diploma mailed to L.A."

"You're not going to walk the stage?"

"Do I have to? It's just a ceremony."

"Exactly! It's a ceremony! A ritual! A symbolic movement to the next phase of life."

Sebastian is surprised that Viola is so flippant about graduation, Viola who's taken so many courses on ancient religions, who first introduced him to Frazer's *The Golden Bough*, who despite her very un-Christian lifestyle still loves to stand in churches, "to feel all those years of history that the building represents," as she once put it to him in a church in Rome, on the last night of their summer trip through Europe. It makes him sad, the thought of her not sitting there next to him in her black cap and gown.

"I don't need a ritual to tell me I've grown up," Viola says.

She enters her kitchen, squeezing past a stack of cardboard boxes, and pulls a bottle of wine from the cupboard.

"I've packed my wine glasses," she says. "But I have a jam jar and a candleholder that I use as cups. Don't worry, I've washed them."

"Sure," Sebastian says.

He's not concerned with how he imbibes his wine. As Viola searches one of the boxes for a wine opener, Sebastian steps towards her desk. In the emptiness of the apartment the whole thing looks like a museum piece, the gray IKEA table, the screwed-on metal legs, the torn office chair, Viola's scuffed up MacBook Pro trailing cords to an ergonomic keyboard, mouse, and external hard drive, a stack of books on Ottoman History, and above them, still taped to the wall, her array of postcards collected from museums, arranged like Sebastian's in a haunting timeline. His eyes are drawn briefly to Waterhouse's *The Magic Circle*.

From the kitchen, he hears the pop of the cork and the lapping sound of wine being poured, and after a moment, Viola joins Sebastian by her desk, the smell of cheap red wine rising around her like a mist. Sebastian takes the candleholder and sips it, his eyes still fixed on the postcards. The wine is harsh on his tongue, sharp and acidic, and yet the taste is nostalgic.

Viola sips her wine and grimaces.

"It's not great, I know," she says. "Bottom shelf Trader Joes."

"It's perfect," Sebastian says.

His eyes move from *The Magic Circle* along the row of postcards and eventually stop at one taped right at the end of the row for freshman year, from London's Guildhall Gallery (another museum that he and Viola visited together): *The Eve of St. Agnes* (1848) by William Holman Hunt. Madeline and Porphyro stand huddled on the painting's right, dressed for the road in their dashing Medieval garb, Madeline's red lips just a thin smile against her pale skin, Porphyro's hand resting on the unchained door, which is open just a crack to reveal the promising world outside. They look briefly back into the still, silent hall, at the men who lie asleep beside their fallen wine jugs and the dogs who look tired, all of them remnants of the small world they will soon leave behind. In the distance, meanwhile, though a set of arches and white columns, the party continues, with men lifting jugs in toasts above their heads, oblivious to the departing youths.

Sebastian reaches out and puts his fingers on the postcard, on Madeline's maroon cloak. He imagines he can feel it, the soft, luxurious fabric, and for a moment it's like he's there with her in that room.

Viola sits down on the sofa, and Sebastian sits next to her, and they place their makeshift wine glasses on the floor by their feet. There's just a small space between their bodies, a few inches of blue upholstery, but to him the gap feels like an ocean, and he wonders how he can cross without drowning, without the candle flame in his heart being snuffed out by crashing waves.

"What are you thinking about?" Viola asks.

The wine on her lips is like lipstick, and it brings out her white skin and her light blue eyes. As she asks the question, her eyebrows narrow and her lips curl into a faint smile, as if she already knows the answer and is following his every thought. Sebastian stares at her crossed legs and at the zipper on her boots and at the way her black skirt hikes up and her bare thighs squeeze together. His heart beats so quickly and wildly that he's afraid the thumping sound will shatter the candleholder and spill wine and broken glass all over the floor.

He thinks of what Walter said and decides now for sure that the professor was wrong. Of course Sebastian knows who Viola is. She has been his one constant throughout the past four years, the only person with whom he's truly been himself and who's truly understood him. After that first party in freshman year, he might never have seen her again, and she might have become one of the hundreds of pretty eyes and heads of hair dissolved into the blurry mosaic of memory. But as it turned out they shared a class (History 4B, Medieval Europe), and so he ran into her again in front of Dwinelle, reading an olive-green copy of Einhard's *Life of Charlemagne,* and after they sat together that day and listened to a lecture on the Carolingians, it was easy for them to slip into a regular friendship, going to Crossroads Dining Hall together and spending their meal points on mediocre food (before gradually developing over the course of the year a taste for the more refined cuisine of Downtown Berkeley or Elmwood), discussing history and art and their favorite European countries, becoming by the end of the year the closest of friends. They may never have, like Walter said, discussed the future or their dreams or ambitions or their visions for what their practical lives might one day look like, but none of those things mattered because they felt so together in the present, and so what need had they of the future?

It's in this instant, with Viola before him like a divine art object, her hair as blond as the room's golden light, her lips as red as wine, her skin as white as marble, her body smelling as it did at The Comstock, the sound of their hearts beating a layered, tandem rhythm, her gentle breath brushing warm against his face and tasting faintly of wine, and only a sliver of IKEA fabric now separating them from consummation, that Sebastian suddenly understands it all. He's aware of nothing else except Viola's physical presence, sight and smell and sound and feeling, hair and lips and skin and heart and breath, their colors flashing like music notes across his eyes. Even his memories of her and of college cease, and for the first time in his life, he's in an eternal present. He and Viola are suspended, no longer aging, like the lovers on Keats's Urn, like Madeline and Porphyro on the postcard on the wall, like any figure in any painting, the young troubadour on the thorny path, Sebastian's reflection in the window of a museum. It's as fragile as glass, and any mistake and the whole thing will shatter, but for that one instant, Sebastian and Viola have accomplished what artists throughout the ages have sought to do—to stop time, to preserve youth, to hold and capture one fleeting, sensory moment.

But then time begins again, and Sebastian feels the moment recede. And so he leans forward, swiftly, suddenly, and kisses Viola on her wine-stained lips.

Her eyes widen with surprise, but she doesn't recoil. Her mouth hangs slightly open, and so she tastes wet and warm.

"Oh, Sebastian," she says, after a moment. "What are you doing…"

Her voice is off-key and breaks apart as it meets the air, clanging unpleasantly like the bell of a clocktower. Suddenly, she looks far away, like someone on a distant shore, while Sebastian paddles his boat furiously against steadily building waves.

She stands to walk away, but Sebastian grabs her hand.

"Wait," he says.

Her skin is soft but cold to the touch, though he doesn't let go, even as panic spreads through his chest. She turns to him, frowning, and because she's standing and he's still sitting, she's like a towering Greek column holding up the ceiling.

"Sebastian—"

He hears in her voice the same dissonance from before, but more pronounced now, as if her voice is composed of two parts, one pressing against the other, both made of glass and about to shatter.

"I have to say something," he says, his heart beating desperately.

He's still seated, still holding her hand in his, and Viola's eyes narrow with fear, as if she already knows what he's going to say. She tries to pull her hand back, but he clings to it.

"Sebastian, no—"

"I love you, Viola."

The words spill out. Viola jerks her hand back, out of Sebastian's grip. She steps away, and her foot kicks the candleholder filled with the remnants of Sebastian's wine. It overturns and somehow shatters. Pieces of broken glass scatter across the hardwood floor like dice, while dark red liquid spreads out in a widening stain.

"Fuck," Viola says.

She fishes a towel out of the nearest cardboard box, and then bends down to mop up the wine. Sebastian reaches out towards her.

"Viola—"

"I got it!" she says, not looking up at him. "I got it."

He watches as she gathers the glass pieces in the towel and strides over to the kitchen, picking up her own jam jar of wine as she does. Somehow, she's got them all, every last shard of glass, and all that's left is a faint red stain on the hardwood floor, like some sinister work of abstract art. Sebastian stares down at the floor. He hears Viola toss the towel into her trash can, and he looks up in time to see her walk over to the edge of the kitchen, where she stops, on the threshold.

"Viola—" he repeats.

"Why did you say that?"

She's angrier than he's ever seen her before, and her voice is a shard of broken glass pressing into his chest.

"Because it's true," Sebastian says. "I love you, Viola. I always have."

"No." She shakes her head. "No, no, you can't do this to me, Sebastian, not now, not when we're about to graduate—"

"Why not now?" Sebastian asks. "When else will we get the chance?"

He steps towards her, but she backs away from him, dancing from his extended hand and back out into her living room, weaving her way through the boxes and over to her desk. Her blond hair is a tangle across her face, and her eyes are narrowed, the blue swirling like a storm.

"We're the same, Viola," he says. "Don't you see? We're perfect for each other. You're the only person who understands me, the only person who sees the world like I do. And it's taken me four years to see, but now I do, clearer than anything, like I'm looking into a mirror—"

"Stop it!" Viola shouts. The walls shake with her thunderous voice, and the dust specks floating in the air swirl about in the sudden gale. "We're not the same!"

Sebastian feels a pain in his chest, Viola's voice pressing the shard of glass deeper, turning it—

"How can you say that?" he asks. "How can you think that?"

"I don't want to be you, Sebastian!" she says. "I don't want us to be the same!"

"But why not? Haven't you been happy with me, these past four years—"

"Of course I've been happy with you! I'm never not

happy with you! All we do is drink and reminisce about freshman year and all the good times we've had—"

"Exactly!" Sebastian says. "That's what I feel too and that's what I think about and that's why we're meant for each other—"

"But I don't want to think about all that!" She steps backwards, over the threshold of dust and into the empty space where her roommate's desk once stood. "I don't want to be reminded of freshman fucking year all the time! That's the past, Sebastian, and that's why we're different. You cling to the past, and you don't want things to change. If you had your way, you would be in college forever. But I'm not like that. I'm ready to move on, ready to travel the world—"

"And I want to travel with you!" Sebastian says. "I want to go with you on your grand tour, like we did back in the summer after freshman year—"

"No!" Viola says. "No, no, Sebastian, no! I don't want it to be like that fucking summer! Don't you understand? I'm not the same person I was back then!"

She sinks to her knees, and the line of dust around her now looks like an impenetrable wall, and Sebastian wonders if she'll suddenly disappear forever, like the desk that was once there.

"You know, I thought about you all the time," she says. Her voice has softened now, but it's still not calming or joyful like before, but wistful and lamenting. "I always imagined a night like tonight, a bottle of wine and a romantic kiss. But I think it was only recently that you even saw me in that way. I thought about it a lot, though, from the day I first met you. So, maybe I did love you Sebastian, maybe once, but…that was in the past."

Sebastian feels his heart slowing to a mournful, tragic cadence.

"What changed?" he asks.

She looks up at him from her knees, still surrounded by the frame of dust.

"I guess I saw who you really were. And after watching you with Fatima, I realized I didn't want to be just another one of your white girls."

Sebastian is stunned. He feels his heart sink inside his chest. How can she say that? Doesn't she understand? She's different from the others. She's not just another girl, white or otherwise. She's Viola. She's his reflection. She may be white, but that doesn't matter to him. Everyone he knew always brought up a woman's goddamn skin color, Fatima and Harry and Imogen and all the rest, but Sebastian always imagined that Viola would be different, that Viola would understand that for him it's not about race, it's about aesthetics, only aesthetics…

He searches for something to say to her, but realizes he has no words left, that his body is as empty and shattered as the wine glass. She was a column, holding up the ceiling, only now she's fallen, and the room has collapsed, and he can feel the apartment and all its memories crumbling to dust, can feel time overtaking even this sacred refuge.

"You should leave," Viola says.

Sebastian doesn't protest. He goes out the door and doesn't even hear it close behind him as he lets his feet carry him down the stairwell. He doesn't hear his footsteps on the stone and he no longer smells the chipped paint and the wet wood. He no longer senses anything. Even the nighttime air of late spring, which should be cool, relaxing, and temperate, feels like nothing. And as he walks down the quiet streets and back towards downtown, no part of him remains at all in the present. Instead, he's in the past, in the Corinthi-an-columned building, amidst the smells of that freshman year party. He's sitting next to Viola on an IKEA sofa. She is staring at him, her blue eyes dilated, and suddenly, in light of what she's told him tonight, the memory of that night is different. Viola leans towards him, she laughs at each of his jokes, she places a hand on his shoulder, she makes a comment about how they're dressed similarly, and Sebastian knows now that she likes him, and he wants nothing more than to lean towards her, to kiss her there, in freshman year, to tell her that he loves her, that he has loved her, that he will love her. But that's not how the memory goes, and he sees himself catch the eye of another girl (white, of course), the girl he'll end up sleeping with that night, the girl whose name he doesn't even remember, whose eye color and hair color he also doesn't even remember, the girl who's just a blurry face in a crowded mosaic, and he wants to yell at his freshman self, to tell him to stop, to go back, that the only person who matters is there on the IKEA sofa—but he can't stop himself, and before he knows it, September of 2007 has become May of 2011, and it's too late to change anything.

CHAPTER TEN

THE VOYAGE OF LIFE: MANHOOD
(1842)

The homeless man is not there. It's the day before the apocalypse, May 20, 2011, and his whiteboard should say 1 DAY TILL THE END. But the selfless prophet has opted to take a much-deserved day of rest, and the space on Sproul Plaza where he and his bucket have been is now empty. In fact, the whole of Sproul Plaza is empty save for Sebastian, who sits on the steps of Sproul Hall, staring with wonder at the sudden void around him. There are still twelve hours left in the world, but from where he sits, everything has already ended. Exams and graduation ceremonies are over, final grades have been turned in, the undergraduates have moved out of their apartments and dorms, the libraries have closed for a week's holiday before the summer semester begins, and the only people who still occasionally wander the stony paths of campus are graduate students and professors, and even they seem to have taken a holiday today, or else are already in their offices, too busy to enjoy the beautiful May sunshine. It's as if Berkeley has on this final day become a museum, to preserve for Sebastian one last memory of his old world.

Sebastian wonders where the homeless man is and how he's preparing for the end. Sebastian himself is, of course, throwing a party. Yesterday, he purchased some cheap wine, Vodka of the Gods, and twelve-packs of PBR and sent out Facebook invitations to all his college friends. He genuinely wanted to invite the homeless man as a guest of honor and is upset now to find the plaza empty. Without that prophet's presence, the party no longer matters. After all, everyone else that he would have liked to see has also already left Berkeley. Imogen has been gone since the beginning of the month (Facebook photos indicate she's on the East Coast, traveling with friends). Harry moved out a week ago, back in with his parents for a few months before his job in Sacramento starts (he and Sebastian shared a stiff, formal goodbye handshake the morning he left). Nate has gone back to Southern California to visit family before starting a summer program in Washington D.C. And Viola, of course, is gone too, having moved out the day after her Ottoman History final. So if not them and if not the homeless man, who is left to mourn with Sebastian the coming of the end of time? A few scattered friends from Cambridge and his summer in D.C., one or two fellow Art History majors, some people from his English and History classes, some sophomores and juniors from Model UN who won't under-stand the significance of the moment and who'll treat the whole thing like a joke? In the end, the party will end up just a tragic anticlimax.

There is one person, of course, who he knows is still in Berkeley, someone he didn't invite to the party. He saw her about a week ago, on the day of the main graduation ceremony, from this very spot, where he took to coming regularly throughout the last two weeks, to sit and ruminate. The Plaza was crowded that day, with capped and gowned students drifting slowly over to Memorial Stadium, and she was among them, making her way through the bodies, walking quickly despite her high heels, attired in her black cap and gown, with a purple stole for Phi Beta Kappa draped around her shoulders.

"Fatima," Sebastian called.

She stopped, just below the steps where he was sitting. He stood up and slowly descended towards her. She was greatly changed from how he remembered her, like a faded painting newly restored. She looked as if she'd just come from the salon, her black hair shining and curled slightly at the ends, and she wore more makeup than usual, her eyes vivid and framed in black eyeliner and mascara. She smelled different too, more alive, more vibrant, like flowers in springtime. Perhaps it was a new shampoo.

"Hey!" she said. "Long time no see."

She looked surprised to see him, but if she was displeased, she hid it well. He hadn't seen her since just after their breakup, and she didn't seem to him like the same person, as if the girl he had dated were somebody else. He felt suddenly uncertain about having called out to her.

"How've you been?" he asked.

"Good," she said, nodding. "I've been good."

They stood awkwardly. Behind her, more students in caps and gowns drifted by, like a river of black water meandering off to the underworld. Sebastian himself was dressed casually, in black jeans and his classic blazer, and he felt distant from the crowd, as if the people graduating were part of some more advanced society that Sebastian had declined to join.

"Are you not going today?" Fatima asked, noting his lack of cap and gown. "It's the official ceremony."

"I went to the Art History one yesterday," Sebastian said. "I think one is enough."

Sebastian didn't think he could handle any more than one block of bland speeches filled with false optimism and delusional attitudes about how the graduating students were now ready for the real world. The Art History ceremony the day before (scheduled at 9 a.m., as if the early hour would reinforce the notion that this was a commencement and not an ending) was more than enough. Held in the Zellerbach Playhouse, where Sebastian had seen many plays and concerts over the past four years (with graduation being the final of these, ultimately as theatrical as any performance), it was a brutal two hours sitting in the overly air-conditioned space in a line of similarly capped and gowned students, applauding for each sentimental speech and then walking across the stage when his own name was called, shaking hands with a professor he'd never met, accepting from him the blank piece of rolled up and ribboned paper meant to stand in for his diploma (the real one would arrive in the mail some time in August), and all the while looking out of the corner of his eye at his father, who was sitting in the audience and doing his best to appear proud. Sebastian couldn't imagine doing all that again on a larger scale.

"Are you heading back to Southern California after graduation?" Sebastian asked Fatima.

"I'm staying in the Bay Area for a few weeks actually," she said. "The job at Pangea starts next month, and my parents want to help me look for apartments."

Sebastian nods. He never actually met Fatima's parents, Muhammad and Khatija Ahmed, despite her repeated insistence that he come to Orange County to visit. They came up to the Bay Area once in the last year, but Sebastian was away at a Model UN conference.

"Also they want to meet Chris," Fatima added.

"Chris?"

"My boyfriend."

"Ah."

She said this with no malice, as if Sebastian were just a casual friend who hadn't yet heard that she had a new boyfriend. Sebastian couldn't help but wonder if "Chris" was a white guy. If he was, then Sebastian envied him.

"Well, I should get going," Fatima said.

"Okay."

He watched her turn to join the black river of students. In a moment, she would disappear, and something in his chest told him he'd likely never see her again.

"Hey, one more thing," he said.

Fatima turned.

"Yeah?"

"I just—I want to say I'm sorry," Sebastian said. "About everything that happened. I don't think I ever actually said it."

Her mascaraed eyes looked fierce against her glowing skin. She frowned and was silent for a long moment.

"Well, at least you said it now," she said.

She gave him one last look, unsmiling and enigmatic, before she disappeared into the crowd. Soon she was lost amidst the river of black-robed bodies.

Now, those bodies are gone, and Sebastian sits on those same steps, staring at the spot where he last saw her. He wonders if he should invite her to his party tonight, and if she'll even come, or if she'll be too busy with "Chris." Sebastian checked Facebook soon after their conversation and found a series of pictures with her and a white guy, someone taller than Sebastian but a little pudgy in the face and stomach and with an already-receding hairline. He and Fatima stood smiling in San Francisco in front of the Ferry Building, his arm draped confidently around her shoulders. It was a cheesy, touristy shot, with no attempt at artistry, but they looked happy and like real adults.

The sound of a bell jars Sebastian out of his reverie. It's the Campanile, chiming out 1 p.m. The ringing is strange, echoing across the empty campus with only Sebastian (and whoever that solitary bell-ringer is) there to hear it. It's as if the world is mocking him, reminding him that even now, hours before the end, when everything is already over, time still marches on.

❀

The party that night is a strange gathering, with the atmosphere of a wake and only about twenty people spread thinly across Sebastian's apartment. About half of them are strangers, having been invited by those that Sebastian does know, but even the latter group are only vague acquaintances of his: Paul Lieberman from his summer program in Cambridge (an English major heading back to Cambridge for grad school), Kevin Liu from his summer program in Washington D.C. (a political science major heading back to D.C. for an unpaid internship with his congressman), Anna Kim from his Art History graduating class (a "post-post-modernist" (her words) heading to New York to "try and make it in the art world"), Amina Ali from Model UN (an engineering student, a junior, and next year's President of UCBMUN), all in all like a room full of someone else's group of friends. It doesn't help that his apartment also feels like a different place without Harry's half of the furniture. Harry's room, which leads out to the balcony, is completely empty, and Sebastian longs for his old roommate's comforting presence, the pedantic tones of another philosophical lecture drifting out above the din of a party.

The one surprising face is Rebecca Chen, last year's Model UN president, returning to Berkeley after a year in Greenville, Mississippi doing Teach for America. She tells Sebastian she heard about the party through Amina and decided to drop by.

"I'm visiting parents for the weekend," she says. "A much needed break from teaching."

"How is it?" Sebastian asks.

Rebecca pours out a large helping of Vodka of the Gods and drinks it one long swig.

"Shitty," she says. "Goddamn, I never thought I'd miss the taste of Trader Joe's vodka."

"Do they not have a Trader Joe's in Greenville?"

"Are you kidding? The nearest one is either in Birmingham or Baton Rouge, each five hours away."

"Jesus."

She gives him a pained and frustrated look, and in it Sebastian can barely recognize the fashionable, optimistic Rebecca Chen of a year ago, she who mentored him through Model UN, who taught him how to leave his life behind in Berkeley, to take the best from every conference, and then to seamlessly return four days later. Now she is tired, dark circles under her eyes, permanent wrinkles on her forehead, her hair frazzled and thinner.

"I fucking hate it, Sebastian," she says.

"Teaching?"

"Adulthood." She looks mournfully across Sebastian's apartment. "I really miss college."

Rebecca moves off to chat with others. Sebastian sinks onto his couch and stares at the bottles of alcohol that line his table. He's not drinking tonight, a decision he didn't premeditate but that he came to as soon as the party began (if Fatima were here, maybe she would be proud). The truth is that the thought of alcohol brings on only bitter memories now, of stumbling through a Chicago club looking for Helena, of puking against a mirror, most of all of Viola, sitting across a table from him with ale-scented breath and wine-red lips. More than that, Sebastian feels that when the world ends in less than two hours, he wants to be sober, fully alert, completely himself. He doesn't want to be too drunk to appreciate the change happening around him, or worse, to black out and wake up the next day and realize that the world ended and that he missed it.

His newfound temperance makes him think of Islam. Three days ago, while wandering Berkeley on one of his solitary, daylong walks, he saw them again, the Muslim Student Association members, praying together outside the MLK building. There were fewer of them than during the semester, but still enough that when they intoned the phrase

"Allahu-Akbar" it echoed across the emptying campus and stirred Sebastian's heart. Later, when he returned home, he pulled out his own prayer rug, which was folded up in his closet and under a pile of old clothes. The mat was his mother's, and he brought it with him to college despite never intending to actually use it. He unfurled it then for the first time, out across the floor of his room, and stared at the mosque woven into the carpet. Its colors were more vivid than he remembered, a deep red sky and an ivory-white dome, with tall columns in the foreground flanking a distant minaret. He'd never thought of Islam possessing anything as wondrous as Western Art, and he'd abandoned the religion largely because he never felt the same rapture that he did staring at a Pre-Raphaelite painting. But as he looked at all the colors woven into that fabric, he realized he'd been wrong, and that even without the religious significance, on a purely aesthetic level, this rug was a work of beauty too, with its geometric-patterned border and its arabesque swirls and golden filigrees, rivaling anything from the European nineteenth century. Memories then flooded back, of his mother teaching him to pray upon the rug, of her putting her forehead down during the sajdah, the orange dupata around her head slipping as she did and causing her dark hair to cascade across her face.

He thought then about the Islamic conception of the end of the world. Eschatology in any religion is a confusing mishmash of traditions, and in Islam it was no different. Sebastian remembered learning a contradictory story about an antichrist known as the Dajjal and a Mahdi savior who will unite the Muslim world and then join forces with a resurrected Jesus and defeat the aforementioned Dajjal, while either at the same time or some time later the angel Israfil will blow a trumpet, either once, twice, or three times, ending time itself, after which God will raise everyone from the dead and judge whether they will go to heaven or hell. But more haunting than any lessons from Sunday Islamic

school were the lines from the Qur'an itself on the subject
of the end of days, from the 75th Sura, "Al-Qiyamah" or
"The Resurrection," which Sebastian looked up and reread
online:

No! I swear by the Day of Resurrection.
No! I swear by the reproachful soul.
What, does man reckon We shall not gather his bones?
Yes indeed; We are able to shape again his fingers.
Nay, but man desires to continue on as a libertine,
asking, 'When shall be the Day of Resurrection?'
But when the sight is dazed
and the moon is eclipsed,
and the sun and moon are brought together,
upon that day man shall say, 'Whiter to flee?'
No indeed: not a refuge!
Upon that day the recourse shall be to thy Lord.
Upon that day man shall be told his former deeds and his
latter;
nay, man shall be a clear proof against himself,
even though he offer his excuses.
Move not thy tongue with it to hasten it;
Ours it is to gather it, and to recite it.
So, when We recite it, follow thou its recitation.
Then Ours it is to explain it.
No indeed; but you love the hasty world,
and leave be the Hereafter.
Upon that day faces shall be radiant,
gazing upon their Lord;
and upon that day faces shall be scowling.
thou mightest think the Calamity has been wreaked on them.
No indeed; when it reaches the clavicles
and it is said, 'Who is an enchanter?'
and he thinks that it is the parting
and leg is intertwined with leg,

upon that day unto thy Lord shall be the driving.
For he confirmed it not, and did not pray,
but he cried it lies, and he turned away,
then he went to his household arrogantly.
Nearer to thee and nearer
then nearer to thee and nearer!
What, does man reckon he shall be left to roam at will?
Was he not a sperm-drop spilled?
Then, he was a blood-clot, and he created and formed,
and He made of him two kinds, male and female.
What, is He not able to quicken the dead?

Sebastian often found Qur'anic syntax incomprehensible, though when he read the verse, the last lines moved him. Of course a religious account of the end of days, enigmatic as it was, would conclude with a discussion of the origin of life. What is the story of destruction if not also a story of creation? What is the end of one world if not the beginning of another?

It's as he's thinking about endings, seated on his IKEA sofa amid the tepid noise of his party, that he sees her, leaning against the far wall of his apartment and staring at him across the room while she carefully sips her drink, which in the clear plastic cup looks as dark-red as blood. She has dark hair, pale skin, blue eyes, and dark-red lipstick and wears jeans, a baggy shirt, and a black leather jacket. He doesn't recognize her and assumes that she came with a friend and that, based on her body language, she doesn't know many people at the party. When she notices Sebastian watching her, she smiles and makes her way over to him, across the semi-crowded room. Slowly, she sits next to him on the IKEA sofa, her eyes fixed on his.

"Not drinking tonight?" she asks.

Sebastian shakes his head.

"Not tonight."

"Might be your last chance…"

Her eyes flash with mirth, a strange optimism that's out of place amidst the melancholy tenor of the evening. Her drink smells sharp and fruity, of cranberry and vodka, and the rim of her cup is stained dark-red from her lipstick.

"You're the host, aren't you?" she asks.

"I am. Sebastian."

"Miranda."

They shake hands and then fall into silence. Miranda smiles at him and runs her hand through her hair, brushing it back behind her ear. It's a nervous habit that Sebastian recognizes immediately, a classic sign of attraction, and a year ago, or even a few months ago, he would have flirted back, and his heart would have raced with that familiar thrill. But now he feels only bitterness as he thinks again of Viola's last words to him. Just another one of his white girls.

Yet what is he supposed to do? There are so many white girls in America, and so many of them are beautiful. Is he really wrong to desire them? All he ever wanted was to live a life of pure aesthetics, to be Dorian Gray or Don Draper. But he realizes now that everyone around him, even Viola, only ever saw him as Othello. And in the end, his desire turned into poison.

He stands from the couch.

"It was nice to meet you," he says to Miranda.

She looks briefly disappointed but then resumes her flirtatious smile, even as Sebastian turns away.

"You should stay and meet me some more!"

Sebastian doesn't turn at the words and instead steps through Harry's empty room and out onto the balcony. He slides the door closed behind him and shivers. The weather is strange tonight, as if it's wintertime rather than May. Cold winds whip at him now, and the balcony railing is like ice as he leans against it. But he stays here, staring down at the empty street below. The Berkeley Rep across the street is closed, there being no performances tonight, and the large glass windows look in on an unlit, empty lobby. Farther down on Shattuck, the multicolored lights shine above PiQ and mingle with the yellow cast upwards from streetlamps, though they only illuminate a deserted corner. No crowds gather outside the bar on the corner to smoke, and no students saunter past Half-Price Books or line up outside the Mexican/Pakistani restaurant. Downtown is as quiet as the campus beyond, which rises up above the skyline. Sebastian is jarred by how different the view looks. In a year, the construction cranes have thrown up an entire building, with sand-colored walls and large, clear glass windows. It looks out of place next to the weathered stone buildings around it, like something from the future.

Sebastian hears the balcony door slide open and sees Miranda emerge into the cold.

"Can I join you?" she asks.

"If you want," Sebastian says.

She steps up beside him and leans against the railing, holding her drink precariously over the edge and parodying Sebastian's ruminative posture by staring out over the quiet city.

"So why exactly is everyone here so serious?" she asks, after a moment. "It's like someone died or something."

"Haven't you heard? The world is ending."

Miranda laughs. "Okay, please explain that to me. Someone said something to me about a homeless guy and a bucket, but I didn't really follow."

Sebastian sighs and looks down at his feet. His leather shoes stand out against the gray concrete. He tries to imagine them rising up and into the heavens.

"Did you ever see the homeless man down on Sproul?" Sebastian asks, looking up. "The one who counted down the days till the end of the world?"

"No, I don't think so. But I've only been here a year."

Sebastian's heart picks up. "Are you a junior transfer too?"

"What? No, I'm a freshman."

A freshman. Of course. She's so young after all, with that bloom in her cheeks and that optimism in her eyes.

"Anyway, what about this homeless guy, then?" Miranda asks.

"He was this old man who would sit out on Sproul Plaza, clean-shaven, long white hair, and he was there every day for the past year, holding up this sign that warned that the end of the world would happen tonight at midnight, May 21, 2011."

Sebastian stares at her, wondering if she'll understand. But her eyes don't change, and she simply shrugs.

"Okay," she says. "But why does that mean you have to be sad? I mean, I hope you know the world isn't actually going to end tonight."

"But you do see why the date is significant, right?"

"No, not really."

"It's end of college!"

"Well, for some people…"

"For me and for every graduating senior, and for most of the people in that room! After tonight, everything will change! There'll be no more parties, no more classes, no more freedom to do or study whatever we want. We have to get jobs, pay the bills, think about our futures, put aside any dreams we might have made here—"

"But doesn't everyone have to do that eventually? You just described becoming an adult."

Sebastian sighs in frustration. Of course she can be glib about it. To her, the end of college is a lifetime from now.

"Look," he says. "You won't really understand it until you're a senior like me, but eventually, college ends up feeling like our society's big practical joke. For four years we're told to dream big, study everything, learn about how great the past was, think about new and interesting things, imagine worlds we never thought possible—and then suddenly it's all taken away and we're told that no, actually, we have to go out into the real world and get a job for a fucking company that makes wires and can't even get a basic mythological reference correct." He's breathing hard, and his voice is echoing out over the balcony railing and down across the empty street. "Do you know those Thomas Cole paintings? *The Voyage of Life?*"

"I don't really know much about art, honestly. I study computer science."

Of course she does.

"Well, they're four panels depicting the stages of life: *Childhood, Youth, Manhood,* and *Old Age.* In each one, our hero journeys in a boat down a river and through a different landscape. *Childhood* and *Youth* are lovely and peaceful, with green all around and blue skies above. And in *Youth,* our hero is young and optimistic and stands at the prow of the boat, pointing to a palace in the distant sky, and it's beautiful and majestic, and it stirs your heart. But then there's *Manhood.* The palace is gone, and the sky is dark, and our hero's boat is tossed about in the waves, and he's older now, huddled and shivering in the rain, and the landscape has turned to rocks and crags, and it's as if all the green in the world has disappeared. And that's how I feel now. Like the palace has disappeared." He's leaning towards her now, and he can feel her breath against his cheek and smell a hint of her flowery perfume. He imagines her standing on the riverbank in *Youth,* waving at him as his boat passes.

She is serious for one more moment before smiling and shaking her head.

"Well, that's all very poetic and everything," she says. "But I really don't think youth goes away because you graduate. That's when life itself begins! When you get to move to a city and get a job and put all those skills you learned in college to use!"

"Is that what you'll do?" Sebastian asks, trying his best not to sound condescending.

"Yes," Miranda says, her eyes beaming. "I'll get a job as

a coder in Silicon Valley, and I'll live in a big apartment in SOMA with all my friends, and we'll throw all kinds of wild parties on our rooftop. You'll be invited of course."

"I'll be ancient by the time you graduate."

"Oh, I doubt that! How old are you?"

"Twenty-two."

"Well, you look great. You could still totally pass for nineteen."

She laughs and holds out her drink, offering it to him.

"So, drink up," she says. "You're not an old man yet."

Sebastian stares at the clear cup in her hand. The drink is the color of blood and smells of cranberry and Vodka of the Gods, but to Sebastian in that moment it's ambrosia, and Miranda is some kind of Prometheus figure, descended from the heavens to offer it to him, this elixir of immortality, this philosopher's stone, this cup of sweet nectar drawn from the Fountain of Youth. Is it really as simple as this, he wonders? Is the secret to staying young really just a mental exercise, a decision to cast aside all doubts and fears and take a drink? Is Miranda really right? Will a simple drink cure of him of his melancholy, and will the palace then materialize for him once again in the Berkeley sky?

He wants to drink it now. He imagines the alcohol sliding down his throat, the sweet taste of the cranberry and the sharp afterthought of the vodka. His head would flood with warmth, his eyes would blur, his skin would feel warm. An old familiar comfort would settle across his heart. With those clouded eyes, under that magical spell, he could stare out at Berkeley and pretend he's still young, that it's still a year ago and that it's Fatima standing next to him. All he has to do is reach out and take the cup and brush his fingers against Miranda's, which must be warm in the cool night air.

But no. He knows it won't work. He knows now that time can't be stopped.

After a moment, the sliding door opens, and a guy

Sebastian doesn't know looks out.

"It's almost time!" the guy says. "Come join us for the countdown!"

Miranda still holds out the cup, but Sebastian turns away and steps back inside. Everyone is gathered in a semi-circle, and when he enters, they cheer. He's taken aback by the spectacle, by how loud even a small group like this one can be and by how warm he feels even in a room full of strangers.

"Sebastian!" someone shouts. "Sebastian Khan! Lead us in a toast!"

Miranda, entering behind him, smiles and holds out the drink. The crowd goes quiet with anticipation. Slowly, Sebastian takes the cup from Miranda's hand, careful not to let his fingers brush against hers. He raises it into the air and considers what to say. He imagines a palace before him slowly disappearing into a stormy sky.

"To the end of the world," he says. "And to the beginning of another."

The crowd cheers, and everyone raises their cups in response. But when they all lean back and drink in one long, collective swig, Sebastian doesn't join them. Instead, he lowers the cup, Miranda's cup, still marked on the rim with her lipstick smear, and hands it wordlessly back to her. She frowns as she takes it and then drinks a sip herself, staring over it at Sebastian through her dark-framed glasses.

"One minute!" someone shouts, looking down at their phone.

Across the room, Sebastian sees the clock on his micro-wave move from 11:58 to 11:59. He imagines the homeless man's whiteboard as a stopwatch now, counting down sixty seconds until everything ends. *Fifty-nine, fifty-eight, fifty-seven.*

Sebastian looks over at Miranda, who stands by his side. She is beautiful, he can't deny that: dark hair, pale skin, blue eyes, red lips, an amalgam of all the girls he's ever been attracted to. And yet he feels like a virgin before her, staring at a woman for the first time in his life.

"Forty-five seconds!" the guy with the phone shouts.

Miranda stares back at Sebastian, a glint in her eye. She's standing closer to him now than she was before, and in the microwave he can see their silhouetted profiles, reflected in the black.

"If you don't kiss me know, you may never get the chance," Miranda says, in a voice that's barely a whisper.

"Thirty seconds!"

But Sebastian doesn't move. He stares at Miranda's dark-red, glossy lips. He imagines a different version of himself, Sebastian Khan from a year ago, someone who would lean forward and kiss her now. Her lips would be warm and soft, and he would taste on them the Vodka of the Gods.

"Fifteen seconds!"

Sebastian looks past Miranda. The small crowd has grown quiet now. Some people have their eyes closed and others grip their friends' hands.

"Ten seconds!" the guy shouts. "Nine! Eight!"

The crowd joins in now, counting down in a unified chant. Sebastian, however, simply listens to each thudding number. He imagines that, across the world, groups of partygoers in other rooms are chanting too, and that their collective voices echo upward to the heavens.

"Seven! Six! Five!"

Miranda has joined the countdown now, but she no longer smiles, and her eyes betray uncertainty, as if she isn't sure anymore that the world won't actually end. The air fills with the scent of cranberry and vodka as she intones each number.

"Four! Three!"

Faces flash before Sebastian, the homeless man, Professor Walter, his mother and father, Nate and Harry, Madeline and faux-Madeline, Lorelei and Rosalind, Juliet and Imogen, Helena and Elena, Fatima, Viola—

AATIF RASHID

"Two!"

All the art he's ever seen now flashes before him, in every medium, museums, textbooks, postcards, iPhones, drunken mirages, images in his head, the pendulum of a clock moving across a timeline of art history, forward and backward and forward through the centuries, *Youth, The Magic Circle, The Poet and the Siren, Octobre, The Rake's Progress, Pilgrimage to the Isle of Cythera, Marriage A-la-Mode, Beata Beatrix, Portrait of a Young Man, The Eve of St. Agnes,* and, finally, *Manhood,* whose dark skies he imagines swirling outside his apartment—

"One!"

Sebastian shuts his eyes and hears the crowd's collective intake of breath. The ensuing silence lasts only for a moment, but in that time Sebastian feels what everyone around him feels. There's a palpable fear in the silence, a fear that perhaps the homeless man was right, and for an instant all their rational skepticism vanishes and there's not a disbeliever among them. Suddenly, Sebastian knows that he doesn't want the world to end, and he hopes with all his heart that the homeless man is wrong.

He keeps his eyes shut. But gradually, he smells vodka and cranberry circling around him, and he tastes them in the air, and he feels too of the warmth of other bodies, and after a moment, he hears the crowd cheer in euphoria, and slowly, he opens his eyes and sees the glow of his mid-century lamp and the lights from the city drifting in from the balcony's glass door and all the colors around him, the blue of the sofa, the gray of the carpet, the egg-shell white of the walls, the browns and blacks and reds and blonds of everyone's hair, the blood-red of the drink that Miranda still holds in her hand—and it's thus, in all those sensory details, that he knows he is alive. And he understands finally that no art, not even the best of paintings, can ever capture such a feeling. It can come close, of course, closer than anything else in the world—but in the end, it's only paint on a canvas, only words on a page, always just a reproduction one degree removed from the real feeling.

In the swirl of jumping and laughing bodies, Sebastian suddenly realizes that Miranda has disappeared. He looks for her, but she's not there, and there's too much noise and movement, too many people bumping into him, clapping him on the shoulders, shoving drinks at him, shouting "We're still here!" and "We're alive!" and toasting to new beginnings. He smells lingering remnants of her vodka and cranberry breath, but he can't find her anywhere.

The party dissipates quickly after the false end of the world. People shake Sebastian's hand and hug him as they trickle out of his apartment. It's not until 12:30 a.m. that he finally does see her, standing by his open front door at the end of his long entryway, about to slip quietly out. He walks quickly over. Her lipstick is gone, perhaps washed away against the tide of several drinks.

"Hey," Sebastian says.

"Hey," Miranda says.

They stand a moment, beside the open door. Outside, the sky is dark, and a cool wind blows down through the open-air hallway. Yellow lights dance in the distance, from cars drifting down empty streets.

"You were right," Sebastian says to Miranda. "The world didn't end."

Miranda smiles and looks down at her feet.

"I told you so," she says.

They stand for another awkward moment before Sebastian reaches out his hand.

"It was good to meet you, Miranda," he says.

"Yeah. Likewise."

They shake hands. Her skin is not as warm as he imagined it would be, not as soft, but it's a real, human presence in the empty hallway.

She leaves, and the door closes with a slow, echoing sound. The laughter of the few remaining guests drifts over from the living room. Miranda's vodka and cranberry scented breath still lingers in the entryway.

Sebastian returns and takes a seat. Only Rebecca and some others from Model UN are left now, reminiscing about the past and drinking the last of the Vodka of the Gods. Sebastian doesn't say much, though, and just lets the others talk. When the vodka is gone, around 1 a.m., they stand to leave, each giving Sebastian a long hug.

When the door slams closed and their voices recede down the hallway, Sebastian is left seated on his sofa amidst the remnants of the party. Empty bottles of vodka and wine are spread out across the room like unlit candles. Clear plastic cups sit precariously on countertops and tables, some half-filled, like libations ready to be poured out as offerings. The square lamp shrouds the room in a jaundiced yellow. A general gloom descends upon the apartment, a silence like that of a religious sanctuary or a mausoleum honoring some fallen hero. Sebastian sits for a moment in that silence before rising to clean up.

On the table, he finds Miranda's cup, amidst empty bottles of Vodka of the Gods. There's nothing left inside, though its rim is still marked with the red imprint of her lips. He stares at them, these red lips, pale reflections of a kiss he never had from her, just a work of art now, to be displayed with all the others in the museum in his head. In a prior world these lips would have been everything to him, the distilled essence of yet another girl. But he feels different now, and he understands that she, along with all the others, is far more than just this image.

Slowly, he rubs his thumb against the cup until the lips are gone.

EPILOGUE

Sebastian Khan stares at his reflection in the window. The wavy black hair, the light-olive skin, the nose and cheekbones and lips—they're all the same as they were four years ago. The figure too is mostly unchanged, five feet, eight inches, one hundred and fifty-five pounds (all that drinking has added ten, but seeing how much others have gained in four years, Sebastian knows it could have been worse), overall still attractive, charming, and mysterious. Only the eyes have seriously changed. They are still dark brown and hypnotic and still swallow up the pupils, but now there is a new melancholy underlying the gaze, a wisdom that wasn't there before.

In staring at his reflection, Sebastian wonders it hasn't changed more. Was there some spell he weaved the last time he was here? Some Dorian-Gray-like pact with the devil of aesthetics to keep his reflection young? If so, then where is the aging painting? Or are the signs that he's older only internal?

Outside the Philadelphia skyline is dark and gray, and crumbling leaves fall from trees. The city is jarringly unchanged from how he remembers it. He arrived here four days ago as part of a month-long trip down the East Coast, to Boston, New York, Philadelphia, and Washington D.C. They're all places he's been before, but he feels the need to see them outside the frame of a Model UN conference, not as a college student but as a "real adult"—and so he's spending the money he made over the summer from working as a waiter at Gather rather than simply swiping the old credit card connected to his father's account, which has ultimately meant staying at cheap hostels and crashing on friends' couches and buying food at supermarkets instead of fancy restaurants and taking Greyhounds and Mega-buses to get from city to city. His father discouraged him from taking the restaurant job ("I didn't pay $100,000 to put you through college so you could end up being a goddamn kitchen wench.") and offered to fund any traveling Sebastian wanted to do. But Sebastian said he wanted to start paying his own way through life. It was a humbling summer working at Gather, being on the other side of one of his favorite bourgeois haunts, and especially one filled with such memories. More than once he thought he saw Fatima enter, but it was just another brown girl with a white boyfriend.

Before Sebastian left for his trip, his father asked him whether waiting tables was now his intended profession. Sebastian didn't dignify his father with a response, but the question lingered in his mind all through Boston and New York, and lingers still as he stands before his reflection in the Philadelphia Museum of Art. He still hates the word "profession," but now it carries more significance than it ever did before. He doesn't want to wait tables his whole life, and he doesn't want to do any of the other things his fellow humanities majors are doing, teaching or joining the Peace Corps or working marketing or recruiting for a tech company or going to law or business school or working in consulting or getting an MFA in something (one impractical degree is enough for now) or even applying to grad school in Art History, since the last thing he wants to do is lock himself in another ivory tower.

The truth is, the only thing Sebastian cares about, the only thing that matters to him, is right here, reflected back at him in the window. If his artistic and literary education will be useful in any way, it will be in the service of this image and to understand the soul below. What he really wants is to create a portrait of himself, something that will capture both image and soul. He snapped a photo earlier on his new iPhone 4S, but it felt far too modern, too crisp and clean. Yet even an old-fashioned portrait is only an image, ultimately too superficial to reveal the truth Sebastian is looking for. Even his reflection in the glass feels like a lie. Perhaps the best portrait, then, has to go beyond an image. Perhaps what he really needs to do is write a novel, tracing his last year of college, from Fatima to Miranda, and in the third person so he can truly look at himself. It would be a mirror too, but different from the window, one that will reveal everything, the way he's hurt those around him, the way he's justified what he's done, the way he's changed, who he really is. It wouldn't be real, of course, just a set of words on a page. But still, even if the whole thing were an exaggeration, even if he made himself taller and more attractive and intelligent and changed his friends' names and amalgamated a bunch of them together and invented whole experiences and wild stories that never happened, it would still at least represent a version of who he once was and express how he now sees the world and himself—a portrait of Sebastian Khan, if not real, at least true.

He steps away from the window and walks across the room's marble floor, to the painting in the adjoining room. Around him drift thin, murmuring crowds, a group of old ladies holding expensive purses, a few uniformed high school girls taking notes for an assignment, an old man in a hat and cane sitting on the sofa in the room's center, and a woman Sebastian's age, glancing briefly up at him as she glides past the nineteenth-century works. Everyone lingers only for a moment next to Sebastian to stare up at the painting before stepping over the threshold into the twentieth-century rooms.

The painting is not how Sebastian remembers it. Couture's once beautiful figures now seem grotesque. The lady in the carriage isn't radiant but foolish, her semi-nakedness a comical exaggeration against the dull colors of the background foliage. Sebastian notices too that her eyes seem closed, as if she's willfully ignorant of the reality of the world around her. And of the four figures that pull the carriage, even the troubadour looks absurd, with his dreamy-eyed expression, his foppish attire, the jester's rouge and makeup on his face. The only wise ones in the whole piece are the crone in the back of the carriage and, something Sebastian's never noticed before, a bearded statue in the middle of the path, looking upon the passing carriage in laughing judgment.

Sebastian shivers. The world suddenly feels cold, and even the heated halls of the museum aren't enough to keep out the gray chill lurking beyond the window.

He lets out a breath and turns from the painting. The next room is more dimly lit, and from here he can see the frightening canvases that line the walls, misshapen human bodies, discordant splashes of color, jagged lines and ugliness everywhere. But something about the room is alluring, as if now there is more truth in there than in all his beloved preceding centuries.

About the Author

Aatif Rashid is a writer living in Los Angeles. His work has appeared in *The Los Angeles Review of Books, The Massachusetts Review, Arcturus*, and *Metaphorosis*, as well as online on Medium. He currently writes regularly for *The Kenyon Review* blog about fiction writing and literature. You can find him on Twitter @Aatif_Rashid and at http://aatifrashid.com.

7.13
BOOKS

CPSIA information can be obtained
at www.ICGtesting.com
Printed in the USA
LVHW041521280619
622667LV00001B/92